SORROW FOR THY SONS

Sorrow For Thy Sons

by
GWYN THOMAS

LAWRENCE & WISHART
LONDON

Lawrence & Wishart Limited
39 Museum Street
London WC1A 1LQ

First published 1986

The text of *Sorrow For Thy Sons* has been prepared for publication by Dai Smith.

This book has been published with the financial support of the Welsh Arts Council.

Photoset in North Wales by
Derek Doyle & Associates, Mold, Clwyd.
Printed and bound in Great Britain by
Oxford University Press

Introduction
by Dai Smith

In late 1980 I went to talk to Gwyn Thomas at his house in the Vale of Glamorgan in order to prepare a profile for the new, and short-lived, Welsh magazine *Arcade*. He had been ill for some time and was visibly low in spirit. Nonetheless, for an old pupil from his schoolmaster days, he rallied and bantered and enthused for a few hours. Our conversation ranged widely but kept returning to the Rhondda of his youth and the style he invented to represent it. The two were inseperable. He acknowledged that some readers had found his deviance from verisimilitude in plots and the exuberant eloquence of his fictional dialogue just too much to accept but his retort was 'only the very best language was good enough for the people I was writing about'. His developed style was a deliberate attempt to show directly the consciousness of fate which underlined the humanity of people not allowed to live as fully as they would have wished. Humour became a chosen mode for him because it established, without any doubt, that an intelligence was at work. Protest could be evaded, even dismissed, in a way that the fingering joke could not be. 'Somebody', he told me, 'ought to analyse my humour. One thing that it proves is that the South Welsh did enlarge understanding. I was only a clue to the great thing that was being achieved – a mountain of achievement that has crumbled away. I think my humour shows the way in which the intellect of the Welsh working class might have developed their world.'

We then fell to talking of why that had not happened. The melancholy was kept at bay by his restless wit. At the end of the afternoon I moved the conversation back to the 1930s and asked what had become of his first novel: *Sorrow For Thy Sons*. It had never been published. It was, he said, 'lost' or 'in a drawer somewhere'. In any case, he remembered it as quite unlike the prose he later wrote and first saw in print in the mid 1940s. It was a savagely etched account of 1930s unemployment. 'Protest inhibits humour,' he concluded. We went out with his wife, Lyn, for a last drink at his pub.

* * *

Gwyn Thomas died in April 1981. He left behind a number of notebooks and manuscripts, many containing unpublished material. It ranged from two-liners to essays to plays to novels. There was no sign of *Sorrow For Thy Sons*. Yet the novel had existed. Its provenance and title first came to light when Gwyn referred to it in his autobiography *A Few Selected Exits* in 1968. He had begun writing it almost immediately after the end of three strained and alienating years at Oxford:

> It was a daft, hallucinated year [1935-36] ... The routine of my days was simple. At night I slept not at all. I would read until dawn, then wake the entire family by putting on a record of the slow movement of Rachmaninov's Second Concerto.
>
> My brothers would come down the stairs in varying stages of grunting rage, wishing to hang Rachmaninov and flog me. I would sleep for about an hour then walk the hill-top paths for two hours, talking to myself ... By the time I

returned to the house the chapter was ready to be decanted on to paper as fast as my sixpenny fountain pen could travel.

The novel was not written in a customary vacuum. Victor Gollancz had advertised a competition for the best novel on unemployment. I felt that as far as this problem was concerned I was the national dipstick. Industrially the valley had the rattle in its throat and I was making some pretty good sounds myself. The book's title was *Sorrow For Thy Sons* which, against the background of my general mood, was almost cheerful.

Gollancz said he liked the fervour of the book, but its facts were so raw, its wrath so pitiless, its commercial prospects were nil unless he could issue a free pair of asbestos underdrawers to every reader. So he had to say no to publication.

The chronology wobbled to accomodate the hyperbole but the basis of Gwyn Thomas' memory was sound. In 1936 Gollancz had announced a competition for 'the best genuinely proletarian novel by a British writer'. Entries had to reach the publisher by August 1937. Gwyn's novel, typed up by Wynne Roberts, a friend from Rhondda and Oxford, had been submitted and in 1983 Lyn Thomas, working through mounds of paper, discovered that yellowing typescript. She re-assembled and re-typed it. Now that it could be read again it could also be seen why Gollancz had rejected it for specific reasons. A later response confirmed this. In the autumn of 1938 Norman Collins of Gollancz had written to the 25 year old author:

I did not read your previous novel myself, but I have gone over the reports which the book received and I can, I think, give at least a hint of what the readers felt.

They were unanimous in praising the power of the novel but felt that its unrelieved 'sordidness' detracted from the picture rather than added to it. One reader said that if there had been anything in it at all which had been pleasant and beautiful it would have heightened the effect of the rest, and another reader made the remark that if only the book had 'the relief of beauty that Rhys Davies can give' it would have been a very fine piece of work indeed.

All three readers commented on the fact that some of the physical descriptions were so realistic as to produce actual nausea in the reader, but it is worth while to remember that, as your audience will be 99 per cent more or less tender-stomached, you will frighten them all away if you write in this fashion.

The advice now sounds like a compliment. Gwyn Thomas's novel had not quite slotted into the 1930s genre of 'proletarian novels'. It was neither naturalistic documentary nor heroic epic, although it was set, recognisably, in the Rhondda of the 1930s, and was a detailed tale of life on the dole and moved, as a climax, to the tremendous marches of January and February 1935 against Part II of the National Government's Unemployment Act, 'direct action' which had forced the government to halt its implementation of new, and reduced, scales of unemployment benefit. These marches were a prime example of a united front from below, and of a potential Popular Front, so desired by Gollancz. And yet it was not a novel that provided easy political succour for the left sympathisers Gollancz wished to reach and influence.

Unlike most novels about the devastated industrial regions of inter-war Britain, and especially those about 'exotic' South Wales, Gwyn Thomas's novel did not deign to introduce or explain his society to outsiders of any kind. He positively rejected the charity of sympathy. His valley was the centre not the margin. Nor was this hubris, but rather a firm understanding of how far 'his people' had had to travel to enable him to be 'a clue to the great thing that was being achieved'. At the same time this certainty was what allowed him to criticise from within, and quite sharply, working-class misery and self-exploitation. *Sorrow For Thy Sons,* though couched mostly in a framework of 'realistic' description, increasingly broke those formal bounds limiting its huge, moral passion. This was as disturbing to 1930s' sensibilities as the assumption that South Wales was a shining example of universality, even in its gloom, not a forlorn sample of forgotten provincialism. Later he would make these things clear and succinct by employing a 'sidling malicious obliquity'. His 1937 novel is not only the missing link in that personal process, it is a central coping stone now restored to the canon of twentieth century Welsh literature and a 'genuinely proletarian novel'.

The three brothers in *Sorrow* – Alf, Herbert and Hugh – are fatherless and motherless as the novel begins in 1931. They are without the ties of work, morality or future aspirations. Their debate concerns the nature of any available human identity in a world apparently, and literally, intent on de-humanising them. The novel is not a tract for its times and thereby becomes a voice for our own. It is not a piece of emotional breast-baring that can testify to the suffering of the 1930s and, in the new social history textbooks, be ticked blandly off against a bucketful of statistics on rising productivity and improving health care. What it does, instead, is to explore self-awareness, discuss choice, explain the necessary displacement from roots and certitude and community that 'coal capitalism' entailed and then, moving beyond that, through dialogue, authorial intervention, and a plot that only encircles itself, the novel declared its allegiance, in a unity of mind and heart, to the significance of a class experience and to the consciousness that comes, albeit like lightning flashes, with that class history. Gwyn Thomas's novel of half a century ago arrives in 1986 like such a flash. It lights up the skies of our lives.

* * *

Gwyn Thomas once said of his friend and mentor, the Rhondda novelist Lewis Jones, that we ought to cherish any dust left from the passing of that astonishing star. The same could be said of Gwyn Thomas himself. From the late 1940s he fashioned a prose whose visceral tickle owed more to the scalpel than the feather duster in order to lay bare the bones of his constant theme: no less than the making and breaking of the South Wales Valleys and their rich political and social culture. He was a prose writer of mordant, inimitable genius whose early work was hailed as such world-wide. New generations need to discover and interpret him for themselves as his books, once again, come back into print.

* * *

Gwyn Thomas was born in the Rhondda in 1913. He was educated at Porth County School and at Oxford University where he read Spanish. In 1933, thanks to a miner's scholarship, he spent six months at the University of Madrid. He taught, subsequently, for the WEA in South Wales before settling to the life of a schoolteacher in Barry, from 1942 until his decision to become a full-time writer and broadcaster in 1962. He was already well known as a prolific novelist and short-story writer but he now concentrated increasingly on writing plays and musicals. Gwyn Thomas died in 1981.

His writings include the fiction: *Where did I Put My Pity?* (1946), *The Dark Philosophers* (1946), *The Alone to The Alone* (1947), *All Things Betray Thee* (1949) and *A Frost on My Frolic* (1953); the plays: *The Keep* (1962) *Sap* (1974) and *The Breakers* (1976); autobiography: *A Few Selected Exits* (1968).

Part One
The Brothers

Alf threw the clothes off himself. The stale air came up in a solid block. He remembered the clothes hadn't been changed since the day his mother died, a month before.

There was a small mirror hanging in the corner of the room. A split ran through the middle of it. Beneath the mirror Alf had scribbled the date on which the breakage had taken place. May 1927. Now it was May 1930. Four years more of pesky rotten luck to go.

Alf stood in front of the mirror. He was short, wide, black of hair, full of mouth. His eyes were dark, full of hardness and filmed over by hours of sleep. He had gone to bed at half-past nine the night before. He had been going to take Gwyneth to a dance, a cheap, smelly, good-for-nothing tanner hop with all the bags and ploughboys of the town making funny motions at one another, waiting for a chance to escape out of earshot of that bellocking, tuneless combination of piano, trombone and cymbals that passed for a band, and out into the cool, shadowy and refuse-gorged recesses of the back lane that separated the dance hall from the river.

But Gwyneth had worked on in the shop. Either the boss had been in a tantrum or there had been a customer who was deaf and dumb or just goddamn difficult. Gwyneth's explanation had been as hard to follow as the windings of that back lane by the dance hall. But she had looked pale. Paler than usual. And usually she had less colour than a corpse. It was that shop she worked in. Alf had spent a lot of time waiting in there, waiting for Gwyneth. The place was never properly lit until they switched on the electric. Alf had never failed to wonder at the fact that one building could keep out so much light.

And that manager, Gwyneth's boss. There was a man for you. Alf blinked into the mirror and called Gwyneth's boss a mingy cow. He never turned the lights up until everybody was groping about in the dark, the girls in the shop cursing flashes because they couldn't keep an eye on the customers and the customers creating blue hell because they couldn't keep an eye on the shop-girls or the materials they were buying. The shop was a millinery store.

Two nights out of every three Gwyneth was all washed out when Alf met her. She couldn't dance, didn't feel like the pictures, drooped if she walked. Altogether Gwyneth was at the bottom of the slope. Alf didn't know quite what to do about it. He liked her. But he was so full of life and blood. Alf was strong and fundamental – like a dog or a kick in the stomach. That fact stared at you from his face, from every line, feature and suggestion of it.

He didn't know exactly what to do about Gwyneth. He might marry her. Get her out of that shop. Give her plenty of time to rest, to get to the seaside or up to the top of the mountains and rub stuff in her face, anything to coax that flat whiteness from around her mouth and eyes.

It gave Alf a bad conscience to see her looking like that when he went out with her. People stared at them. Damn people. Alf snapped his teeth. He always got fits of bitter windy anger when he got out of bed and walked about the bedroom, or stood in front of the mirror in his shirt. Must be dreams that hadn't quite left his mind and were soaring restlessly around trying to find a way out. Damn people! Perhaps they thought he had something to do with the way Gwyneth looked. That was a joke. Alf pressed on the bare balls of his feet, as if pressing out all the joke's rich juices. As if he had something to do with it! He hadn't touched her. Kissed her, sure. So many times it made him sick to think how many. A wonder both of them hadn't choked.

Gwyneth had funny lips, twisted a bit, made her talk like a woman who's hiring a maid. That wasn't her fault. Gwyneth was too fond of hard work to think of hiring a maid. It was a touch of paralysis she had had as a kid that made her talk funny like that. Screwed her lips up into a curious shape, gave Alf the itch to be always touching them with his. But more than that, nothing.

He had behaved like a deacon, a good deacon, not one of the sort that goes ramming around as soon as the chapel's back is turned. And Alf had built up a reputation as one of the most mobile and destructive units in the town's love-life. Hadn't touched her. He respected her, wanted to give her his pay, the whole lot, just keep enough back for fags, a bob on the greyhounds and one or two little extras. He wanted to carry things for her, and daft things like that.

Alf looked out of the window. Houses faced him; grey, drab, sickening little cots they were. Beetle traps. Anything from six to eight people living in each, treading on one another's shirt tails, bawling into one another's ears that this was a hell of a life because there wasn't enough room to move about in, not enough food to fill your bag without filching somebody else's, not enough rest or peace or satisfaction to give your mind or soul anything but a feeling they were full of sand, gritty to the teeth and being torn to bits by the tiny, ruthless, biting little particles every time they moved.

And everything the people in those houses said was heard as plain as a gramophone record by the people next door, because the walls that divided them were like tissue paper. Wet tissue paper, waiting to fold up and make one decent, unbroken chicken run of the whole block. Alf stared at the houses opposite for a full minute. Beetle traps to be sure. There wasn't any other name for them. Hundreds of them, stretching for a good half mile up the street, interrupted at intervals of a hundred yards to permit side streets to shoot off hastily, scrambling downhill on one side, uphill on the other, as if in a hurry to get away from the main road which was the model of all evils.

Alf's window was open. He leaned forward, his expanded chest resting on the window top. The sky was light, but not fully. The morning was still very early.

Alf leaned further out of the window. The morning air was cold. It was always cold when it came down from the hills. It came from somewhere beyond the hills, the sea maybe or the rear side of heaven itself, emitting cold blasts to cool the hot sin reproduced through the earth at night. Alf felt no curiosity about what lay beyond the hills. He'd have traded all the seas in the world for just a yard of the valleys' green slopes. His life was there, in those slopes. Beneath them, he had worked since his fourteenth birthday, getting coal for other men to use, and other men to profit by.

Above them, he had lain, through the evenings and nights of ten summers, with the twenty-five different women towards whom his passion had arisen and his pocket had grown generous. The valley he looked out at he loved. In it was contained every mortal thing he had ever caressed and wished to hold as his own for as long as he should live.

In the house opposite there were a few gas lights burning. There was no need for gas lights. There was light enough from the morning for anyone to find his way around. But winter was not long over,. The habit of putting the light on when they came down to prepare themselves for work stuck with some people till May was out. Alf thought there might be something more in that proverb about casting clouts than met the eye. That was something you noticed about the valley. So little met the eye, but God! the things that were there, things a fellow'd never dream about unless he were crazy and went in for imagining things that would land him, soon or late, in the darkest den of the County Asylum.

Those houses there that he was staring at, just those three nearest him, with the lamppost in the middle, standing up with its broken, guttering mantle, like the light of the world. In the first there was that old couple, cheerfully starving to death on ten shillings a week old age and six bob from the parish, just because some clown of a vote-scraping, careerist councillor had told them once that if they'd hitch their stars, votes and faith to his rumbling political wagon, they'd soon be having an old age pension of a pound a week. They looked forward to that day and the redness that shone in their cheeks was not of health, but of hope. They argued that when the pension went up to a pound, that amount, on top of the little savings they already had by them, would be enough to see them on easy street.

Alf promised that on the day the old couple packed in on account of the emptiness between their ribs, he'd call in and revive the bodies and lay upon them a wreath of those flowers, the most beautiful and perfumed that grew in the valley. Demagogue's Delight … red in the centre, white and yellow around.

Then there was the house next to that in which the old couple lived. A girl lived there, about twenty-eight years old, with legs like telegraph poles, varicose veined, lumpy shoulders that sloped irresponsibly, eyes that were weak and peering from her face as if she was constantly staring into the night. People said that her lover of ten years back

— 15 —

had left her in the dark, and that expression she wore was her way of expecting him back. He never came back. Some maintained he had never gone away. Others that he had never even lived. Others that it was just as well if he hadn't because she'd have worn him down to a thin thread of his virginal self.

The girl had no control. The way she spoke showed that. Every sentence she uttered gaped with an adenoidal looseness, and the language she used was the sort that came up from the drains and went out with the tide every morning. She couldn't read or write. Alf had tried her just to make sure. He had offered her a newspaper to read. She said she didn't need it. She had just been. He explained he wanted her to read it. She called him a bloody cleversticks of hell, rolled the paper into a tight, tampy ball and flung it in Alf's face, causing his eye to smart for hours.

A strong girl, but loose in mind and body. Nobody had bothered to marry her, but she had borne three children as a token of her willingness. This had been exaggerated into a legend. Annie, the legend ran, had bastards so regularly you could set your clocks by her. They had put her away for a spell in the workhouse hospital. The authorities explained, christianly, to Annie's parents that all they wanted to do was to keep her under observation, read her a group of inspiring texts and tracts on the subject of self-discipline and control, and get her to submit her life to a few general directives more wholesome than the driving rain of animal lust that had been beating in her face and blinding her eyes from the day of her birth.

Her parents had consented. They were normal, kindly, chapel-going people, contented toilers, without a trace of perversion or revolutionary unorthodoxy in any part of their family records, but, as the good minister put it to them, the family records of the proletariat do not stretch back so far, except in shadow form in the account books of the coalowners.

Annie was removed to the hospital. After the birth of her second child, they promoted her to the position of a maidservant. She was made to scrub to the point of lily-whiteness more floors than she had ever seen before, and when that work was done she was closeted either with an improving book which she couldn't read, or with a garrulous uplifter of the masses whose talk, twisted into skeins of silky metaphors, Annie was either too stupid to understand or too dog-tired to hear.

That got on Annie's nerves. The inmates revolted against the sound of her running like mad through the corridors at night, whimpering like a curlew, then screaming and weeping with the profound and painful sex-hunger that burned like a bush fire in every pint of her blood. A callous and sophisticated male attendant satisfied her at last, then, in the fullness of his own satisfaction, gave the Master and Matron ten good and widely different reasons why Annie should be sent home. Annie went home. The workhouse forgot her. She did not forget the workhouse. She roamed the mountains, happy and licentious, like a wildcat, keeping her eyes on her paws, sharpening her claws on the small grey pebbles littered on the mountain paths, ready to fight for her freedom and draw blood in accordance with the laws of nature.

Alf looked at the drawn blinds of Annie's house. A light showed through the fanlight above the yellow-painted front door. That would be Annie's father preparing for work. Annie's father had a reputation for always being the first at the pit-head. For twenty years he had begun every working day by getting to the pit-head twenty minutes before it was necessary. This had pleased the manager who, as far as the men in his employ were concerned, would have been willing to stake his life on the correctness of the axiom that dawns abed and daylight slumber were not meant for man alive. He dealt mercilessly with late-comers. He met them at the pit-head with the words: 'Back to your sloth, sluggard!' Some of the men, thinking that 'sloth' was a dirty word for a wife, had done him damage. But Annie's father made up for these exceptions. The manager had had a paragraph put in the local paper, celebrating his twenty years of eager service with the colliery company. Annie's father had expressed his gratitude for that gesture during the following ten years by turning up for work thirty minutes earlier than was necessary.

In the house next to Annie's lived a man and wife, with a lodger. Alf knew the husband well. He had a bent for natural studies. He had taken Alf for walks along the mountains and lanes, pointing out plants that killed, herbs that cured and other plants that made you so sick in the stomach and dizzy in the head you didn't care whether you lived or died.

This husband was a pretty anaemic fellow for all his knowledge of herbs. Alf believed his wife wasn't giving him enough to eat. Alf told him that with his exact knowledge of the countryside he ought to go on a diet of birds' nest and see if it would stiffen him up any. The husband said that wouldn't be fair on the birds. Alf answered that a bird's life, like a miner's life, was so chock full of injustices, big and small, the addition of one more crime wouldn't hurt.

The husband stuck to his point. He loved nature more than himself. Alf told him if he loved it much more birds would start nesting in his hair. The wife was a robust woman, with a throat as deep and as resonant as a pit shaft. Alf thought that if you fell down that woman's throat you'd come to no harm, because her inside was full of the sunlight she got down her every time she swallowed, and you'd come up as the first line of a sentimental song. She was a crack hand at sentimental songs.

At every bi-monthly concert of the Legion (Women's Branch), held to finance a yearly trip to the West coast with a Bacchanalian romp on the sands, she sang, 'God send you back to me' with such husky sincerity that she could draw tears with her first bar of the accompaniment, even before she had opened her mouth. Some of the more wry-minded members of the Legion thought it wasn't fair on God, the way she sang that song, because even if it lay within His powers to grant her request, He wouldn't know who to send back, her husband or the lodger.

She was active in politics. She bustled on every committee entrusted with distributing boots, shoes or shirts under the Distressed Areas charity schemes. There was always a substantial flow of people into her parlour. She didn't think too highly of her supplicants. She viewed them, one and all, as the agents of their own decline and corruption, stirring out of their wilderness only to feast on the good hearts of the charitable. There was an accumulation of stuff in the parlour, piles of boot-boxes and flannels.

There had been a scandal. She had been accused of selling the stuff for her own benefit at cut rates. The shopkeepers had started the scandal. It had taken root among some of the unemployed who were fed up and angry with charity ramps, and ready to instigate a blood-bath for the cleansing of those responsible.

The lodger was a rare specimen. He, too, was a local politician. He had developed his chest muscles to compensate for a weakness in the left leg which he dragged behind him, the result of an accident in the pit. He had enough fresh air and leisure to put the finishing touches to his philosophy and chest development. There was hair on both chest and philosophy. He was a rigid constitutionalist. He preached the gospel that in the constitution there was a big blank space into which Socialism, if necessary, could be written. He'd expand his chest lungs with one deep breath and cool off his temper with the outgoing blast which lasted anything from thirty seconds to a minute.

Alf had always felt he'd like to strangle the fellow, if only he had stronger fingers. He had advised Bob, the husband, to do the strangling, because the lodger's devotion to Bob's wife was as well known as the war memorial. But Bob was bloodless. His fingers were weaker even than Alf's, and with the lodger's record lung expansion nothing short of a pair of tightly tied trusses around his neck would succeed in stopping his breath for good. Bob was not discontented. He had worked and walked all the passion out of his system. Alf wondered whether he'd go on living like that until he died. He supposed he would.

When something like nature got into a fellow's mind, it was harder to get rid of than a disease or a birthmark. It was like a blotter. Any interest he might have in the work he did, any hatred he might have felt for those who did him wrong, got soaked into it. Alf saw the light being lit in Bob's house. That would be Bob or the lodger. Bob's wife took it easy. She never left her bed until nine o'clock in the morning.

Beyond the houses was a brook. It sprang from the heart of the mountain, red with iron, red, some made out, with the blood of the Celts who had crawled away to die in the mountain's heart, away from the bludgeonings of either Roman legionaries or Saxon coalowners. At intervals, the brook ran up against a high piled barricade of empty rusted tins and festering offal. Around the barricades played children.

Beyond the brook was a maze of red brick houses. The houses had looked beautiful on the day of their completion. From that day forward, their decline dated. In one of these houses Gwyneth lived and coughed badly two nights out of three. She lived with her father, who read the Great Book of Martyrs right through once a year, blamed the agnosticism of his father for his failure to cope with football pools, filled his stomach with the cheapest beer going once a week, and shivered with a kind of ague once a fortnight.

Still standing by the window, Alf stood on his toes and craned his neck, trying to catch a glimpse of those houses beyond the brook where Gwyneth lived. The houses opposite were too high. He was too short. His toes ached. A splinter from the wooden floor went into his big toe. He plucked it without interest. Jones the ostler from up the road passed by with his stick that had a piece of loose clicketing metal on the end of it. That would make the time about half past four. Alf felt like shouting to Jones to see why in the name of the holy Joe he didn't get a nail from somewhere in the colliery and put that bit of metal right. It had been clicketing and getting on people's nerves for five years or more. But Jones was a bit deaf, and as obstinate as some of the horses it was his job to feed underground. The metal would keep on clicketing until Jones passed over or the stick crumbled.

Alf looked under the dressing-table for his stockings. He remembered he had left them downstairs. He went out on to the landing. He opened the door of the nearest bedroom. Hugh's bed was empty. He passed downstairs. There was a passage way eight feet long from the stair bottom to the front door, furnished with four oblong pieces of coconut matting, one very frayed in the centre. Between the mats, the linoleum looked stained and dusty. The house needed cleaning.

The middle room was cold and dreary. It had never been much used. The walls were damp. Black, damp-proof paper had been laid on underneath the ordinary flowered paper. Patches of black showed around the flowers. Hugh had called the room 'Gangrene Hall'. Wherever Hugh might be, he was never far from the truth. On the walls of the room hung pictures of many relatives. Most of the relatives were dead. You could tell that from their pictures. They looked as if they had sprung from nowhere into mature life, for the single purpose of being photographed, then back to the cool silence of the void to burn their high-collared coats and do a double somersault out of their stiff fly-black collars.

Alf's mother had insisted that they keep these portraits. While she lived, they had been scattered throughout the house. From the kitchen to the front bedroom there had been a considerable camp-following of uncles, aunts, grandfathers and grandmothers. The practice of ancestor worship was implicit in every breath and step you took. After the mother's death Alf and Hugh had collected the blood relations and put them in a heap on the middle room table. Alf got the paraffin oil in which to soak them. Hugh had the matches with which to set them roaring with eloquent flame.

Hugh had composed a little funeral speech that covered the whole issue. But Herbert had interposed. Herbert was the eldest of the three brothers. Herbert was a legalist, as became the manager of a grocery branch shop. Herbert was conscious of his blood. He saw each portrait as a wood and paper extension of his own veins. He had made a speech about vandalism that had made Alf laugh and Hugh retch. He was all for the replacement of the pictures on their original nails. Alf had torn the nails out. They compromised. Fresh nails were fixed in the walls of the middle room. Now all of the twenty photographs hung there. Between the lot, Hugh reckoned that there were enough side-whiskers to provide the valley's one hundred and fifty thousand natives with hair shirts down to their knees, and that would be for the best because hair shirts could not tickle very much more than flannel, and hair shirts, combined with poor wages, were one thing likely to get the whole one hundred and fifty thousand kicking up hell. Herbert had objected to the word 'hell'. Hugh had objected to Herbert. The matter ended there.

The middle room was dark. The window gave out on to the back paving which was shadowed by the pantry, a white-limed projection from the kitchen. Very little light came into the middle room. One had to go very close to the relatives to make out their features. No one went very close, save Alf and Hugh. They went not to stare and study but to hiss.

The door leading to the kitchen was closed. Alf pulled at the latch. It was stiff, stubborn. He tugged at it. The point of the latch was knife-sharp. It almost opened the tip of his finger. One of the mourners at Alf's mother's funeral had drawn blood on that latch. He had said it was a bad omen. There was going to be a death in the house. Alf told him there had been a death in the house, and what did he expect for his money? The mourner said that only went to show. There had been much talk of tearing the latch off and fixing a knob there instead. Alf gave the latch another tug. The door opened.

Alf noticed that the kitchen fire was still lit. It had sunk low. There was a kettle pressed down on it. Two towels, dirty, were hung from a brass bar, thick and running just below the mantel shelf.

Hugh was sitting by the table, dressed in a blue pullover, a pair of navy blue serge trousers. He wore no collar. His tie was slung over the back of the chair on which he sat. Around him on the table was a druidic circle of books. Open in front of him was a notebook of closely written notes. He was staring at it emptily. His eyes looked very tired. His hands were propped under his chin. Near his left elbow was a cup and saucer. The cup was half full of tea. He emptied it as Alf came into the room.

'Hullo, Hugh.'

'Hullo, Alf,'

'Been up all night?'

'Mm.'

'Tired?'

'Feel as if I'd been walked over.'

'What you want to stay up for?'

'Didn't feel sleepy. Exams in two months.'

'Two months is a long time.'

'Not to get through all this stuff.'

'Looks a lot.'

'It is.'

'What is it?'

'This thing I'm doing now?'

'Aye.'

'Religious Wars.'

'How can wars be religious?'

'Catholics against Protestants.'

'Those boys spent a lot of time fighting.'

'That's the way their religion took them.'

'Funny religion … But it's still the same. Look at these deacons around here. If there's a penny shortage in the funds, there's hell to play with the whole lot of them.'

'The world isn't good enough for them. They want to make it worse.'

'They're making a damn good job of it.'

'That's what they get paid for.'

'We should have been preachers, Hugh.'

'What for?'

'Good money. People bringing you stuff all the time because they think you're collecting the tickets at the back door for heaven, and every time you go away to preach you get free grub, free lodge, everything in your lap.'

'What's the use of that? We wouldn't believe in the stuff

we'd be preaching.'

'I don't believe in the coal I dig either, but it comes to the surface all the same and I get paid for it. What's the tea like, Hugh?'

'Stewed all to blazes.'

'You always get tea like that. How do you manage it?'

'I never empty the old leaves out. I put a fresh lot in the pot.'

'That's some system. You'll be killing somebody with it one day.'

'I like it strong.'

'Strong! That's poison. Your stomach must be looking like the floor of a stable.'

'Feels like it.'

'No wonder. Is the tea warm?'

'So-so.'

Alf got himself a cup and saucer from the sideboard. On the two top shelves of the sideboard hung a variety of forty-five jugs, some plain, some coloured, all unused. Hugh looked up at them.

'What did Mam want with all those jugs, Alf?'

'She was afraid she'd run short.'

'Only an earthquake could have made her run short of jugs. There's more there than you'd need to start a soup-kitchen.'

'Perhaps she had seen an earthquake. Perhaps she had wanted to start a soup-kitchen. There's kids around here needing soup. God knows what might have been at the back of her mind.'

'Seems sort of funny to be talking about her like this, don't it?'

'Aye. She was all right.'

'All right.'

'Everything she made was just so. She knew us backwards. Though I wish to Christ she had taught you to make tea. This stuff's a scandal, Hugh.'

'Don't drink it. Throw it in the grate.'

'And start a fire?'

'You better stop walking about in your shirt like that, you'll be catching something sure, walking about bare.'

'I was just going to look for my trousers.'

Alf went to the small recess beneath the stairs. He rummaged in a discoloured, creaking basket. He came out dragging a pair of working trousers behind him. The belt on it jangled.

'These trousers are wet. No shape on things since Mam went.'

Hugh looked across at him.

'What are you putting those things on for, Alf? Going gardening?'

'Gardening! Don't be so bloody daft. That's what comes of staying up all night getting facts on Catholics. I'm going to work, of course. I work in the pit. You remember me. I'm Alf.'

'I remember. But you finished work yesterday.'

'Yesterday?'

'A week ago you started your week's notice.'

'A week's notice?'

' 'Course. Don't you remember?'

'God help. So I do. What made me forget a thing like that anyway?'

'You must have been thinking about something else.'

'I was. I was thinking about Gwyneth, and the people living over the road.'

'Annie?'

'Annie and Bob and the old couple.'

'You did a lot of thinking.'

'About everything except my job. How in the name of Jesus did I come to forget about that? I knew about it all right. Yet it didn't even cross my mind.'

'You were sleepy. When a fellow's sleepy he don't think of anything much.'

'That goes for me all right. I can get out of bed and walk about, stare at the mountain, sing a bit, even talk, but I don't wake proper. Got to put my head under the tap before I wake proper.'

'How are you now? Waking or sleeping?'

'I'm awake. I don't need a tap this morning … Hell! Only now I'm realising it.'

'What?'

'I might not work in that pit again.'

'Good riddance to the bloody thing. You're better off out of it, Alf. Honest you are.'

'That's the only work I've ever known. Nine years I've spent there.'

'Start something else. You're not a crock or anything like that.'

'Something else? Such as what now?'

'Oh, something. Anything's better than the pit. What did you stand to get out of it? You get a leg torn off in the conveyor. You get a broken back maybe. Or if you're lucky, you might even last it out and manage to get old in it, and your skin gets as full of blue marks as a bit of that cheese.'

'I didn't earn bad money. Better than the seventeen bob I'll get on the dole anyway.'

'Seventeen bob. Doesn't sound much.'

'It isn't much. I could spend nearly all that much on fags.'

'Herbert'll cut down our fag allowance.'

'I was thinking about Herbert.'

'Thinking what?'

'He threw his weight about before. You know the way he talks about sacrificing to keep you in school.'

'It's he wanted me to stay in school. What's he talking about?'

'Don't ask Herbert that. He's so full of his own importance and his little schemes, he probably says lies to himself in his sleep. But he'll be a hell of a sight worse if I'm out of a job for long.'

'You'll get something else, Alf. Sure you will.'

'There's lots of other fellows around here. They're young, too. And strong. They said that and believed it, just like you are now. But that hasn't stopped some of them from being on the dole for three, four, five years.'

'They haven't tried perhaps?'

'Tried. Like hell they try. But it just doesn't get them anywhere. All over the shop there's pits closing down. These bloody owners must be going into the banana business. There's no jobs around here, that's all.'

'There's other places.'

'Don't want them.'

'Why not?'

'I was born here.'

'That don't mean to say you're going to die here.'

'I might be unlucky. I might not die at all. You know that placard that soft-looking bloke with the bowler over his ears carries around on a Saturday night?'

'Millions now living may never die?'

'He looks as if he'd pack in any minute. That bowler'll smother him. It slips down lower every time I see him, like one of those things what do you call them ... ice ... glashes.'

'Glaciers.'

'That's right. Millions now living might never die. I might be one of them. But as long as I live, it's here I'm staying. Not that I'm sentimental, but nobody's going to drive me out of this valley. If a fellow can't find a job in the place where he was born and where he wants to be, they can all go to hell, Herbert included.'

'Herbert's sure to go to hell.'

'He'd start a new grocery branch there.'

'He wouldn't give tick to the devil.'

'Herbert takes after his grandfather.'

'Never knew him.'

'I didn't. His picture's in there. He looks a bumptious sort of sod.'

Alf went to the door. He leaned forward and looked up.

'Going to be a nice day.'

'What's the odds.'

'Oh, just glad it isn't raining, that's all.'

Alf trembled and closed the door. He was frowning. When he frowned his face became very heavy, dark and contemplative. There were notable streaks of oiliness in his hair. Alf used bottles and bottles of olive oil on his hair.

Hugh took the spoon from the saucer by his side, and scooped the sugar from the bottom of the cup. Drops of cold tea fell from the spoon on to the written pages of his notebook. They fell on the name of Luther and he thought that was just as well. He munched the sugar slowly and felt sure his teeth would ache after it. They always did when he ate something sweet.

'Put your trousers on, Alf, you're shivering.'

Alf threw his working trousers back on to the basket he had taken it from. Stains of coal-dust showed on the light blue shirt, the sleeve of which hung over the side of the basket.

'Where do you keep those old grey trousers of yours, Hugh?'

'On the nail behind the door. Under the mac. The one with the torn collar.'

'How do you tear the collars of your mac like that?'

'It's the hooks we hang them on in school.'

'Oh.'

Alf found the grey trousers. He put them on and walked to the fire. He stirred the bottom bar. The fire collapsed. The kettle rattled and spilled its water, hissing. He held it in his hand, looked at Hugh, seeming to be tracing some connection between the washed-out look on Hugh's face and the taste on the tea.

He sat down in the armchair that stood on the right of the fire. It was a hard, square-looking chair. It had been presented to Mr Evans, Alf's father, ten years before, by the members of the local Friendly Benefit whose president he had been. The members had been grateful to Mr Evans for never having even tried to swindle them. Mr Evans had been proud of the chair. He had tricked it out with scores of nails and old bits of iron to make it more solid. He had done that.

Alf swore he could never sit in it without feeling he was starting a long stretch in jail. Only a man who made a cult of honesty like Mr Evans could have contrived such a chair. Sitting on it without a cushion, Alf and Hugh had proved that it made your buttocks look like Good Friday. There were two cushions on it. The cushions were substantial and embroidered with drawings of shepherds and sheep, two shepherds to one sheep on the top cushion, and one shepherd to two sheep on the bottom.

Alf kept the first one at the bottom because it was fairer on the second shepherd, who must have been wasting his time helping his pal keep an eye on one sheep. The cushions had come as presents to the three brothers from two maiden aunts who lived higher up the valley in an elaborate enough hillside villa. They owned ten houses between them. The younger one had written a paper for the Young People's Society on why rents should be reduced, and made sure when she wasn't reading the paper that her sister saw to it that they weren't. Herbert visited them sometimes.

Alf shifted about on his cushions.

'When we burn this damn chair we'll get a couple of nice soft sandbags to sit on here. They couldn't be tougher than these things. Come closer to the fire, Hugh. You must be freezing over there.'

'I'm all right. There isn't a fire anyway.'

'I'll get some coal now. I'll build it up.'

'Don't look so worried, Alf. You look as if you got a snake stuck in each ear.'

'It's rotten.'

'What is?'

'That pit, closing down just at this time.'

'It was only a matter of waiting. Haven't they been saying for years the thing wasn't paying? It's a wonder it kept going so long.'

'Every time there'd be a bit of trouble, they'd say it was going to close. That was their way of keeping us quiet. They never ran it at a loss. That bastard of a manager never did anything for charity in his life except get born. We never really thought it would finish. It was one of the best pits in the area.'

'Don't worry about it, Alf. One day we'll laugh at all this.'

'Tell me how long we got to wait before we start laughing.'

'If I go on to college, I'll be finished in about four years. I'll get a good job. Then everything will be all right.'

'Four years … After waiting that time, we'll have to spend another four years tickling each other to get the way of laughing back into our system. No. You don't get what I'm driving at exactly. I had made plans.'

'Plans?'

'I was thinking of getting married.'

'Married? I didn't know.'

'I didn't either till I got out of bed this morning.'

'Fellows get married on the dole.'

'And other fellows get cramp in the water.'

'What does that mean?'

'No marrying on the dole for me.'

'You get extra if you're married.'

'You ought to be a politician, Hugh. You know every bloody thing. You get extra. How much? You might as well get married to a camel. That'd be a good idea if there were enough camels to go round. No, I wouldn't do that to Gwyneth. She wants the best. She's delicate. I'll have to wait a bit. I'll have to see what happens.'

'That's the best.'

'Go to bed, Hugh, you sound half dead.'

'I could go to sleep on the table a treat.'

'Don't do that. Herbert would sweep you up with the crumbs and feed you to the birds. I'm going up the tip.'

'Up the tip! What you going up the tip for?'

'Walk. It's a nice day. That tea made me feel a bit sick. And I got a feeling there's a lot of things going to make me feel sick pretty soon.'

'I'll come up with you.'

'Get some sleep.'

'I'm going to school at half-past eight. It'll be that in no time. Might as well get some fresh air. There isn't any in the bedroom.'

'You never open the window.'

'No fear. That woman next door starts talking to herself at seven o'clock and doesn't stop until she wakes me up.'

'What does she talk about? She looks like a half-wit.'

'Her first husband.'

'Never knew she had one.'

'Two.'

'People do more things behind my back here ... Or is it my back's always turned? What does she say about her first husband?'

'He had a lot of money.'

'And her second husband squirted it all against the wall.'

'That's about it.'

'Widows always say the same lies. Maybe they read the

same books. There's only one woman around here who says the truth and that's Annie over the road.'

'She doesn't say anything.'

'She's welcome.'

Hugh pushed his chair back and screwed his face up as he stretched his legs.

'Cramp like hell.'

Alf got his coat from the back of the chair. Hugh had thrown his onto a pile of newspapers on the sofa. He put it on. It was short for him. He had grown out of it. He pulled it down sharply to make it seem longer. Alf told him it would be easier if he walked about with his legs bent.

Alf went up to the top of the back garden with a bucket in his hand, to get some coal. The coal-shed was small, ramshackle, made from bits of tea-chest covered over with felting. Twice it had been blown down by heavy winds. Hugh said that another couple of falls would see it getting the idea and springing back into shape after every collapse. The bucket Alf carried had a cardboard bottom. The tin bucket had been kicked out by kids who passed through the back lane on their way to the elementary school, two hundred yards up the road. The kids dawdled on their way to school thinking out new tricks to play on the full ashbuckets that stood outside each back door waiting for the ashman.

The cardboard bottom fell out of the bucket as Alf carried the coal down to the house. He cursed like a maniac. The lumps scattered over the narrow path. He flung the bucket from him. It landed with a crash on the shed that had been built on to the house. Anything the brothers wanted to throw out of the house, a chair with three legs, a cup without a handle, a mirror without a glass, a mattress that had gone to the devil or the bugs, went into the shed, as the first stage of its journey to the refuse incinerator.

Alf whispered the last half-dozen of his curses. It was too early in the morning to go bawling blasphemies. He heard one of the upper windows of the house next door being opened. It opened with a stiff, painful squeak. The tenant of the house, an Apostolic, a man with thin features, a bald head and eyes full either of conscience or disease, put his head out and looked around. When he caught sight of Alf, he put his fingers to his lips and shh'd.

'What's the matter with you?' The vigour in Alf's voice deepened it a few tones. When the Apostolic spoke, his voice sounded like the window he had opened. There was a squeaky painfulness about it.

'I heard foul language, brother.'

'That was me, brother.'

'You?'

'I said me.'

'Your tongue is not as clean as the morning.'

'You try handling that bloody bucket.'

'I've handled sin.'

'What's that like?'

'Worse.'

'Has it got a cardboard bottom?'

'Wouldn't know that.'

'Tell me when you find out. It makes all the difference.'

The Apostolic withdrew.

Alf collected as many of the lumps of coal as he could in his hands and carried them down. He threw them without order on to the fire. He said that there might be enough fire under them to make them burn, but he was giving them their chance and that was the most they could expect. He couldn't be bothered to look for firewood.

* * *

Alf and Hugh left the house by the back way. They walked down the back lane in silence towards the road which led up to the tip. The back lane was hard walking. Lumps of stone projected from the hard-stamped earth. Small heaps of slag and small coal had been shovelled against the wall on either side. A dog ran past them and made for some sheep who were nosing at a small tuft of green that grew at the base of a wireless aerial. Alf grinned.

'A coalowner closes a pit and I can't get married. That dog chases those sheep and they can't eat grass. What's worse?'

Hugh yawned.

'Don't know. I haven't been either yet.'

'I can't say I know much about unemployment so far. But I think the sheep get the best of it.'

'Don't see it. They just keep them and kill them.'

'And they leave them alone while they're waiting. They get a bit of peace, more than we get.'

Emerging from the back lane, they passed the policeman's house. It was one of the biggest and best houses in that neighbourhood. It stood on its own, separate from the three streets that flew away from it. It had a name, not a number. It was surrounded by a red brick wall, eight feet high. There was a Union Jack flying in the back yard of the house. Alf looked up at the pieces of broken glass that had been embedded into the concrete at the top of the wall.

'I remember the time when that house belonged to the schoolmaster.'

'So do I. I'm old enough to remember that.'

'What did he look like then?'

'Big fellow. Fat. He couldn't walk far without sitting down.'

'He had gout, or a rupture or something. That's why he always had to limp about. There was always a slit in the back of his coat to give his arse plenty of room to move about. There was talk once of painting the countries of the Empire on the seat of his trousers to save the

Education Committee the price of a globe, but they found they'd have to use part of his stomach to get Australia in. He said he didn't want no convict hanging around his navel. He was the headmaster of the school for twenty years.'

'How'd he get that job?'

'God knows. He didn't have any diplomas or letters or anything. He was as ignorant as hell. The boys in school the same time as me was as dull as sledges, but he couldn't teach us anything. He did a bit with Welsh poetry. That's how he kept the job. He got a good screw for telling us the wrong way to spell and leathering Jesus out of us every time we got to the damn school a bit late or forgot to call him "Sir". He built that house.'

'Nice house.'

'All right. Schoolmasters live in smaller houses now and police sergeants take over the classy places. That's the way of it. Policemen are the most important people around here now. Teachers used to beat us up for not going to school. Now policemen beat us up for not going to work. Bloody daft.'

'What's he got that flag flying for?'

'Might be the washing.'

'It's a Union Jack.'

'He's a great patriot, that policeman.'

'What's he patriotic about?'

'God knows. He was talking to me and a couple of the chaps down on the corner there one night by the fish shop. He was boosting the army up. Said it was a bloody great life. Plenty of fresh air and Christ knows what else. I told him about our Uncle Will.'

'The one that ate the fish and died black in the face?'

'It might have been the fish. He always looked pretty black in the face to me. He never shaved until somebody failed to acknowledge him in the street. Then he'd off with the lot. That was Uncle Will. The place was cleaner for his passing. He joined the army and he told us fresh air was the only thing there was plenty of. That's what I told the policeman. He didn't like that. He said Uncle Will was a bloody Red.'

'What did you say?'

'I said maybe, but Uncle Will could tell fresh air when he saw it. That was about the only thing he could tell when he saw it. Will was slower than a mule at catching on to things, unless it was something liable to turn his stomach. Then he was quicker than a sheep-dog. There never was such a chap as Will for having his guts up. He was lucky he lived in times when there was plenty of food about. If he was alive now he'd starve to death in a week. The policeman didn't like what I said about the army. But he didn't give up. He'd talk your elbow off, that chap. He's not as backward as he looks. He'd make a bloody good spy. That's probably what he is, anyway. He started to advertise the navy then. He recited a poem.'

'A poem. What for?'

'Ask him. A poem about thirty feet long. Never thought he'd finish. It would make a damn good roof ladder if it was straightened out. It was about some ship sinking.'

'The *Birkenhead*?'

'I didn't catch the name. He kept helping himself to a packet of chips Joe Mansfield had in his hand. Policemen put the fear of hell into Joe. He pinched some communion cups from the chapel where his father is caretaker and he's been like that ever since. He was too frightened to eat. It made me laugh to see him. When the poem was finished, the copper gave a list of all the victories our navy had won at sea. I never knew there was so much sea to fight on. He kept spouting names and dates for more than ten minutes. Sounded like a football fixture card.'

'Did he get any recruits?'

'Fred Evans told him he thought it was a lot of bloody lies, and he told Fred there were special places in jail for fellows who said things like that.'

'He must be crazy.'

'I told you he was a patriot. He organises the Boy Scouts around here. He gets hold of all the little half-wits he can and gets them to buy yellow mufflers to put round their necks. That makes them Cubs, makes them something worse if their luck's out or the colour runs, and it gets him promotion.'

'We better join the Cubs, Alf.'

'We might come to worse than that.'

'Look at all the broken glass he's got running around the wall.'

'When the schoolmaster was living there there wasn't any broken glass. The schoolmaster might have been as dull as a jimmy, but at least he trusted people. He didn't act as if he thought everybody was going to burgle his house or cut his throat, like this fellow. Things gets worse. People get worse with them. When everybody had good money and jobs were safe, people understood each other. There was more sympathy and understanding about than people could use. Now a couple of pits close down and people that were kissing each other ten years ago get as mean and rotten as rats. It's "Look after yourself and bugger your neighbour before he buggers you". Makes me sick. Broken glass on walls. There you have it, all summed up nice and pretty in a nutshell. I saw a little kid climbing over that wall there to get a ball he had kicked over. He almost ripped his kneecap off on the damn stuff. He fell down. The policeman came out and stood there like a lighthouse taking the poor little devil's name and address while the blood was flowing over the kid's boots and stockings on to the pavement.'

'Makes you want to kick somebody in the face.'

'Make sure it's the right face, that's all. I noticed the kid trooping around in the Boy Scouts now. That's the way converts are made.'

The tip came into sight. The tip's bulk was enormous. It had been growing steadily ever since the day it was discovered that the appearance of mountains could be ruined by depositing rubble on their slopes. The tip's side was pitted with holes where the men had dug during the strikes. Over the older parts of the tip a thin down of grass was growing.

The two brothers came level with an old ramshackle building, fronted by a wall with an iron gate let into it. The gate had been imposing once, in the boom days. It looked sluttish now. Its iron bars had been bent or broken by the joint animal effort of many boys at play who had found the joy of genuine sport in despoiling the property of the colliery company. The gate hung tipsily on its hinges. The building, for a time, had been a fan, supplying air to a level that had been closed down as redundant four or five years since. The machinery had been removed and sold as scrap. One half of the building had been demolished, leaving exposed two large cast-iron boilers now going fast to absolute rust.

Looked at from a distance they were brilliant yellow. Most of the roof tiles had been taken away. The wooden rafters had been allowed to stay, some to be kicked in by crawling boys, others to be chopped down for firewood, if you were lucky enough to do the job undisturbed with the policeman living so near. In every stone of the building there was a sermon about decay.

The management of the colliery had been pressed to go forward with the demolition and remove the building root and crop. The management had replied that it didn't like being pressed, which was true. The management did all the pressing that was necessary, on the necks of their employees, with an eye to seeing the blood squirt from their ears. Also, they had found that demolitions were costly as well as negative. They decided to leave half the fan in existence and surround it with a wire fence, barbed wire, just to prove by this epigrammatic gesture that fans may come and fans may go, but proprietary rights go on for ever.

The manager, living in a twelve-roomed mansion on the other side of the valley, heat and lighting free, never had occasion to notice that what was left of the fan had become an eyesore. The fan had become a headless ghost. Some people claimed that still, on quiet nights, they could hear the pulsing beat of its machinery. They had heard that beat for twenty years until it had become a part of their sleep. On quiet nights, their sorrowful imaginings forgot that when levels become redundant, machines as well as men are crowded out of use.

One section of the barbed wire had been torn up. Half a dozen fellows were rounded up for the offence. Three of them said they didn't have the strength to do it not even if they wanted to. Their faces and bodies, whipped by all the forms of emaciation, looked as if they were telling the truth and they were believed. The other three had said that they had done it and would do it again if they had the chance. They had worked in the level which the fan had supplied. When the fan closed they had lost their work for good. When they saw the derelict fan being fenced round it seemed to them like turning the dagger in the wound. They were the words used by one of the defendants to the magistrate. The magistrate said that daggers and wounds were not things to be discussed in a British court, at least not as metaphors. As facts they could be discussed freely. But not as metaphors. Metaphors were powder barrels of disaffection. They exploded under one's nose. The three men were fined fifty shillings each, and damages on top.

But the torn up section of the fencing was never replaced. In the roof of the abandoned fan birds nested and whitened the crumbling walls. Around the walls, in recesses where the furnaces had once sent their hot blasts to the boilers, boys and girls worked up their heat with little kisses, and precarious dreams of nest-building. There was still a door leading into that part of the building that remained standing. It was a good door. Why it had not been torn away and stolen long since was a mystery. Some were waiting for the building to crumble and save them the trouble of tearing the door away.

Those who followed that line of thought, surprised to find that crumbling is a process on a par with eternity, had either given up hope, or taken courses in philosophy in the Workmen's Institute to break the back of the waiting period. Others, more practical and less given to staring at the eternal, waited for the policeman to crumble. When that happened they'd steal the whole building and use the material to build a row of pigsties, at rents within the reach of the working population. Across the door there was an elaborate sign: 'Trespassers will be prosecuted.' This notice had been affixed since the abandonment of the fan. A visitor to the Distressed Areas, unfamiliar with the mechanics of social decay, had described the notice as the four most unnecessary words he had ever seen.

A pathway, six feet broad, fairly smooth, apart from a few furrows worn in the soft surface by the rainwaters, led obliquely to the tip. It ended a hundred feet above the level of the town, at the gate of a whitewashed cottage. The cottage itself was small, one room down and two up. It had the appearance of largeness, given to it by a series of outhouses, made loosely of wood and zinc, that the tenant had thrown up around it. The cottage garden was well tended and flourishing. Some years before the larger part of the vegetable crop had been pilfered by the youths who roamed the tip at night in search of love or silence, and came to their homes hungry enough in the stomach or sick enough in the mind to steal anything.

The gardener was a man who liked vegetables. Also, he had five children, whose appetites made him wonder if it was possible for a man to breed locusts. This year, in self-defence, he had strengthened and heightened the fences. The cottage was hardly to be seen from the ascending pathway.

Alf knew the tenant, Tom Forbes, well. Tom was a Somerset man who worked in the engine-house at the top of the tip. Tom was a solitary, whiskered, drawly sort of man, who took a long time to laugh or think but once started laughed too much to think. Tom rented the cottage from the coal company. He admitted that the five shillings he paid weekly for it was a swindle, but Tom remembered the squires of Somersetshire and never probed very deeply into the rent question. His instincts were still rural. He looked upon the eight hours he spent daily pushing trams of rubble and emptying them as a mechanical gesture that had no meaning.

It was the hours he spent gardening or teaching his children to garden that he regarded as his chief link with living. He was grateful to the cottage for giving him as near an approach to solitude as you could get in the valley if you didn't have the money to buy a farm. It kept him safely from that sprawl of closely regimented streets in the valley-bed below. For that, Tom was very glad.

He resented the pathway that led from his cottage down to the streets. Tom looked on the streets as something that sprang from the convergence of whores and hooligans. He wanted no truck with them. He cursed the pathway for an intrusion. It commemorated the death of his first child. The undertaker had hinted that the bearers who'd volunteered to carry the coffin down the rough slopes of the tip stood a middling chance of getting their necks broken. Tom had suggested carrying the coffin himself rather than have a path made. It was only a little coffin. The undertaker stood his ground and held out for a path. It wouldn't be fit or proper for a man to go carrying a coffin by himself as if it were a sack of bran. You could get a good price for a sack of bran; you couldn't for a corpse. It had no value at all, except as the centre point of a very interesting ceremony.

The undertaker won. The path was roughed out. Since then it had been broadened and stamped smooth and hard by thousands of evening walkers. Tom's children were growing up. They had brought him some sadness. From the oldest to the youngest they had hated the cottage. Their instincts were not his. The pits, stacks and streets of the mining valley were all they had ever known from birth. When Tom rumbled in their ears of the paradisal peace and placidity of the countryside he had left as a boy, of the beauty and security of living simply by the crops one raised from the earth, they laughed at what they thought was a bungling effort on his part to pull their legs.

They kept their eyes fixed on the streets below, where their schoolmates lived and played, where civilisation, in the form of a standardised squalor that tasted sour at first but sweet when you had a bellyfull, made life safer and easier. The two oldest boys had already left home. One was married and lived in the valley and the other had left the district. Once gone, they had never returned. It was the completeness of their treachery that made Tom ache.

Tom blamed it on the pathway. If that had never been built he might have kept them by his side. They had gone, as absolutely as that first child, for whom the path had been built, had gone. The three remaining children were growing up. Soon, the pathway would plunge its hook into their hearts and minds. It would take them, too. And Tom would be left alone, with his whiskers, his fences, his vegetables and the necessity of doing work that sickened him, and paying five shilllings rent per week on a house that only his own efforts had made inhabitable.

At the gate of Tom's cottage, Alf and Hugh stopped and looked backwards towards the place they had come from. They had walked fast up the path. Both were out of breath. Hugh turned out one of his coat pockets. In his hand he held a dirty litter of spent match sticks and old papers. He searched among them for a smokeable cigarette butt. He found none. Alf passed him a cigarette. Hugh struck a match on a flat reddish stone beneath his feet. Still stooping, he pushed his right stocking into his shoe to hide a hole. Alf counted the cigarettes left in his packet and put them back into an inside pocket.

'That'll be five thousand fags you owe me, now, Hugh.'

'You ought to give up counting, Alf. It'll wear you down. Might be years before I'm able to buy my own.'

'I'll keep on counting. It's good training for the day when I might have nothing to count any more.'

'I'll pay you back, Alf, every cent and fag I've had off you. I'll pay you back twice over.'

'What are you bothering about that for?'

'I'm serious. We're good friends, Alf, me and you. I want to do something to show that. But it seems I'll have to wait such a hell of a long time before I can do anything to show that I can be as good to you as you've been to me ... '

'Oh, arsehole.'

Hugh opened his mouth wide and wearily. He was too tired even to make a sound with it. Across the valley the sun was up, yellow and strong, standing immediately above a crane which surmounted a tip, a small conical tip, newer and neater than the one on which they were standing. Hugh's face muscles stiffened at the apex of his silent yawn. His mind was muzzy with sleeplessness. His impressions were vividly conceived, then instantly blurred and distorted. He imagined his face to have been transformed into a large black hole. At the back of that hole there was a powerful suction, drawing the sun towards him. If his face didn't shut, he might swallow the sun.

He put his cigarette out. He belched. He was sorry for the ten cups of deathly stale tea he had drunk during the night. He could feel the walls of his stomach getting leather-soled. He sat down on the piece of flat reddish rock. It would make a mess on the seat of his flannel trousers. That powdery sort of stone always did. But he'd leave the powder on. He could use it to prove to the boys at school that he had spent the night rolling about the side of a mountain with some girl. The boys wouldn't believe it. They classed Hugh as a sexless hermit. But he might believe it and that would make him feel less lonely.

He looked up at Alf. He noticed how straight Alf's back was, how thick his shoulders were, making him look shorter than he was. Alf had his head thrown back and his nostrils stretched as if he was doing breathing exercises. His eyes were fixed in front of him, staring, if at anything, at the rough scaly patch of mountain, pitted with outcrop workings and pimpled with tree stumps, that separated the conical tip from the topmost terrace. That was an ugly mountain, opposite. Hugh had no great love for it. He plucked the leg of Alf's trousers.

'You look like a picture I once saw. A Red Indian looking from the top of a hill at the lost land of his fathers.'

'Lost land. That's about it, I'm damned. Lost it is, by the look of it. Look at that fan. You ever seen anything that looked like a corner of a graveyard?'

'It's in a state. It makes you want to go down on your knees and pray for a new dose of life to pump into things. But there's nobody buried there. That's one good thing. Unless the druids once used it to bury their dead.'

'Nobody buried there? I don't know. A chap can be buried in a place before he's dead. When I was a kid, that fan was the centre of life for me. There were six or seven of us, all about the same age. The fan was our home from home. We used to take our food up there to eat. We used to know the ins and outs of that engine-house better than Hayward himself. Hayward was the chap who used to work there. He was deaf, and a bit religious, especially when he was on the night-shift and had no company. He could recite the Sermon on the Mount faster than any man I ever knew. Every time he recited it, he'd ask whether he was taking it too fast or too slow, because his hearing made him a bad judge.

'If I wanted to get in his good books, I'd tell him he said it just right, not too brown on either side. When there was nothing to get from him, I told him the truth. I told him he took it so fast you could not tell the Sermon from the Mount unless you kept your ear to the ground. But he never slowed it up. He was a good sort, old Hayward. Pure and good all through, like home-made toffee. He loved that fan. He died about two months after it closed. His life ended with the fan. That's something that damned manager would never understand. What profits are to him, that engine-house and stoke-hole were to Hayward.

'Can you imagine the manager living without profits? Not on the tail of your shirt he wouldn't. He'd go and fly himself at half-mast from his flag-pole just to get out of the misery. That's how it was with Hayward. D'you remember that stoke-hole? We'd sit there for hours, especially in the winter. The iron plates on the floor were always warm. We always felt like fresh loaves. There were beetles there the size of your finger. We used to catch them and put them in Joe Mansfield's hair. No wonder he grew up with a hell of a stutter. It's a wonder he could talk at all between those beetles and the communion cups he stole. He never had a chance …

'It was when old Hayward was feeding the fires we got out biggest treat. He'd make us stand far back. The fires splashed a lot. Hayward said Joe Mansfield was the sort of kid who'd get himself set aflame just to be a nuisance. There was something funny about the way Hayward used to feed the fires. It wasn't like a feller giving coal to flames. He didn't chuck it in as if that was the job he was paid for and didn't give a damn how he did it. He'd stretch his arms out as far as they'd go without being scorched and pour it in gently as if the furnance had a delicate stomach. Like a mother giving food to a kid.'

Alf glanced down. Hugh was dozing. Alf touched him with his foot. Hugh opened his eyes.

'Hullo, Alf.'

'Welcome home.'

'I dozed off.'

'Do you want to go down?'

'Let's go up a bit further. Funny. I had the idea I'd been sleeping for about an hour.'

'That's because you're very tired. It wasn't more than a couple of minutes.'

Alongside Tom's cottage ran the incline. It was steeper, more slippery than the pathway. They took it more slowly, Hugh walking a few yards behind Alf. The metal rails were polished white. Alf tried walking on them and slipped off every two feet or so. Between the metals lay the wire rope, strong, twisted, waiting to be tightened.

At the top of the incline was a flat run of a quarter mile to the engine-house, a many-sided structure, built of light grey stone, fitted with a good variety of iron stairs and doors. From a distance it looked like a fort. From close up, it did not look like an engine-house.

They did not follow the metals. They branched to the left and entered a quarry. Part of the quarry was still worked. They passed the powder-house, a squat, solid little hut. There was a notice on the door, in Welsh and English, telling children to keep their fingers to themselves. This applied only to the powder. It didn't prevent children from falling over the top of the quarry once in a while and breaking their limbs. This was not minded. What was minded was that they should not become familiar with the meaning and power of explosives. Alf and Hugh kept their eyes on the top layer of rock above them. It overhung dangerously. Hugh asked Alf why they didn't blast it.

'Leaving it like that is as good a way as any of keeping off trespassers.'

'These people got trespassers on the brain.'

'That's to prove they've got a brain.'

'I take back what I said.'

'Don't bother. There's nobody listening.'

They made their way out of the quarry by climbing a narrow, twisting path, rich with sheep's leavings. Hugh tried treading carefully to keep his shoes clean. Alf told him not to be so particular. The sheep couldn't help it, he said. They chewed grass all day. Whoever paid the piper called the tune. At the top of the quarry they came to a green tableland. On one side lay the top's most recent growth, wonderfully high and steep. On the other side the ground fell away sharply, down towards a thin straggle of houses built on a bleak slope. Along the edge of this tableland the two brothers walked steadily, for an hour.

* * *

When they got back down to the valley, the first children were on their way to school, in ones and twos, mostly in twos, clutching each others' hands, the younger ones staring around them solemnly, curiously, as if they had just been born.

Alf said it was a bit too early to see the ashbucket kickers at work. He couldn't remember ever having done anything like that himself. He wanted to see exactly how they got to work. There was also an idea in his mind that he'd like to see them kicking the daylights out of the policeman's bucket, which was something more than a bucket. It was a hygienic container with a handle on each side. In that neighbourhood it looked odd. By some it was mistaken for a milk-churn. By very few was it mistaken for a hygenic container. The ashman had his doubts about it. It was so easy to lift he couldn't bring himself to believe it was an ashbucket.

Herbert was having breakfast when Hugh and Alf got into the house. Herbert was taller than either of his brothers. He had a long, healthy, tightly-fleshed face. There was a ready made smile in constant wait around his mouth. His teeth were big and jagged, but cleaned like a religion. They were two shades whiter than Hugh's, three shades whiter than Alf's. Herbert was proud of his teeth but his gums bled often from the painful scrubbing he gave them. He paid half a crown for his toothbrush.

Alf said that with false teeth getting cheaper every day, or every other day at the outside, that price was a scandal. He added that you could always tell the age of a horse by the price he paid for his toothbrush. When Alf made statements like that there was to be seen a blanched and furious tightening of the flesh on Herbert's face, and in Herbert's mind there would spring to birth a feeling that there was no end to his hatred of Alf.

Herbert was plucking the tin cap from a milk bottle. He held the bottle far away from him, afraid of having the milk spilt on his blue shirt, with the semi-stiff collar and cuffs, or on his uncreasable green tie or on his navy blue trousers with the pin stripe. Herbert kept his clothes for years. When he discarded them they walked, head up, dignified, to the grave. His hair, less black than Alf's, rather darker than Hugh's, was parted and brushed in accordance with the advertisements. It was never otherwise, except when he slept and even then it was only a small minority section of hairs that cast away from their moorings of heavy, greasy fixative and deviated from the discipline imposed on them by Herbert. Alf maintained that he'd rather be a beggar in the house of the Lord than a hair on the head of Herbert.

The coal Alf had put on the fire before going up the tip had caught. It was flaming fiercely. It was good house-coal, crumbly and quick burning. Alf sat down on the iron-fitted chair that spoke in its creaks of his father's honesty. He looked at the black and white check pattern on Herbert's braces and thought it was a shame Herbert had to put a coat on and hide it.

Herbert sprinkled more cornflakes into a glass dish. He added some sugar and milk. He stood up to eat it. He liked giving the impression that he never had time enough to sit. Hugh poured out tea for the three of them. It was fresh. Herbert had made it just before they came in. Herbert looked at the back of Hugh's collar. It was engrained with dirt. Herbert blew his breath out loudly to show he was disgusted. Alf told him that if he didn't eat something more solid than cornflakes for breakfast he'd be having attacks of wind like that permanently, instead of in short bursts.

'That wasn't an attack of wind,' Herbert stirred his cornflakes into the milk. He would have thrown the dish at Alf with pleasure.

'Sounds like it to me. When you talk even, it sounds like an attack of wind to me.'

'Some people like the way I talk.'

'I know who they are. That's because they were born dumb.'

'I was looking at Hugh's collar.'

'It's too big for him, that's all. His neck will get fatter. Then it'll fit.'

'I wasn't looking at the size. It's the state of it. It's filthy. He looks as if he's been rolling about in the dirt.'

— 50 —

He turned to Hugh.

'Have you been rolling about in the dirt, Hugh?'

Hugh stood propped against the mantelpiece, sipping his tea.

'What the hell do you think I am, a snake? Why should I go rolling about?'

'We ask many questions, Hugh. We get few replies.'

'You sound like that headmaster of ours. You should have gone in for teaching, Herb.'

'I would probably have made a good teacher.'

'You're saying it, not me.'

'When did you change that shirt last?'

'God knows. Studying history gives me enough dates to remember, don't it?'

'It's a disgrace. You'll be dirtying the walls of the school if you go about in that thing much longer. Why don't you spruce up?'

'What have I to look dressed up about? When I'm not in school, I'm in the house here working. You talk as if I'm a bloody ambassador.'

'You'll be growing up to look like a tramp.'

Alf kicked off the shoe he had unlaced. He looked up, puzzled.

'What's wrong with Hugh looking like a tramp?'

'Having two tramps in the family pulls one's reputation down.'

'You're making me out to be a tramp?'

'You are not very particular about the way you go around. The girls you've knocked about with are the worse bags in the place, and the language you use on the road is enough to blow the roof off a chapel.'

'That's why I use it. I haven't seen any roofs blowing off yet. It must be a matter of patience or I'm not using the right words.'

'There are some people who don't believe you're my brother.'

'They make up for it by believing in a lot of things that are a hell of a sight funnier than that. You're not very proud of me, that's it.'

'I'm ashamed of you.'

'Herbert, you're a stuck-up bastard.'

'I've got a decent job. I mean to keep it. I'll do that in my own way, and when I tell Hugh his shirt is ready to walk off him, it means he ought to change it.'

Hugh looked at himself in the mirror.

'It's pretty black, fair play.'

'Black? It makes me think it's going to rain.'

'It might. This is a rainy place. You know what they call it in geography books?'

'No.'

'The piss-pot of Glamorgan.'

'Your language is getting worse than Alf's.'

'I do French. I still think Alf's language is better. It's nearer the bone and it's sweeter.'

'Change your shirt.'

'Where do I find one?'

'Wear one of those that Dad left.'

'A flannel one?'

'Why not?'

'And laugh myself to death through tickling. No fear. Those shirts are torture. No wonder Dad never cheated anybody. He was always too busy trying to keep himself from being driven daft by that flannel. When I'm wearing one of those things all I need is a couple of pence in my boots and I'll feel like a bloody monk.'

'Wear one of mine then. But keep it somewhere near the colour it starts off with. You work on shirts like a strong dye.'

'I'll do my best. Where do I find it?'

'Bottom drawer of chest in my room.'

'Will it make me look as neat as you?'

'If you put it on properly.'

'God help. They'll be treating me like a new boy in school. I'll probably have ten old friendships to make all over again. I'll go change it.'

'Wash first.'

'What for? I always wash last. It's easier.'

'Haven't you got any respect for other people's property?'

'No.'

'Start having some. If you go fooling with my shirts with your hands as black as that, that bottom drawer'll be looking as if a horse has been trampling over it.'

'How would a horse get up them stairs. It's too narrow.'

Hugh swilled briefly under the tap. He rubbed a bar of red carbolic soap into his face. Herbert passed him out a towel. It was a thick bath towel and not too dry. Herbert got a lot of them from the shop. They were free gifts. The one he handed to Hugh had only a few more days to go before starting to smell. Hugh's wrists and neck were ringed with black suds.

'When you wash clean, Hugh, I'll hand you a dry towel. Not before. A kid would wash cleaner than you do!'

'There's such a thing as paying too high a price for a dry towel. I'll put plenty of soap on.'

'You gave the bucket a good wash.'

'We ought to have a bathroom. I'd have a good wash then.'

'Who'd wash the bathroom?'

'Let the rain in.'

Hugh took his shirt off. He held it in his hands, examining it, whistling perplexedly as he fingered the dirtier parts of it.

'Good wheatfield going to ruin on those cuffs. If hard times come we'll follow up that idea. I've seen allotments on the side of the mountain with less dirt than there is in this shirt.'

'Pity whoever'll have to wash it.'

'I read somewhere pity was the rust on the hinges of the human intellect.'

'You read the wrong things.'

'We don't pick what we read. The books are set for us. We got to read them or pip.'

'You won't pip, will you Hugh?'

'Me? No. I can't fail. I'll have a good time when I'm forty.'

Hugh stood in his vest, collecting what books he needed and packing them into a worn leather satchel that had lost all its original shape. College was his next step, and college students used cases, not satchels. The satchel bulged with the books he had put in, history textbooks for the most part. They had bulk if not truth.

He fastened the satchel straps as best he could. He had had the straps repaired countless times. He hoped they'd hold. If they didn't and those books went tumbling into the gutter, he doubted whether he'd have the moral courage to pick them up again. He shook the teapot to see if there was any tea left. It was empty. He went upstairs to get a clean shirt.

Herbert finished off the flakes by lifting the glass dish to his lips and draining off what milk there was left. He opened a drawer in the china-laden sideboard and took out a newly-laundered white shop-coat. He handled it carefully with a bare minimum of fingering to obviate stains and any disturbance of the creases. Herbert had a virgin's fondness for pure white. The black suit he had worn at the funerals of his father and mother had depressed him far more than either of the deaths.

He shared Alf's indifference to death. To Herbert the dying of human beings resembled the depletion of the shop's stock. If the shopkeeper had gumption, without which he may as well jump in the canal and play ducks and drakes with the barges, he'd see to it that the stock was renewed and worsened or improved as the demands of the business required. Herbert placed the coat in a small attaché case. He fastened the clips of the case expertly, both at once. Alf's head was sunk down on his chest. He was stroking with his right hand the cuts and callouses of his left. He spoke to Herbert without lifting his head.

'You make too much fuss of Hugh. He doesn't like it. You ought to know that.'

'Somebody's got to look after him. Would you?'

'No. I don't think so. I find looking after myself is a job that gets beyond me.'

'There you are then.'

'You're acting father, that's it.'

'As far as Hugh's concerned.'

'You were cut out to be a father, Herb. I can't think of anything worse to tell you.'

'That's praise, only you don't know it.'

'I didn't, or you wouldn't have heard it.'

There was a pause. Herbert took his coat and waistcoat from a clothes-hanger and put them on. He brushed a final gloss on to his hair, brushing lightly and delicately to avoid having any loose strands of hair falling on his shoulders. His hair was naturally dry and brittle. It had a tendency to fall out. The passing of five years would see him more than thin on the top.

He stood in front of the mirror for half a minute, staring at himself, pulling his chin in and straightening himself. Alf wondered how often Herbert had done that and what was the point of it. He noticed that Herbert had the deliberate pontifical look he always had when he had something to say. Alf waited for him to say it.

'Look Alf … '

'Aye.'

'About your job.'

'What about it? I got a feeling I know what you're going to say.'

'You finished working your notice yesterday?'

'I know. Though I didn't remember it when I woke up. Sleep puts a fellow off his guard.'

'You're unemployed from today on.'

'Don't make it sound so bloody pitiful. It doesn't hit you. People keep on buying groceries whether the pits are open or not.'

'It's pretty serious for you.'

'More serious than you imagine.'

'You should have taken that factory job Uncle Henry found for you in London. It was good of him to put himself out for you like that. He said there'd be a slump in the coal business.'

'He said that after he'd taken his investments from the pits here and sunk them in that factory. Uncle Henry! There's a smarmy old sod for you! But I forgot. You like him. You would. Well I don't. I'd rot before I'd go to London. I told Uncle Henry just exactly what he could do with his job and if he did, he must still be having a painful time of it.'

'He's got a good head.'

'And what lies under it is probably the same stuff as they sweep off the roads and put on gardens. When I get a new set of nails in my shoes, I'll trample on his face.'

'That sort of talk never got anybody anywhere.'

'That sort of uncle never got anybody anywhere. But what are we worrying about anyway? The pit might start again soon. You know how these managers are. They get frightened when they lose a market and sit down and wait for the end.'

'I was talking to the manager last night. He's president of the tennis club. We had a yearly meeting last night. He was there. He gave a guinea.'

'Robbing Peter to pay the tennis club.'

'He's leaving the district.'

'For good?'

'He's got a new job in Scotland. Same company.'

'What did he say about our pit?'

'It won't open again.'

'He said that?'

'I was standing right next to him.'

'You might have had the decency to stand further away from the fellow than that. Well, if he said that, it must be true.'

'So you'll be unemployed for a spell.'

'That's what I was thinking. What do you suggest I ought to do about it? Start wasting my shoe leather tramping about the other pits asking for a start?'

'You'll be spending quite a lot of time in the house.'

'That's likely.'

'The house is pretty dusty.'

'I'd noticed that.'

'I'd been thinking of getting a girl in to do the cleaning. A young girl. Two days a week. Pay her about half a crown.'

'You should have made it three days and brought it up to three bob. Then she could really have started furnishing the house.'

'There's no need for you to laugh at everything I say.'

'It isn't what you say, Herb, it's the way you say it. You tell me the simplest bloody things as if you're letting me in on a secret. That must be the tone you use when you tell your customers the price of bacon is up again.'

'The price of bacon is not up again.'

'It will be. No, Herb. I wasn't laughing at you. That's my way. You're too touchy. It's those people you knock about with. They make you like that. Bank clerks and managers and typists. Pansies and half-wits, the lot of them. I've often thought if there was some way of letting off a bomb under that tennis pavillion, it would be a damn good way of celebrating May Day ... Go on, get a girl. It'll be all right to hear a girl's voice in this house

— 57 —

again and there'll be a bit of shape on the place. It's looking like a pawnshop.'

'But I was thinking. You'll be in all the time.'

'Are you trying to tell me the kid wouldn't be safe in the house? That's a nice way to talk. I'm no Mormon. If Methodism was good enough for the old man, it's good enough for me. I may be a little loose when the mood's on, but that's only when there's no rain or dew on the grass and everything's dry. I got a girl anyway. Don't forget that.'

'I didn't mean it that way. I wasn't looking at it from that point of view.'

'When you weren't doing that, Herb, you were safe in the shawl.'

'The girl would have to be paid.'

'There are people around here keeping girls without paying them. But let's say we are more honest.'

'We'll say that. But with you unemployed we won't have as much money coming in, will we?'

'That's true. Unless they give one pound ten on the dole to bring it up with what I was earning in the pit and that's about as likely as that preacher up the road there kicking God from his pulpit.'

'The payments on that furniture we bought come pretty heavy.'

'That was your idea, not mine. This is the only room downstairs I ever use.'

'It makes the home look better, doesn't it?'

'Only a war could have made it look worse than that horsehair stuff we had before.'

'With you out of work I'll have to make all the payments myself.'

'Do that and you can keep it. That'll be some satisfaction. When you get married that'll be the beginning of a home for you.'

'Thank you, Alf.'

'Thank the colliery company. It's they are putting me on the insurance, damn them.'

'But the payments will come a bit heavy for a bit. We might not be able to afford a girl to do the housework.'

'That's so. I can't decide who's the unluckiest. The girl who won't get the job or us poor devils who'll have to live here without her help.'

'I was thinking … Now that you'll have so much time on your hands, you could do a bit of cleaning and tidying.'

'Wait a minute, Herbert. I don't want to miss this. You mean you want me to be a skivvy?'

'Just keep the place in order.'

'Wash dishes, for instance?'

'If you like.'

'Make meals?'

'That would be fine.'

'Make beds?'

'That would be a real help.'

'Scrub floors?'

'Mm.'

'You go to hell. For eight years and more I've worked underground. That's the trade I know. That's finished with, it seems. It's a pity, but it's happening to thousands. It doesn't qualify me as a housemaid. I've got pride, more pride than you, though it doesn't show in the same places. So, until I find another job, I'll just look around and take it easy.'

'All right. I thought it was a good idea. That's the only reason I had for mentioning it.'

'It was a good idea all right. Only trouble was that it was born too soon. Put it back where you found it and let it ripen.'

Hugh came down from upstairs. Herbert's shirt and collar fitted him well. He had taken special care to get the collar to sit properly. The expression on his face lay midway between pride, bewilderment and regretful self-consciousness. Alf examined him.

'Dressed up like that, it's a safe bet you'll end up in a horseshow or a meeting of the Baptist Union.'

'That's what I thought.'

'You'll pass.'

Hugh took his satchel under his left arm and went through the door. Herbert put on his hat, a slate grey velour, picked up his case and followed him. The shop he managed was not far from Hugh's school.

Alf did not move from his chair for ten or fifteen minutes after they left. Through the window he could see a branch of the apple tree next door. It had come to blossom. Hugh had called the blossom beautiful. He had read out a verse of poetry to prove it, but it was the wrong verse and proved nothing.

Alf was thinking that in a few days, around about the middle of May, the blossoms would fall and then there'd be a devil of a mess on the ground around about. In all these pretty things there was a catch somewhere. There was Gwyneth. Pretty, but all the same, she had skin that looked like the wax of a candle, and spat blood into her handkerchief.

The kitchen was very quiet. Alf wondered if the following day, and the day after, would be just like this. Most likely. There was nothing to make them any different. He rubbed his stockinged feet on the hearth mat to make a noise, but the noise he made was so like silence he gave it up. Outside, on the back paving, a cat was pushing an empty salmon tin around.

Alf got up from his chair, sharply. He wanted something to do, badly. He felt like digging a garden. There was no garden to dig. The patch at the back of the house was a lawn. During his father's lifetime chickens had been kept there. There was, it was said, some element in the soil that bound the chickens up tighter than a cask and interfered with their laying. Alf had suggested kicking them in the rear until they got more fertile, but his father would not hear of coercion or unkindness in any shape or form. There was, he said, something to be admired in every creature that was awake at the very first peeping of the dawn. When the old man died the chickens had been dispensed with, the fences taken down and the cots burned.

Alf roamed from one room to the other. He rubbed his hands together. His callouses were itching. He had noticed that they did this often whenever he was at a dead end in anything. As he walked he kept his eyes on the floor. He wanted to avoid looking at either the furniture or the pictures on the wall. The thoughts they gave him tasted nasty. His stockinged feet gave out no sound on the linoleum or the mats. He padded like a cat.

He thought he'd go out on to the back paving and have a turn at nosing around the salmon tin. It might give him some ideas about a new job. He returned to the kitchen to put his shoes on. He recalled what he had said to Herbert about having pride. He thought now that that was a pretty foolish thing to have said. There was no sense in it. What did he have to be proud about? Not much. Not very much.

He took the food from the kitchen table into the pantry. He put it down any shape, on the first empty space on the first shelf that came to hand. He felt as if he was betraying himself. That was only a pang. He forgot it as he looked more closely at the shelves in front of him and saw the chaos of them; a trail of white sugar from a split sugar bag over a half eaten joint of beef; a jam jar leaning on its side and in danger of spilling the contents over a wedge-shaped slice of American cheese on a plate that was stamped with enough dark, distinct fingermarks to keep the police forces of two continents busy for a twelvemonth; a half dozen empty cornflake packets, taking up a lot of room that couldn't be spared in that dark corner behind the door; three or four of Herbert's toothbrushes, worn thin and discarded, but never thrown out. Alf cleared them out. He arranged the food in orderly heaps and deliberate groups. He got some satisfaction from it.

He poured some hot water into a bowl. He soaped it profusely, working up a thick lather with his hands. He turned his shirt collar down and washed himself. Then he washed all the dirty dishes he could find. Alf discovered the pattern of them only after he had cleaned them. As he proceeded to wipe the second bowlful of dishes, his expression was meditative, as if he were trying not to commit himself too deeply to the job he was doing.

With the dishes out of the way, he sat down again. He was still restless, but couldn't decide to get on with the cleaning he had begun. That would be selling out to Herbert. He stretched his hand behind the chair and groped for a portable gramophone that stood in the corner. Herbert had got the gramophone for a countless number of cigarette coupons. It was a harsh little instrument, unsteady and inefficient. It had driven Alf to say that the most harmful thing about smoking was the gifts you got with the coupons.

He pulled the gramophone up and put it on a chair by his side. The records, a dozen and no more, with torn covers and multicoloured labels, were on the sideboard. He picked out the noisiest tenor he could find, not because he liked tenors but the song the tenor was singing was about pagans, and he wanted to provide the hymn-singing Apostolic next door with as much competition as possible. The needle was not firmly fixed in the socket. It made the natural tremolo in the tenor's voice sound ten times worse. He sounded as if he were singing in a storm.

Alf knocked him off, for pity's sake. He kicked up the

corner of one of the coconut mats. Between the mats and the linoleum, sheets of newspaper were spread. The newspaper print could not be seen for the veil of dust, stamped with the pattern of the mat that overspread it. Alf decided, Herbert or no Herbert, pride or no pride, there was something to be said for keeping a place clean. He took the mats up. Of the newspaper he made a bundle and threw it on the fire. He hoped the flames would set the chimney on fire. That would bring the policeman out nosing and handing out summonses. That would suit Alf. It would be like a long, cool drink to him to cuss a policeman up in heaps.

He swept the floor violently. The dust clouds mounted like frightened horses. The kitchen was hot. Alf was sweating. He rubbed the dirt into his face. Being clean sickened him. He got the bucketful of lukewarm water. He splashed the soaked floor cloth over every inch of the stained, yellow-green linoleum. He washed even the legs of the table and the chairs. His trouser legs were soaking wet, but he didn't mind that. He wanted the place to smell like a soap factory. It was something to do; it was work. It would stop him developing piles sitting around street corners talking about Christ knows what with God knows who.

And if Gwyneth went ill and wanted some help around the house, he'd know how to give it. He lifted his trouser legs and wiped the water that streamed down his calf with the wrung floor cloth. Two streets away the church bells started to ring. Alf clenched his teeth and started a buzzing in his ears to keep out the sound of the church bells. He had no love for them. They made him think of Sunday mornings and empty streets … He hated empty streets.

He knew the bell ringer, a brainless, servile clodge of a man with shoulders rounded and mad to worship; an age-long inveterate blackleg and eater of toffees in paper.

The bell continued to ring. Somebody being mourned or buried or something. Alf wrapped the floor cloth around the bar of soap and plunged it in the water. He wanted to marry Gwyneth and bury the bell ringer. He hummed a piece of that song about pagans the tenor had failed to get through owing to that shake in the needle. He found himself off key. That was funny. Usually he hummed in tune. He didn't have his mind on the song … something new had come into his life. Being without a job. He was trying his best not to make up his mind about what he thought of it.

* * *

The Labour Exchange was a church hall. The windows were Gothic, its paintwork faded green, and its general layout a series of angular errors. It had been built through the good offices and chequebooks of three men. The late colliery manager who had worn his moustache from ear to ear and used it as a measuring rule, had starved his wife and noted in his memobook the exact sum he had saved by doing so, and would willingly have bought a new memobook in which to note down the exact sum he'd have saved by starving the whole of humanity. Had he had the chance he'd have done that willingly. Himself he had never starved. He had imagined himself as the central point in British coal production and responsible for the maintenance of glowing hearths up and down the land. His stomach had been of such a size as to justify that thought. With his whiskers and his waddle he had bestridden the community like a roosting Pasha, putting the fear of God into children and the fear of the sack into their elders, thus being one of the first men ever to put God in a sack and use it to beat all sense and powers of resistance from the heads of his employees.

The second of the church hall founders was a bailiff, a clever, oily and opportunist fellow who had shed his scruples with his milk teeth. In the slaughterhouse of South Wales he was the first slaughterer. He wore yellow gloves. Some said he wore them to dazzle his victims. Others made the reason the desire to hide the blood that stuck to his fingers in the course of smashing up a minimum of two houses a week. For every five families he evicted, he contributed a guinea to the building fund of the Cottage Hospital. He had a tortured, ill body and thought he might need the hospital one day. Otherwise he would have sunk his contribution in new houses for people, at higher rents, whom he had driven from their original homes. The hospital had named a ward after him. They were still seeking his permission to name a new disease after him.

The third of the founders was another local boy who had made good by buying goods to sell at a profit. He had made a fortune and wore it as clumsily as a small boy wears his father's trousers. He was a leading speaker in religious conferences but not because he was sympathetic to religion. He couldn't be. He had sold so many things as bacon which he knew had never seen the inside or outside of a pig, that he had grown to suspect that by the same law of dissimulation, the Holy Ghost might turn out to be none other than the hairy butt-end of a rat's tail. But he saw that the people who assembled, for better or for worse or just the free tea, in religious conferences, had a large and powerful say in determining the philosophy of the masses, which should be, as he saw it, just enough as was necessary to give the masses a love of humble stability, and a consciousness of the fact that their grocery account books should be kept clean, paid up, fastened with a bit of string, hung up on the same hook where it could be found and never used as toilet paper until the last page had been filled. His best speech, kept in mothballs during the winter months, rehearsed privately during the spring and scattered like patent manure over South Wales from July to the end of August, was one which referred to Wales as 'the gallant little heart of Britain'.

He had once said 'sweetbread' instead of 'heart', but had withdrawn that on the advice of the man who managed his dairy department, as being too technical, especially for his vegetarian admirers, who were many, the mass of his customers being too poor to buy meat, except when a pit pony was taken from the pit to die and be sliced up at three ha'p'orth a pound. He went on to say that the valves of the little heart were the men of public vision and enterprise, (himself, the bailiff and the manager) who, giving the metaphor a wry neck, a north eye and a limp, were the medicated paraffin that flowed through the bowels of the South Wales proletariat keeping them sweet and wholesome.

These men were the triumvirate upon whose social activities three-quarters of the community's misery was founded and upon whose charities the church hall had been built.

Political meetings had always been banned from it. The vicar's consent was necessary before it could be used and he had laid down that only activities conducive to the spreading of happiness among the poor could find a place in the church hall. In that way the church hall had won its position as the largest single opium den in the western half of the world. Hallelujah oratorios and cretinous children's cantatas, staged for the benefit of this chapel or that, had been performed there plentifully, each performance chipping off with sharp-edged precision a good inch of the town's political consciousness, each of the inches being presented in turns as a triumphant little keepsake to the three patriarchal founders as a tribute to the strategical gifts they had shown to realise the kingdom of Heaven on Earth.

The vicar had not demurred when the government converted the hall into a Labour Exchange. Three thousand men, drawn from a two mile radius, signed there. The vicar said that this was the finest use to which the hall had ever been put. He conceived of the dole as a great spreader of happiness. The vicar had known only one intellectual doubt in the course of his life. This was when he doubted his possession of an intellect, a doubt which had remained with him, giving his face a puzzled, lost-on-the-mountain look that was construed by his parishioners as saintliness. So, having accommodated himself in the body of coal-capitalism he was the sort of optimist who would credit a swarm of plague-ridden rats with spreading happiness.

There was another element that determined the vicar's attitude to the use of the church hall as a Labour Exchange. He was the son of a labourer. He had grown up from boyhood to believe that there was some natural correspondence between excessive labour and low wages. His father's toil had been so excessive as to make him stoop like a victim of curvature. That had been just as well, because his father's wages were so low it would have been impossible to count them standing up straight. It had always been necessary to get very close to the floor to get them in the right perspective.

On entering the church the vicar had found himself getting three or four times what his father had earned doing a hundredth part of the work his father had performed. That had troubled him. His living was the gift of a class to which he was a stranger, but his conscience was the product of the class from which he had sprung. Each tried to vomit the other out of its system and the poor vicar found himself as often as not roasting on a spit kindled by that struggle.

He saw the work he did as being too small, the salary

he got for it too high. He had played with the idea of digging his parishioners' gardens. The parishioners had rejected that. It put their domestic lives under surveillance. They admired the church only from a distance. Later, he had speculated on handing back some part of his salary to the church. The elders of the church had opposed that with tooth, nail and edicts. It was impossible, they said, to detect anything godly in a man who didn't earn three or four times as much as they did. Moreover he had married the fast and frivolous daughter of a tradesman, who developed hyperthyroid tendencies and was cursed with a desire to keep on changing the furniture. This weakness took up all he earned and a little more on the side borrowed from her father.

The last of the vicar's doubts vanished with the coming of large-scale unemployment. As little as he did for his salary, he now saw thousands of men trooping three days a week into the church hall and getting what seemed to be enough to live on (hyperthyroid symptoms apart) for actually doing less work than composing a sermon. The vicar plastered that fact like a healing ointment over the red, painful dermatitis that beset his conscience, and in the fullness of time his conscience was healed and proof against the cowardly temptation to look at things in the light of abstract justice. He hauled the name and substance of Unemployment Insurance on high. He set it beside the Trinity and worshipped all four as the motive forces of what good there is on earth.

* * *

Inside the Exchange, Alf completed the formalities of his first signing. He did it dourly, either growling or snapping the replies he made to the clerk's questions. The clerk was a slight, sandy-haired, cheerful fellow. He had been unemployed himself before getting the clerking job. He was sympathetic.

Alf turned away from the box. There were four queues of men waiting to sign. The closing down of Alf's pit had meant a big influx of custom. Two or three younger clerks were rushing about hurriedly with forms in their hands. Alf made his way round them, glancing, as he walked, at various notices concerning new employment and bits of regulations that hung on the wall. He promised himself to read them one day. One day when the light wasn't so bad and the print of the notices was bigger. Men suffering with pit-blindness would never get to know the regulations. Alf thought it would be funny never to get the hang of this dole business, to be in it, say, ten years, and still be doing things arse-backwards.

The windows of the hall were unwashed, murky. One or two lights were burning above the clerks' heads. There was a notice requesting silence in one of the far corners. The notice seemed to have got under the men's skin. In that corner the noise was deafening. There was an argument going on. Everybody was talking. Alf could only see one fellow listening. He was wearing a fading yellow seaman's jumper and had a wooden leg. He used the wooden leg to hammer home the other people's points. Alf wanted to see exactly how he did it. He had never realised that a wooden leg could be lifted. He paused to watch. A stout clerk with a protruding pair of lips and a house-proud expression told him to keep moving outward if he didn't mind, because the place was getting more congested than a lungful of phlegm. Alf looked at the clerk's watch chain which was almost big enough to make the clerk's waistcoat look like a slave pen had it not been for the man's manifest self-satisfaction.

Alf muttered that he couldn't get out of the bloody place fast enough, if it was all the same to them. The clerk said that was enough of that. The Exchange superintendent opened the door of the ante-room where he was installed. The superintendent was a tight, short individual with a broad parting in the middle of his hair, gold-rimmed spectacles, spats on his shoes and a Civil Service voice. He had spent years clerking about in the Health Department of the County Hall before graduating to the superintendency. The lines of his face were those of an autocrat, a little autocrat who had got his ideas on authority from reading lives of the Russian Emperors, but in his eyes there was fear and distrust of the men who filed through the Exchange three days a week.

He pointed his finger at the far corner where the noise was. According to what he had read of despots, this should have produced the effect of silence. It did not. The argument in the corner became more complicated. There was a search going on for the fellow who had started it to see if he could do anything to get it straightened out. The superintendent stamped on the floor, making the fountain pens in his waistcoat pocket to tremble. He wore rubber soles. The stamp accomplished nothing. He tried shouting. The first shout went wrong. His throat seemed to be full of blotting paper. He tried again, with a clear throat. He asked what they thought the place was, a bear garden? The man with the wooden leg said yes as loudly as he could. The superintendent went back into his ante-room. He sent out a lean young clerk with a submissive face, fresh from the School Certificate class, to deal personally with the arguers.

Alf recognised a lot of men he knew in the queue. Most of those who had been unemployed a long while were reading newspapers, three or four squinting at each copy, some reading aloud, others mumbling, others staring. One man, taller than those around him, with a red, broad, happy face, wearing a white muffler loosely, and the coat, waistcoat and trousers of three different suits making him look like a meeting of friends, was reading in a strained, piping voice, a report of a banquet that had been thrown the night before at the Guildhall. His voice came down, hard and suddenly, like a passionate, unpremeditated kiss, upon any word connoting luxury. Somebody asked him didn't he ever stop thinking of his guts. Somebody else shouted to him to shut his bloody mouth or they'd all be trying to be Mayor.

Alf grinned. The big man's voice did not stop. Alf found his way to the door. Outside the Exchange was a courtyard. It was covered with gravel and dangerous to slip on. Flanking one of the walls were four trees, stunted, miserable and sapless in appearance. They looked as if they only needed the gift of motion to make them swing into line with the army of unemployable and file into the church hall to do their signing. The bark of their trunks was scrofulous and gashed deeply with a legion of initials cut out idly by men waiting their turn in the queue and taking shelter from the rain. About their leaves there was a suggestion of yellow undernourishedness.

He left the trees alone. He decided that wretchedness, in plants as well as in men, was a predetermined and necessary element. The trees had been planted during the war by the local Volunteer Reserves, to commemorate the valour of the local Volunteer Reserves. Those Reserves had been the only laughable thing that had ever happened in the courtyard of the church hall. They were tradesmen running to stomach, and elderly teachers drunk for the most part with cheap history readings. They were a comical undisciplined crew. Their instructor had been an ex-sergeant major, a rheumaticky dotard whose military experience went back to the time of the Roman invasion, when he had betrayed Caractacus to the enemy, developing, with the upward march of history, into being the town's leading flag-wagger on all royal occasions or whenever there was a flag to wag. He had passed out during a royal visit. He had a flag-pole stuck in the middle of his waistcoat for two hours under a hot sun. He had been struck down by a fit.

Alf passed through the courtyard. Under the trees, Bob was waiting, Bob was the nature-lover who lived over the road from Alf. He had worked in the same place as Alf. They had finished together. They passed through the gates that led out from the courtyard. They turned left up a stony lane. The queue of waiting men stretched the length of this lane, four or five deep.

Bob was taller than Alf. He wore a grey suit with very narrow trousers, which, with his thinness, made him look like a stepper. Grey was the colour of his eyes and skin. His nose was hooked, prominent and blue-veined. His way of walking betrayed his love of silence. He stooped as if preparing not to listen to something. Whenever he raised his eyes from the ground and watched the people or buildings they passed, it was with a contemplative disgust. Whenever he did so, he spat away the little spittle there was around his lips.

Bob had never been a Christian or a drinking man. There was a dryness about his person from top to bottom. His voice when he spoke sounded like the crackling of twigs beneath the feet of a solitary walker in an empty wood. His voice when he sang was even sadder. it had been known to make people look around for the corpse.

At the end of the lane the two friends turned right and began descending the hill that led down into the town. By 'town' was meant that fraction of the town that was built on the flat. One street of shops, bordered by two streets of houses culminating on the east side in a square where were situated the town's largest buildings. Those buildings had been built mainly at the turn of the century in the pure passionate morning of super-profits in the coal industry. They were infamously ugly, their buildings having been concerned to convince the world that their way of doing business was going to last for ever and a judgment day. The buildings were prolific of high rateable values, obscure bailiffs' offices where money-lending transactions took place, filled with clerks of petty-bourgeois leanings and ladies' hairdressing salons of shady status. The centre of the square was given over to a public lavatory with a flat roof on which the judges and other officials sat whenever the town had a carnival.

Alf felt in his pocket. He found some liquorice sweets that had fallen through the lining. He handed two to Bob, telling him to dust the tobacco from them. Bob put them into his mouth undusted. He said liquorice and tobacco mixed were good for the stomach. Alf said God help, removed the tobacco crumbs from the sweets he had kept for himself, then threw both crumbs and sweets into the gutter.

'What d'you do that for, Alf?'

'What?'

'Throw those lossins into the gutter like that?'

'I'm going off sweets for good.'

'Thought you liked them.'

'I do. I used to eat as much as two bob's worth a week. Can't do it now. Got to make this bloody dole last as long as possible.'

'Worrying about that already?'

'Not exactly ... D'you see that gang up there this morning?'

'Thousands of them.'

'Never thought there was so many.'

'We live and learn.'

'Call that living?'

'It's learning.'

'What a bloody thing to learn! Thousands of them. Thank God we weren't at the end of that queue.'

'That's the only thing we got to thank God for so far. It's a pretty small mercy.'

'Too small to make a fuss about.'

'Mm.'

Bob went into a public lavatory. But Alf waited outside looking at a bus timetable that was framed on the lavatory wall. A man in his fifties wearing an old bowler, a dark suit and sloppy shoes, came up to him. He asked Alf the way to a place eight miles up the valley. Alf pointed to a bus standing in the square. He told the man to take it. It would get him to the place in about twenty minutes.

'Hell. No,' said the man. 'You might as well ask me to buy the bus as take a ride in it. I haven't got a penny.'

'Neither have I, my friend.'

'You better take the bus.'

'Is that a joke?'

'Take it as you please.'

'I'll laugh at it later on.'

The man pulled his bowler further down on to his brow and smiled.

'These last two days I been looking about a bit.'

'There's nothing much to see about here.'

'I've been walking from Monmouthshire.'

'Monmouth as bad as here?'

'Worse.'

'God help.'

'People are more lively here.'

'They would be if they had a chance. What are you doing walking all that distance?'

'Looking for work.'

'You won't find any here.'

'Funny. I remember a time when you couldn't see these valleys for work. You only had to open your mouth and you had a job.'

'Open your mouth now and you lose your job.'

'As bad as that?'

'The exchange is up there on the top. Go take a look at it. It's like shearing day on a bloody sheep ranch. When they get the shearing finished they'll get enough wool to go round everybody's eyes.'

'Don't tell me to look at a Labour Exchange. The damn things have been making me sick for the last three years. But for real luxury you have to go to the casual ward of a workhouse.'

'Bad?'

'Hell. Look at my hands.'

'They're blistered.'

'That's for chopping wood at two workhouses. What for? A lousy bed and slices of bread and marge thicker than the mattress I slept on. And a mug of cocoa. I mustn't forget the cocoa. Judging by the taste in my mouth it'll never forget me.'

'You should have stuck to the dole. It's easier.'

'I'm hoping my luck will turn. What's left of my family's in this valley somewhere.'

'Hope you'll find them, chum.'

'Which way's it to that place I told you?'

Alf pointed out the road. Without a word of parting the man in the bowler sloped off. He looked very respectable from the back. Alf took it for granted that there was something wrong with him.

Bob came slowly out of the lavatory.

'What you been doing all the time in there, Bob? Having a penn'orth?'

'Thinking.'

'That's some place to think.'

'It was empty and quiet. The sight of those white porcelain stalls always get me thinking.'

'What about?'

'Everything ought to be white like those stalls.'

'You can't turn the whole place into a bog-house. People got to eat and sleep and work somewhere.'

'I know. That's a pity that is. Then I start thinking about Carmarthen and the country. That's where I was born.'

'Never been there.'

' 'S alright in the country, Alf, honest. Wish I was back there.'

'Why'd you come away?'

'My father came. I was just a kid.'

'There was better money here. He was right to come. I reckon that people who work on farms are slaves. Rotten wages, no pleasures, nothing. Early to bed and out of the bloody thing you get before you've had time to go to sleep. And three times to chapel on Sunday. That's some life. Your old man did right to come here.'

'I wonder what he'd say if he saw all these pits closing down?'

'Whatever he said they'd keep on closing them down. The blokes who own them are either deaf or living in London.'

'What if all the pits close?'

'They'll turn every house into a Labour Exchange.'

'People won't stand for that.'

'They'll stand for anything. You saw them this morning. We get used to it. In a couple of months we'll have forgotten about work, and we'll be gabbling and laughing just like those other chaps.'

'No. If all the pits close, people'll get fed up. They'll start going back to the fields they came from.'

'What good will that do them?'

'They'll be safe.'

'You can go to the cemetery and be safe.'

They entered into the street of shops. On the corner there was a conclave of older tradesmen, all hatless and looking very busy, discussing the week's events. They were, to all intents and purposes, the Chamber of Trade, and the week had brought them nothing to discuss except the closing down of the main colliery. Their main conversation, judging by appearances, was dismal. One of them was speaking about the turning of the tide. The rest looked as if the tide was cold and already up to their chins, freezing from their minds all hope of it receding. Alf pointed to them.

'What'll you bet that half of those won't be sold up for rates inside a year?'

'They'll get on the council and there won't be no rates.'

'Carmarthen is just the right place for you, Bob. They can't all get on the council. The council isn't Barry Island. There's only room for about thirty on it.'

'Right'o. Why shouldn't they all be sold up then? They've done alright out of us. They can't grumble.'

'They all grumble though, and they'll grumble altogether. That's why people listen to them. We grumble the wrong way. We do it behind our hands or under the bedclothes. Nobody listens. No wonder we get in a hell of a mess … I don't like this street. What are we doing here? Do you want anything, Bob?'

'Aye bacon. Half a pound. Lean.'

'Why don't your missus do the shopping? I bet you'll bring the wrong kind of bacon and get a row.'

'That's right, too. She's busy today.'

'What at?'

'Getting boots and old clothes for kids whose fathers been on the dole a long time.'

'She still on that game?'

'What do you mean, game?'

'Nothing.'

'She's gone to Cardiff. Some people down there been collecting packets of old clothes to send up the valleys.'

'More germs than charities in those packets.'

'They're washed. Lily seen them being washed.'

'Don't believe it. There's a kid next door but one to us. He got an old suit. It was dirty when he had it. It only started to fit him when he put some of his own dirt on it to fill up the gaps. Even now he looks as if he's crawled into it from below. He wasn't a shapely kid to start off with and now not even his old man will nod to him on the road.'

'You can't blame Lily. She does her best. She's off all day and night.'

'I'm not blaming her, Bob. I'm talking about principles. That's the safest thing to talk about in this street. Talk about something else and the shopkeepers board their fronts up and expect a riot … How do you know what diseases come around to us in these parcels of clothes? Maybe it's part of a plan. Maybe they think that a valley full of people out of work is a damn nuisance that ought to be put a stop to. So they decide to thin the ranks by filling us full of new diseases. You ought to mention that to Lily.'

'She wouldn't listen. You know how she is. She thinks she's doing good.'

'As long as me and a couple more don't think so, we got a fighting chance of coming out alive.'

'Here's the shop. Bacon. Eightpence and tenpence. Dear. Now if I was living in the country there wouldn't be prices like that. You kill the pig and you get it for nothing.'

'You get it for nothing here, too, if you kill the shopkeeper.'

'I got to get it lean. Lily'll send it back if it isn't lean.'

'The eightpenny looks the leanest. Tell Lily it's the tenpenny and spend the tuppence on fags.'

'Do you think the eightpenny's lean enough?'

'You worry about that bacon as if it's a new kid you're having. Can't you eat fat bacon?'

'It isn't me. Lily likes it lean for Roger.'

'The lodger?'

'Aye. He can't stand fat bacon.'

'No wonder. He's the nearest approach to white bacon I've seen. Is he still working?'

'He finished same time as us. Everybody's finishing. It's only the rats they're leaving in that pit.'

'They better stay there. No dole for them.'

'Will Roger get any compensation for his leg?'

'No. The company's handing everything over to the banks.'

'And Roger's gammy leg gets lost in the post.'

'That's it.'

'I didn't see him in the Exchange.'

'He signs this afternoon. He's in Cardiff with Lily this morning.'

'With Lily! He takes your wife to Cardiff and you come down here worrying your guts out whether the bacon you're getting for him is lean enough. That's free trade that is. You'll be losing Lily one of these days. You've spent too much time looking at trees, Bob. You believe in the spring. You think things may change, but they'll be the same as ever a year from now. They won't. People are not trees. They never come back to where they started. They can never find their way back.'

'I don't follow you, Alf. Sometimes you talk like the Bible.'

'God help.'

'Honest you do. What you mean by saying "We're not trees and never come back"?'

'Roger's a snake. You ought to wrap something around his neck.'

'I thought of that. His neck's too big. I couldn't find anything big enough to go around.'

'You never thought of tying two things together.'

'Roger's not so bad when you get to know him, bumptious as he is. But he knows a lot and can manage people. He's a big help to Lily.'

'I'll bet he is.'

'He won't be long out of a job.'

'He's scraped the backside of everybody around here who's got jobs to give away. It's a wonder he stayed in the pit so long.'

They came up alongside a large, sombre, double-front

shop, 'Owens Millinery'. In the vestibule of the shop, rolls of matting and linoleums were stuck up for exhibition. A very tall man, bordering on sixty, with pince-nez and false teeth in constant view, stood in the vestibule stroking one of the rolls, looking very pleased with the feel of it. Alf jerked his finger at him.

'That's Owens. He's a bastard.'

'I don't know anything about bastards.'

'I'm saying he is.'

'Right'o.'

'He ought to have a roll of his own matting stuffed up his date.'

'You can't do that.'

'That what they said to the first fellow that ever died. It didn't stop him.'

'What are you stopping for. You don't want millinery. Come on, Alf.'

'Wait a bit. That's where Gwyneth works, in Owens.'

'Can you see her?'

'No.'

In the right-hand window of Owens' shop a girl was teasing into shape the flounces of the blouse worn by a dummy. The girl and the dummy might have been sisters. The dummy's lips were redder. But the wide open eyes, the waxiness and the suggestion of iron-starved immobility were the same in both. All the shops seemed to be empty of customers. The street itself was full, full of men like themselves parading back and fro incessantly, stopping in front of shop windows, partly to see their reflections, partly to look at goods the prices of which would have swallowed two weeks dole in one gulp, partly to rest their feet which were sick and tired and itching.

'Come on, Bob. Don't let's go back down that street or we'll be getting the habit like those fellows. I haven't felt as bad as this since I stood in the wet grass listening to the preacher praying for fifteen minutes when my mother was buried. If the grass didn't give you a cold, the preacher did … Somebody ought to put a bloody big gravestone over this street and start singing 'Lead Kindly Light'. It would keep off the rain and we could all go to sleep. Let's walk towards them streets on the mountain. There's a collection of fat cows up there that'll get you thinking about those fields and farms you knew when you were a kid.'

They made their way through a narrow, cobbled back street. At one part they had to squeeze through a small space between the scoured window-sill of a house and a GWR haulage cart. The carter was carrying boxes marked 'Condensed Milk. Sweden.' from the goods station on to the cart. Alf shouted across to him.

'Any chance of a start, chum?'

'Jesus Christ, no.' The carter gasped it out. He was too old for the job. He was doubled up over the box he was carrying. He looked as if he might be suffering with a hernia. Alf waved his hand to him and turned to Bob.

'He's bad, that chap. You can see that by him. But he won't give up till he drops down dead. I hope he lets us know when he does. It would be just the sort of job for us.'

From some of the houses they passed there was the sound of music; from others the sound of children, being fed, washed or leathered. From most of the houses there was only silence.

*　*　*

The County School Hugh attended looked very old without being so. The buildings in which the colliery companies kept their clerks and paid their employees looked much more solid and much more sumptuous. The school had looked dingy from the day of its foundation. There were so many self-made grocers, drapers, coal merchants and trade union officials on the County Council whose guiding axiom was that life is the best school and hardship the best university, that no public comment had ever been made on the fact that the County School looked more like the corner of a slum than the headquarters of higher education in the valley.

The stonework had the appearance of having been brought there against its will. The school was fronted with a patch of grass that had never been trimmed. This was called the lawn and served no purpose. It was planted with about forty fir trees, very small, with a suggestion of fright and embarrassment in their bearing. Fitted with caps and bags they'd have passed for new boys.

The windows of the school were high and many-paned. They were fitted with cords. There was something wrong with the mechanism the cords were supposed to operate. The windows never opened. One boy, who valued fresh air above culture and who, considering the school's general curriculum, wasn't far wrong, tried to hang himself on one of the cords as a protest against the lack of ventilation. He had been dissuaded and had later taken a diploma in Swedish drill.

Every six months the council's surveyor came round. He was a very old, abstracted sort of man. The boys called him Willie. His head was totally bald, and shinier than human flesh had a right to be. Every time he was led into every room by the assistant head, who invited him to try the ropes, to prove for himself that they didn't work. Willie would swing about on the ropes like a sailor while the boys laughed into their desks. Sometimes he'd caused a cord to snap, sometimes he'd give himself a crick in the neck, but never did he make any impression on those windows.

He'd say it was funny, but they had worked all right the first time he had tried them. That had been twenty years ago. Willie always wore the frock coat he had worn when the school was opened. He kept it on because he said it brought him good luck. The coat had been black. It was going green. Hugh believed that if Willie had been a bit shorter, and the grass a bit longer and the green on his coat a bit greener, Willie could get lost in the grass and never be seen again.

Hugh sat in his form-room. It was a small melancholy room. There was a big open grate, badly tarnished, taking up almost the whole of one side. During the winters when the fires were lit, the heat all went up the chimney. It had occured to many, during periods of cold, that the classes could conveniently be held in the grate and the rest of the room set on fire for warmth.

The walls of the room were in a bad condition. The cream-coloured plaster seemed to have been made without whatever it is that keeps plaster in place. It had crumbled away in large patches. Whenever Willie came, his attention was always drawn to it. He'd always say that the climate of this country was the builder's foe. Whenever there were boys in the room at the time of his visit, he'd turn to them and tell them never to forget that the rich suffered as well as the poor. Willie would end his visit by acting like an architect and surveyor. He'd take his umbrella, ram it against the wall and bring down a piece of plaster the size of his head, tell one of the boys to clean up the mess, then remark to the assistant head as he left that plastering was expensive when he was a boy and still was, whatever people might say about the County Council.

The two worst scars on the wall, deep, ugly and caused by Willie's prodding, reminded Hugh of a fellow he had seen lying on the side of the incline, up on the slack-tip after being dragged along by a journey of runaway trams, the flesh torn away from the thigh, showing the bone. These scars the caretaker had tried to hide from view by hanging pictures over them. One was a picture of Bishop

Morgan, the translator of the Bible into Welsh, looking as if he was only half-way through the translation. The other was a Hogarth print. It was broken away from the frame and curled up at the bottom.

Hugh had his chair propped against the wall beneath the portrait of Bishop Morgan. Between his shoulders and the wall he had fixed a copy of a history of modern Europe to stop the plaster sinking into his coat. By his side sat his friend, Lloyd, whose shoulders were nearly as wide as the armchair he sat on. Lloyd wore a dark suit, too big for him. His khaki shirt was too small for him. He left it unbuttoned at the neck. He wore a flowered tie, clumsily knotted, which made the collar of his shirt more shapeless than it might have been. His hair in the back fell over his collar. In the front it fell over his eyes.

Four of their classmates were sitting at their desks in the back of the room. One was mumbling, trying to memorise two stanzas of poetry he had underlined. He kept staring angrily at the others as if they were distracting him. The second was sharpening a pencil that was already sharp. He was killing time and he had already killed one inch of the pencil. At intervals he bent over the little pile of wooden splinters and powdered graphite and blew it towards Lloyd. Each time he did it Lloyd took a look at his trousers, brushed them carefully and asked him to blow it at somebody else for a change. The pencil sharpener, who had a weak mouth and a tidy collar, took no notice.

The third of the group, George, smaller than his companions, carrotty-haired, pouty-faced, depressed, impoverished-looking, was staring at the Hogarth print, as if it contained some reference to himself that he couldn't fathom. He had scarcely any eyebrows. His eyes were weak, watery and distrustful. He was past seventeen. He didn't look as if he had grown up. He had been on short rations throughout his adolescence. That hadn't helped him any. The fourth boy, Wilf, fitted himself into a corner. He was reading a detective novel. He held it up high, hiding his face. His hands were white, podgy. He was all hair-cream, rolls of fat and skin blemishes. His father was an accountant with a pull in Conservative politics.

Hugh was reading a French novel. The book dealt with a family of farmers whose land was going to pieces. Hugh was sorry for them and didn't seem to get into the swing of the story. He thought the author was a farmer himself and given to slowness or it might mean that he was to blame in giving a wrong meaning to some of the French words, and putting the story into a wrong light. That was the fault of the dictionary he used. It was small, abridged and cost two and six. Every word that involved a forward step for man was omitted. He and Lloyd had saved up to buy a good one, somewhere around the ten shilling mark. They had saved what they could of their pocket money for three weeks, and the ten shillings coming not an inch nearer, decided it would be just as easy on their pockets if they started to save for the vault of a bank, and contented themselves with the half-crown's worth of ommission they now used.

One of the characters in the novel was given to going around in a farm cart. Without the help of his dictionary, which had no help to give, Hugh had translated 'farm cart' as bath chair and wondered where the character had got his injuries from. The French master, who spent so much of his time referring to the University of Paris, where he had spent a year on the proceeds of a memorial scholarship, as his spiritual home, that he didn't have much leisure left over to teach anybody French, had a good big dictionary which would have given the boys all the encouragement they needed to get through their tests without consulting him.

He had refused to part with the dictionary. The

children of the working class, from the poorest mousehole of which he had sprung, were, according to him, either vandals or half-wits. Were he to hand his dictionary over to them it would probably come back in the form of two covers and the list of abbreviations at the end. He had been strengthened in this idea, not many weeks before, by catching Lloyd tearing handfuls of leaves from a school hymn-book to clean his shoes which he had dirtied playing football in the muddy, insufficient patch behind the school that served as a football field. Lloyd had asked him if he was expected to use his shirt. The French master had said why not.

Hugh tossed the French novel on to the window. They were all waiting for the mid-morning recess bell. There was about ten minutes to go. He started to whistle a melody of moonlight that had been a popular item with the workers' carnivals that had thronged the sunlit streets of the valley during the strike of 1926. The boy who was trying to memorise poetry sighed, as if this was the last straw, took his glasses off and put them on the desk in front of him.

'Sorry, Epsom,' said Hugh.

They called the boy with the spectacles 'Epsom' because he held that if a chap didn't always keep himself regular with opening medicine or two lots of prunes a day, he couldn't study a stitch. Hugh leaned forward. The book he had been leaning against dropped to the floor. He stood up and walked to the window.

'It's bad for you, Epsom.'

'What is?'

'Learning all that poetry. Worst thing out.'

'What's the matter with it?'

'Too rich for you. All rich foods are binding.'

'You're thinking about cheese.'

'What poem you learning?'

'Spenser.'

'You're talking about cheese! After forty pages of Spenser you'll be as tight as a cask. You'll need a fourpenny packet of salts a day to do anything with yourself.'

'Constipation isn't a joke, Hugh.'

'There aren't any jokes. It just depends where you are standing at the time. Ask Wilf.'

Wilf was the boy in the corner, the Conservative's son.

'Wilf ought to know. He's the only one here who looks as if he knows anything about rich foods. How about it, Wilf?'

'I'm all right,' said Wilf, sounding as if he was talking in his sleep at the bottom of a deep well.

'There you are,' said Epsom, beating with a thin index finger on the desk as if proving a point.

'I think poetry's bad for you,' said Hugh.

'That's daft. Because you don't like it … '

'Have you ever seen fairies, sprites?'

'Plenty.'

'You ought to take those glasses off for good and come back to normal. Where did you ever see them?'

'On the hillsides.'

'Where exactly?'

'In this valley, not a mile from here.'

'When?'

'Oh, I was a kid.'

'See? That was before the slump. They've had plenty of chance to starve to death since then. Look, Epsom. We can't keep cats around here any more, let alone fairies. What did they look like anyhow?'

'Women.'

'Nice women?'

'Better than I ever seen on the road.'

'You go to chapel. You're prejudiced. You don't walk on the right roads. You miss the nice women.'

'I tell you I saw them. They were playing.'

'Do you know what you saw?'

'Spirits.'

'Oh hell, no. They were the ghosts of women who used to work in the mines, before those Acts came in. You've read about them in that industrial history book. My grandmother was one of them. They used to saddle her just like a horse. She used to pull trams. She died like that. That's what you saw, Epsom. Ghosts. Women who had such lousy lives when they were living, they came back to make up for lost time.'

'Why should I see them and nobody else?'

'That's all these things you take to clear your inside. You're liable to see anything. When you're empty all the time.'

'I'll have the last laugh.'

'After what you'll have to go through to get it it won't be much pleasure.'

Epsom resumed his reading. Through the window, Hugh watched the caretaker striding about with the broom on his shoulder looking for somewhere to sweep. Hugh turned away and sat down again. He leaned towards Lloyd's chair and started to run his fingers over Lloyd's trousers. Lloyd grunted and pulled his chair away.

'Stop doing that, Hugh. You could fancy you're trying to get off with me, or something.'

'I was just feeling the stuff in your trousers.'

'I was afraid somebody would start getting anxious about that. It comes to something when a fellow can't wear a new suit without being pawed about as if he was a woman.'

'I wasn't pawing, honest, Lloydie. It's nice stuff. Best suit I ever seen on you .'

'Only one other you ever did see on me and that was shrunk when it heard the rain on the window. My mother bought it on a stall in the market. But this one's better.'

'No comparison, boy. You look as swanky as Wilf.'

'Who'd want to?'

'All you want now is a haircut.'

'I'll wait till the exam's over.'

'That's two months.'

'The barber in our street's having a slack time. I want to keep him busy for a week.'

'He'll probably adopt you and do a spreadover job of it.'

'A bit big this suit is.'

'Ready-made, eh?'

'No, it's my uncle's.'

'Your uncle's. Thought it was yours. Is he lending it to you?'

'No, he bought this suit to get married in.'

'It's pretty dark for a wedding, isn't it?'

'He's a pretty dark chap.'

'His wife dead or something?'

'No. She ran away to North Wales a couple of days before they were due to meet the preacher.'

'That's a queer thing to do.'

'She's got nerves. She's been funny ever since she was a kid. She must have been frightened of my uncle.'

'What did he do?'

'Oh, he's a cokum sort of bloke. He wanted to get married bad and he had the suit ready and some furniture bought and everything. He thought it was a pity not to get married just because Sarah had had a fit of twitching and taken a train to the place where she was born. So he looked around a bit to see if there was anybody else willing to marry him. He made some pretty good offers. To anybody who'd marry him inside a month he offered lifelong devotion. To anybody who'd marry him straight away without fooling about whether they loved him or not he offered a bonus on top of the devotion. But the girls must have been busy around that time. Nobody answered. So he got drunk for a week. When he got sober he tried to borrow enough money to go North and look for Sarah. Nobody'd lend him any. He sold his wedding suit to my mother for fifteen bob. He used that for train fare. If he finds her and decides to marry her up there, he'll send a pound to my mother and I send the suit back!'

'What's the chance you'll be able to keep it?'

'Don't know. He'll probably settle to marry Sarah just when the suit's starting to fit me.'

They heard quick steps coming along the corridor. Epsom, nearest the door, said, 'The boss!' Hugh got his book from the window sill, and put his head into it. Wilf slipped his novel into the desk and started to scribble on some blank foolscap paper in front of him. George, the boy with the ginger hair, did not bother to take his eyes off the Hogarth print.

The door was flung open. The headmaster, with one stride, was a yard and a half inside the room, fidgeting about on his feet and rolling his head from side to side as if he didn't want to miss anything. He was a man in his forties, restless, energetic. Outside school he was a lay preacher, using violent metaphors and quotations from the Early Church Fathers to propagate a mild socialism. His mouth twisted up slightly when he spoke. He pronounced every syllable and used many, taking much time over everything he said. He looked across at Hugh.

'You boys look very lazy.'

'Free period, Sir,' said Hugh.

'You are using it well, I trust?'

'Yes, Sir,' said Wilf, bending low over his scribbling, puckering his brow and poking his tongue out, trying to look as if he needed a rest. The head looked towards Wilf, pleased. He had latterly been in conference with Wilf's father. He had his eye on burying the Church Fathers in nameless graves and his mild socialism along with them, and joining the Conservative Association. That would bring him closer to promotion to a headmastership in some less barbarous part of the country where violent metaphors still had some novelty. He stepped backward towards the door, saying, 'Yes ... yes!' agreeing mainly with himself. He half closed the door and opened it again.

'I almost forgot, boys. Very important announcement. I want all the senior boys to assemble in the main hall after recess. We have a visitor. A real leader of Welsh thought. A man for whom I personally have much respect. He will advise you as to your future. He will speak on careers for those about to leave school. Very important. A leader of Welsh thought. Bring as many chairs into the hall as possible. Most of you can sit on the floor.'

Lloyd hadn't changed his position. His head was still drooping over his chest. He didn't like the headmaster. The headmaster didn't like him.

'What's the matter with you, Lloyd?'

'Nothing, Sir.'

'You're wearing a very hang-dog look.'

'I was reading this book.'

'Time enough for that when I've finished speaking. What's the matter with your hair?'

'A bit long, Sir, that's all, Sir.'

'Long! You'll be hiding the rest of the form shortly if it gets much longer.' The headmaster laughed, stagily, throwing his body back from the thighs. The headmaster stopped his laughter abruptly. He didn't believe in wasting too much of the precious sound. He had a notion that his style of laughing would go down well with the Conservative Association.

'Your hair makes you look disreputable, Lloyd. Why don't you comb it, boy? You know, we could probably manage to lend you a comb if it came to the worst.'

Wilf bestirred himself to join in the laughter again. No laughter came.

The headmaster went on, 'Yes, Lloyd. I advise you particularly to come into the main hall after recess. I cannot think of any boy in the school who stands more in need of advice about the future than you. Spruce up. Look respectable. Walk on life, or life will walk on you.'

Wilf scribbled that aphorism on his foolscap and nodded at the headmaster to show that he had taken it whole.

'That's all I have to say to you, Lloyd. Listen carefully to what our visitor has to say. Walk on life and use your comb.'

The headmaster slammed the door as he went out. The recess bell started to ring. Lloyd threw his book against the wall, savagely.

'Combs, uh? One day I'll use a comb on that bastard in a place where he won't like it.'

'It's all right, Lloydie,' said Hugh, 'don't pay any attention to the coon. One day he'll get so important he'll blow up and we'll help the caretaker sweep him down the sink.'

'Ever since he came to the bloody school, he's been on to me. What's a chap's hair got to do with the way he studies. I get ninepence a week pocket money. If he expects me to spend any of that on haircuts he got another thought coming to him fast. When he was my age I bet he went around with his hair in curlers. And as for this fat sow, Wilf ...'

Wilf took up his novel and got lost in it. Lloyd climbed over the front benches and knocked it out of his hand.

'Wilf, you're a fat sow.'

'What have I done now?'

'You know what you've done. Whenever that bloody maniac comes in here bawling and prancing, you side with him, don't you?'

'What's wrong with that? I'll do as I please. You can't

bully me, Lloyd. You get away.'

'Of all the podgy, rotten … Look, you. We're supposed to stand together. Don't suppose your old man told you that an injury to one is an injury to all. No. Your old man's too prosperous for that. He's probably the fellow that does all the injuring, I wouldn't doubt. When the boss comes in here and starts getting funny about the way I look, you laugh until you nearly bust. Perhaps he pays you for it, or strokes you on the head when he comes to supper with your old man. If he does, that just shows you got a good eye for business. But I don't like people laughing at me. When that headmaster does it he comes closer to having his stomach kicked than he thinks. But I don't do it, see. I want a reference off him, a good one. So I keep quiet. So you join in the laughing again and you can watch out for your stomach. The same goes for your old man. I don't like him either.'

Hugh took Lloyd by the arm.

'Come on, Lloydie, for God's sake. Recess'll be over by the time you finish chopsin'. Come on up the bog.'

They went out together. Epsom and George followed them. Wilf and the pencil-sharpener remained in the room, smiling self-consciously at each other.

The senior boys' lavatory stood on the fringe of the school yard, behind the main building. When Hugh and Lloyd got there, there were fifteen or twenty boys standing about inside, either smoking or trying to borrow cigarettes. Epsom had a full packet. He loaned some to Lloyd. Hugh had some of his own. George didn't smoke. He stood near Hugh, looking very forlorn, holding his neck stiffly, as if he had a boil beneath his collar. Lloyd was moping and frowning at some rhymes that had been scribbled on the whitewashed walls of the compartment against which he was leaning.

In the opposite corner was a group of five boys, big-framed, loutish, silent fellows, some spitting their phlegm at a target. The target was a spider's web, looking decayed and rumpled, hanging from a projection in the wall. The game was to shatter the fabric of the web with a direct hit. The marksmanship was bad. The wall, for a yard around the web was spattered. Every time one of the group started to spit, there was a steering away and a ducking of heads by his companions. Lloyd blew the smoke contemptuously from this mouth towards the smokers.

'What those fellows need is a lung disease and two spider's webs. Then they'd be happy!'

'They get the place a bad name,' said Hugh.

'We'll report them to Willie. He'll build them a special gob-gallery ... The bell gone yet?'

'About a minute to go.'

'I'll be glad to see this place a bit emptier. I remember a time when only about six fellows in the whole school used to smoke. That was in the days when all the chapels were full. God was on the side of the righteous because it was possible then to have a nice quiet chat up here. Now we're kept too busy scraping somebody else's phlegm out of our ears to know what anybody's talking about. I won't be sorry to leave.'

The bell rang, jerkily.

'That caretaker swings about on the bell-rope like an ape. Why don't he give the thing a smooth, even tug?'

The boys started to file out leisurely. Epsom dapped his cigarette and blew the black end of it carefully to make sure that it was dead. He put the stub in the inside pocket of his coat. He stretched his arms and yawned. His eyes were watery. He wiped them with his sleeves.

'When these exams are over I'll go to bed early again. I'm not sleeping so well these days. When I lie in bed with my eyes open, I get frightened like I used to when I was small.'

'P'raps there's a war coming that'll stop us getting old

so that we're having our second childhood in advance.'

'My mother bought me some nerve tonic for a week. It was too dear to go on buying it. She wrote away to the firm that makes it saying I was so improved she didn't recognise me. She thought that might get them to send a free supply. They didn't bite.' Epsom touched Lloyd on the shoulder.

'Coming down, Lloydie?'

'What for?'

'Hear the visitor, this leader of Welsh thought.'

'What about it, Hugh?'

'I don't think there's any such chap. Five fags to one it's just the boss with an artificial moustache and a disguised voice leading a double life or something. You going down, Epsom?'

'Might as well. I don't want to get into any rows.'

'No. That's right. He can't think any worse of me and Lloydie if we don't come down at all.'

Epsom went, wiping the smell of tobacco from his fingers with his handkerchief, a small piece of linen with a lace border and a hole in the centre. It was the only handkerchief Epsom had. Nobody had even seen him with another. Little George made no move to go down. He remained with Hugh and Lloydie, standing motionless on the same spot, looking exactly the same as ever, silent, stiff-necked, forlorn.

Hugh stared at George's face from the side. There were no half measures about the pinched melancholy of George's face. If it had been caught between the walls of two back streets and crushed, the juices wouldn't have been squeezed from it more completely. He was standing between Lloyd and Hugh. The contrast made the pallor and dejection all the more noticeable. They were big-bodied, dark, fiercely proud and self-conscious, both of them. They resembled each other like brothers. At a distance Lloyd would have passed for Hugh.

George was six inches shorter than either of them. The extreme fairness of his complexion suggested that he was already half rubbed out and was waiting only for a hand callous enough to go on with the rubbing for him to vanish altogether. He had only lately taken to long trousers. He wore them awkwardly, as if conscious of making an overstatement. He had been at school with Hugh and Lloyd for close on six years. To them he had been closest. Not even to them had he said during all that time anything which might have brought his character into the full light of day for inspection. George was a little book, pocket-size, clasped and unreadable.

Hugh was puzzled. He was wondering why it was that George had not gone down into the main hall with Epsom. George had Epsom's dread of squabbles with the headmaster. Today, George didn't seem to care. Hugh couldn't make it out. Lloyd's cigarette was burned down to its last few strands of life. He had fixed it to the top of a rusty looking pin. He sucked at it violently without getting any smoke from it. He put the pin back behind his lapel and flicked the stub over the lavatory wall.

'If there's anybody on the other side of that wall, I hope that tod'll fall down his neck. I'd like to see somebody on fire. Will the surveyor, for instance. It'd be a pleasure watching a bloke like Willie burning to death. He hangs about the place like a religion that doesn't make sense any more and the effect he has on people's a devil of a sight worse.'

'Leave Willie alone, he's harmless.'

'Let's sing then.'

'Whistle, Lloydie, for God's sake. Your voice hasn't come right since it broke.'

'Since my voice broke! I been explaining to my mother that I run out of fags on Monday and I got to cadge my way through the rest of the week. That hadn't left me much time to train my voice for anything else. What'll I whistle?'

'Make it something soft.'

'That national anthem?'

'God forbid.'

'A hymn?'

'Over my dead body.'

'That's what hymns are for.'

'Whistle something light.'

Lloyd started off on a piece of opera he had heard on a neighbour's gramophone. The piece was a quintet. Lloyd tried to work in all the parts. He found himself stuck up to the neck in melodies and counter-melodies. Hugh told him to stop before he blew himself up. Lloyd drew his lips in, dry and breathless from the whistling.

'What's this chap talking about, Hugh?'

'This visitor?'

'Aye.'

'The future.'

'What is he? A soothsayer?'

'He's going to advise us about jobs.'

'We'll need some advice. I see the pit in your place closed down this week.'

'My brother Alf finished.'

'For good?'

'It won't open again.'

'It was a big pit.'

'One of the best in the valley.'

'When we were kids we wrote essays on what the valleys must have looked like before there were any pits here. You remember. Paradise. All trees. Shepherds. Clear brooks. Druids. Blood-sacrifice. Nature worship. Un-smoky skies. Perfect peace and more than perfect beauty. I won a prize for writing an essay on those lines. Then they realised that I had taken the whole damn lot, commas and all, from a book published by the

Cymmrodorion Society, and I had to give back as much of the prize money as I hadn't spent. That was in the days when there was some point in being dishonest. We're not kids any more. Five years from now, God and the Sultan willing, we'll be teaching ... around here, I hope. We'll be setting essays for kids to write. What'll we give them? "What did this valley look like when there were pits?" '

'What would you really like to be when you grow up, Lloydie?'

'Married. I'm looking forward to the day when I'll be able to stay in the house on Sunday night and read instead of ramming about the High Street like a dog in heat.'

'No, serious. What would you like to be?'

'Serious? Well ... I'd like to be alive and able to alter whatever I am. That's all.'

'That's a lot. What about you, George?'

George shifted about uneasily on one foot. His lips moved but he said nothing. Hugh went on, in a louder tone than before. He was trying to cheer George up.

'I know George wants to be a teacher. He's always on about it. You want to be a teacher, don't you George?'

'I won't be a teacher.' George's voice was cracked and full of self-pity. 'I won't be anything much by the look of it.'

'Don't be daft, George. Or p'raps you're ill. You've been looking funny all the week. You worry too much. You got nothing to worry about. You'll pass your Higher easy and you'll have a scholarship. You'll cheer up then.'

'No, I won't. I'm not trying my Higher and I won't need any scholarship.'

'What are you talking about?'

'I'm leaving next week.'

'Leaving? Leaving the place?'

'The school.'

'What for?'

'Work.'

'You're working now, ain't you?'

'Not earning, though.'

'What you going to work at?'

'My uncle got me a job as clerk in the bus depot.'

'A clerk in the bus depot? That's no sort of job for you, George. There's something better than that for you. What right's your uncle got to do a thing like that. He's got a nerve, taking you out of school. Somebody ought to tell him.'

'He's doing me a favour.'

'I don't see it. Can you see it, Lloydie?'

'I think it's dirty.'

'Me too. It isn't fair on you, George.'

'There's nothing fair. My father's been unemployed three years. We're six in a family. I'm the oldest. My old man's on all day about the sacrifices he's making to keep me here. I get sick of hearing it. Suppose he's right in a way. We can't always be thinking of ourselves. My mother and father think I'd be better off working in a job.'

'And you're leaving next week?'

'Next Monday.'

'And in two months you'd have finished school.'

'In four years I'd have finished college. Four years. My mother and father might be dead by then. They wouldn't get much pleasure out of seeing me put my first pay on their tombstones.'

'George, you look like a kid and talk like an old man.'

'Christ,' said Lloyd, savage, disgruntled, 'between cadging fags and having to pay back our parents in hard cash for the pleasure of having been born to cadge from them, it's a wonder we don't all grow beards and go blind.'

* * *

The main hall of the school was a summary of all the

forms of dinginess that went to make up the whole. On the window sills were pots of artifical flowers. The botanist on the staff had said the flowers would surely die were it not for the fact that every morning four hundred boys crammed into the hall and gave off their oxygen as they let go at the morning hymn of thanksgiving. Nobody knew whether that was a joke or not, because the botanist had false teeth that slipped about, made him contort his features and made it hard to know whether he was in earnest or not.

The flowers had been fashioned in the shape of tulips, cornflowers and dahlias. When new, their colours had been varied and interesting. Now there was a common veil of dust covering them all. The flowerpots were ordinary kitchen jugs with the handles knocked off. They were ugly, graceless.

There were three recesses let into the wall at the lower end of the room. They were deep, dark. In them had been placed busts of the leading poets. One of the boys, with eyes like a hawk and great faith in his own powers of divination, had made them out to be Shakespeare, Milton and Byron, made in cheap plaster, and victimised by neglect and wind erosion. They were chipped and unrecognisable, like the texts of their works that were used throughout the school. Below the busts was a black painted board full of gold lettering. This was the Roll of Honour of schoolboys who had served in the Great War. Many boys had stared at that board during the blank intervals that often occurred in the course of the early morning assembly, and learned its contents off by heart, being able after three or four years of school life to recite it off without a pause.

The headmaster's dais was not a success. It was a hollow, moveable platform, standing not more than six inches from the ground. Its area was six feet by six feet. Half of that was taken up by a table in which was placed a large mahogany book rest. On that rest were the Bible and hymn-book, torn and over-thumbed, which the headmaster used for the morning service. Both books had dozens of pages torn away from them. More than once the headmaster had been forced to stop in the middle of a rolling Biblical passage when he found that the page next to the one from which he was reading was not there to be read from.

He was a resourceful man. Either he'd conclude the unfinished passage with something in the same vein and metre made up out of his own head, garnished with sprigs of Thomas à Kempis, or he'd abandon the text altogether and flash off into a blinding, half-blasphemous attack on all those 'Vandals, Visigoths, Hooligans and others' who tore the page out of sacred books, which were not only sacred, but in view of the superior binding, costly, and use those pages for what dark closet purposes he could not guess at.

The headmaster had never liked the dais. He was not a tall man. There was not much of him to be seen above the table. That he thought unfair to the boys. He considered he cut a good figure seen fairly from top to bottom. Seen only in respect of stomach, head and shoulders, he didn't even impress his wife.

Hugh pushed open the swing doors that led into the main hall. They were stiff and heavy. He had to put his shoulder to them. They squeaked. Hugh could see the headmaster rising from his chair on the platform to see where the noise was coming from. Hugh held the swing door, open to let George come in. Lloyd followed quickly. He let the swing door back with a jolt. Hugh looked around. The air in the room was staler than it had been in the lavatory. That was always so. Hugh put it down to the fact that the general level of thought and talk was mountains higher in the lavatory than it ever was in the main hall.

Hugh kept on searching with his eyes. He was looking for the best place to sit. Some of the boys were on seats grouped along the walls. The majority were massed in the centre of the room, sitting cross-legged, strained and uncomfortable. There was an empty space between two bookcases near to the entrance to the headmaster's private room. It looked as if it had been newly swept. Hugh made for it. He had it in the back of his mind that to sit on any part of that floor except those that had just been given the brush was to make a permanent mess of one's trousers. Besides, if the visitor got slowed up and dull in his talk, there were always those books in their cases to look at. They were so dull the visitor couldn't be worse.

Hugh sat down. George took his place a yard away. Lloyd, never very graceful, and awkward as a camel when he had to pick his way through a score or more of outstretched legs, was in trouble. Hugh had a feeling that Lloyd was going to trip over somebody before he got to the bookcases. Lloyd did that. He came down with a crash on a boy who was wearing a mauve suit, double-breasted waistcoat, with a pair of gold-rimmed spectacles and a pair of glacé-kid shoes that caught the sun. He had been sitting bolt upright before Lloyd tumbled on him. Now he was half-raised from the floor, running his hand hurriedly over the sleeves and body of his jacket, brushing away the wisps of wood, fluff and dirt that clung to it.

Lloyd was bent over him, resting on one hand, looking at his other to see if there were any splinters and letting out a violent murmured rat-tat-tat of curses. The noise had made the visitor pause in his remarks. The headmaster was on his feet, his hand on the visitor's shoulder and murder in his grey North Welsh eyes. He was trying to catch Lloyd's attention. Lloyd was more concerned with the splinters that might have got embedded in the palms of his hands. The headmaster shouted, his voice a graded series of fine mordant edges, 'A little quiet and order in the back, if you don't mind.'

Lloyd crawled towards the bookcases, winking, as he went, at Epsom, who had managed to find himself an armchair beneath the clock and was gazing with a candid objectivity, his chin resting on his weak fists, at the tawdry paper flowers clumped together in their kitchen jugs. Lloyd got between Hugh and George. The headmaster on the platform glanced at the visitor as if expecting thanks for having driven an evil spirit from the assembly. He resumed his seat. The visitor began to speak again. The full light from the window behind played on him. That gave him an appearance of authority which was almost destroyed by the droning, devitalised complacency of his voice. His accent had a base of Oxford with a seasoning of Aberystwyth.

He was a big man, in his fifties. His suit was handsomely tailored. It made the headmaster's suit look like a coal-sack. His hair was half grey and heavily waved on the sides and back, as if designed to play up the idea of total maturity. His face was white, broad, benign and perfectly shaven. The smoothness of his skin impressed many of the boys more than anything the man might say. The sight of the down on their own faces, the sight of frequent stubble on the cheek and chin of their fathers had grown to look normal to them. Such smoothness as this man's must indicate especially high prophetic gifts.

Hugh tried to guess how long the visitor had been speaking. The clock above Epsom's head told him nothing. Either it had stopped an hour before or several days before. The caretaker treated the clock in the same anarchist fashion as he treated most other things about the school. There'd come a time, he'd say, when chitted about the need for winding the clock up once in a while, the time of handing in of cheques, when we'd have to do without clocks whether we liked it or not, and no bloody headmaster was going to tell him any different. No headmaster ever did and the clock was wound only when the caretaker could get somebody to put the ladder against the wall for him.

The visitor seemed to have got into his stride. It was hard to follow what he was saying from the back of the hall where Hugh was sitting. He kept on putting a coloured silk handkerchief up to his mouth as if wanting to spit and not daring to. Between that and the natural muffledness of his voice, Hugh would have preferred to hear a good ventriloquist doing an act. Lloyd was whispering in Hugh's ear that the floor was hard as flint. Hugh asked him if he could follow what the visitor was saying.

'No fear,' said Lloyd, 'that's one good thing about sitting on this bloody floor, you are so busy trying to be comfortable and picking splinters out of your leg, you don't have to listen to anybody.'

'How long has he been talking?'

'About thirty years. He don't sound as if he ever stopped, except to get shaved and combed … God! I bet that bloke's spent some time in barbers' shops.'

'I bet.'

'Maybe he keeps one.'

'Wouldn't he surprised. He looks pretty spick.'

'Pretty what?'

'Spick. Spick and span.'

'Oh that? This whispering is hard work. We ought to ask the visitor to let himself down to a whisper while we talk out loud. I can't see that he's saying much that's important. Those boys down the front look worried to death.'

The visitor was pausing. He didn't appear to be out of breath. He was bending over the table, swinging his big, well-prepared head from left to right, doing the same with the outstretched index of his right hand and smiling as if he had adopted every one of the one hundred and fifty boys present. When he started to speak again, there was a deliberate benevolence in his voice that caused a softening in the faces of the boys.

'Now I come to what is the essential part of my message to you. You are being given a good education. Use it to the best of your abilities. Become citizens of that world of opportunity which is around us. Most of you were born in this valley. Its hills have been your horizon. Do not let that be so for ever. Have courage to look beyond the hills. I am not asking you to sacrifice your local patriotism. Oh dear, no.'

The visitor laughed as if he had said something ridiculous. The dour look on the faces of his listeners did not alter. They saw no joke in what had been said.

'Oh dear, no. To love one's birthplace is a grand and noble thing. But these things must be looked at, my young friends, not in the light of any sentimental loyalties, but in the light of your future welfare, your future happiness. That is the important thing. Let me give you a word of warning. These valleys were once prosperous. Their prosperity is waning and will, I fear, continue to wane. They will not, I fear, continue to afford facilities in the future to absorb you all when you have finished school and college. Do not let that daunt you. There are trouble-makers in these valleys, trouble-makers whose activities account for so much of the discontent and industrial idleness to be seen here, who will try to sow the seed of discontent in your hearts merely because you might fail to find employment in the towns where you were born. Pay no attention to these. Being themselves worthless and unsuccessful they try to poison others with their worthless doctrine of failure. I ask you again, look beyond the hills that have cradled you since birth. Take the world in your stride. This valley may appear large and all-embracing to you. Is it?'

He laughed again. 'Is it? No. Seen against that vast comity of nation we call the Empire, it is but a speck, an infinitesimal, insignificant speck. You are the sons of the Empire. The Empire was formed by your forefathers to give you succour. Take it and the traditions of our land and the Empire wll not fail you. Do not lose heart if an occasional pit happens to close down here. New worlds are being opened up in Canada, Australia, South Africa. There your hopes should lie. There your opportunities are being born. Train yourselves to take them with both hands when the time comes. Thank you.'

The headmaster led the clapping, standing up to it. The clapping was patchy. The brunt of it fell on the younger boys who did very well, some beating the floor with their fists to increase the volume. George clapped three times, looking as if his hands were cold.

'What do you think of it, Lloyd?' said Hugh.

'All shucklenuts. That fellow ought to have a chat with my old man. That would be a debate for you. My old man would tear that visitor's trousers off.'

'What's wrong with your old man?'

'That's the point. There's nothing wrong with him. He's all right. He's one of the trouble-makers that bloke was talking about just now. Trouble-makers ... makes himself sound like God Almighty in *Paradise Lost* talking like that. My old man helped to organise the 1921 strike. Took him a year to get his job back. My old man would die for the Miners' Federation. That's all he's ever believed in. He's made sacrifices for it. Trouble-makers be damned! My old man wouldn't hurt a fly. And what about George there? Why doesn't he stand up and say something? How does leaving school before time and working in a bus depot square with all this talk about opportunities of Empire?'

The only sounds in the room were Lloyd's voice, excited and hard, and the noises made by the boys as they started to change their positions on the floor. The visitor was chatting quietly to the headmaster. The headmaster was not listening. He was staring fixedly at the bookcases under which Lloyd and Hugh were sitting. Hugh told Lloyd to shut up.

The headmaster stood up to address the assembly. He hoped they had all listened attentively and respectfully to what had been said. He instinctively repeated some of the Primrose catchwords that had run thematically through the visitor's speech: 'Be brave', 'New worlds, new lives, new opportunites', 'Be brave', 'Avoid discontent', 'Be loyal', 'Be brave'.

Like most chairmen who do not know what the chair is for, the headmaster got into a rut. He wound up by saying that literature on colonial appointments would soon be forthcoming. He recommended a thorough reading of it to the older lads. With a flourish of his hands he ordered the assembly back to their classrooms. The visitor was fidgety. He was anxious to get on to the next school where he was scheduled to speak. The headmaster got him his bowler hat and overcoat. The visitor put them on, adjusting his bowler in one of the classroom windows and pulling his overcoat down on his shoulders from the inside.

Such nattiness made even Willie's frock tail coat look a thing of shame. The juvenile section of the audience was impressed. Some of the boys gaped and shuffled till they almost stopped in their tracks, seeming as if they wanted to bend down and kiss the hem of the visitor's overcoat in the hope of a cure or increased good fortune in the years to come. A group of assistant masters shepherded the boys from the exits. The visitor took his leave, solemnly, without losing, even for a second, the professional smile that appeared to cover his whole body.

Hugh, Lloyd and George crossed the hall slowly, Hugh leading on their way back to the crumbling classroom.

The headmaster beckoned to them. They stopped, George looking a little frightened. The head shouted: 'You there! Into my room, please.'

The headmaster's room was medium-sized and cosy. Around the wall were placed eight or nine bees-waxed, brilliant dining chairs. The walls were hung with paintings of quiet tone, mostly prints from Italian originals. Above the mantelshelf was a framed facsimile of a few lines from a moth-eaten medieval document. The headmaster was a confirmed and skilful paleographer. He found the facsimile handy to mystify his clients. The table in the centre of the room was untidy with a litter of papers and pens.

The three boys came into the room nervously. They sat down on the three chairs nearest to the door. Hugh sensed something solid and half-satisfied in the deep tick of the expensive clock above the fire. His own ears had grown accustomed to the sound of the cheap alarm clocks they used at home. He liked the pictures on the walls. If he went to bed without supper, he usually managed to see things like that in his sleep. Lloyd was looking surlier than ever.

'I wish he'd hurry.'

'He knows we're waiting. That's why he's dawdling.'

'What does he want us for?'

'This'll give him a chance to show he doesn't like us.'

'He's been showing that without a stop for the last four years.'

'He wants us to burn it into our brains.'

'He'll want branding irons for that.'

'He's probably got some.'

'Maybe that's what's keeping him so long. He's outside, heating them up.'

'I'd like to burn one particular word on his back.'

'He's fireproof. You'd have to paint it on.'

'It would still be the best word to describe him. Got a mirror?'

'No. What do you want it for?'

'Try to get a bit of shape on my hair. P'raps that'll make him feel a bit sweeter to the three of us.'

'Lloydie, you'd need a mirror, two servants and a week off to get any shape on your hair. He'll be along in a minute.'

George felt in the pockets of his waistcoat. He drew out a small round mirror with a tin back on which was printed an advertisement slogan that was being circulated by a local brewery. He passed it over to Lloyd. Lloyd laughed, said he'd changed his mind about it and held the mirror in a sunbeam, causing a little circle of light to dance about at the opposite end of the room. He asked Hugh if he didn't think it was pretty. Hugh agreed. It was. Lloyd had a funny mind for watching things dance.

The headmaster came in. He closed the door behind him and walked over to the fireplace. There was a small fire in the grate.

'You first, Williams. Your conduct, too, has been at fault. But you are a special case. You will be leaving us soon. Next week, I understand. Your father was up to see me a few days ago. He explained the matter to me. Pity. Great pity. With better chances you would have done well. But don't grieve, Williams. A bus depot is not the end of the world. The beginning will be humble, but it is the stiff upward climb that gives life its bitter-sweet tang.' The headmaster rolled his tongue around his mouth. He was enjoying the tang for all it was worth. 'That's all, Williams, you can go.'

George left the room, glancing anxiously back at Lloyd and Hugh before he closed the door. The head took his eyes from the two boys. He walked around the table, gathering up the pens and papers as slowly as it could possibly be done.

Hugh bit his lips and pressed his hands against his knees, wondering whether there was any moral to be drawn from this demonstration of silent tidying. The scene reminded him of a little Miracle play the boys of the lower school had put on to celebrate Good Friday. But the boys of the lower school had never been as dumb as this. The livelier actors had pointed their performance with bursts of laughter.

The headmaster picked the last sheets of paper from the table and placed them at the bottom of the substantial sheaf he held in his hand. He placed them all in a bureau that stood by the window. The table was now clear. He went back to the table.

'Evans, Lloyd, your conduct has made me quite sick. I have tried my best to understand you boys and to make allowances for any strange elements in your psychology, but I have found nothing in any textbook on psychological research that leads me to understand or tolerate the vicious way in which you have consistently underminded authority. When you came to the Sixth Form I made you both prefects. That was to bring out in you a sense of responsibility which would have served you well in later life. The very next day I found you both smoking in the lavatory and trying to get the other boys to pledge themselves to a campaign for the removal of the tobacco tax. Such interest in politics reflects no credit on either of you.

'Your work, according to reports, has been uniformly good. That surprises me. If it hadn't been, I would certainly have taken strong action with the pair of you. I wish to be fair. I wish to do nothing that might prejudice your chances of entering into decent professions. You both come from poor families. Out of consideration for them, I will be lenient with you. But here is a word of warning for you. You might think that by passing examinations you enable yourselves to find a profitable place in society. Society expects more from you than that. It asks that you be tractable and reasonable. It has no place for slouching, rebellious oafs; and that, Evans and

Lloyd, is what you seem determined to be.

'If you want to succeed you will have to temper yourselves into a finer metal and lay aside the mannerisms of your fathers and brothers who work in the pits. Education is not merely a matter of reading books. It is a matter of changing personality. Your personalities need changing badly. You are persistently impolite and insubordinate. You, in particular, Lloyd, have a mania for identifying history with the coal strikes that have taken place in your lifetime. The way you wear your hair is, I take it, your way of protesting that we haven't had a strike for the last four years. Get that nonsense out of your head.

'If you had been living twenty years ago you would have had cause to complain. As it is, you get your education free. You get a maintenance grant of ten shillings a week because your father is unemployed. You should learn the lesson of gratitude, my boy. You might have learnt something if you had presented yourself in hall this morning in time to hear the whole of what our visitor had to say. You strolled in ten to fifteen minutes late. You caused injury to boys smaller than yourselves by falling over them, you kept up a constant chatter while the lecture was in progress, and helped the visitor go away with the impression that we are running a school for renegades and hoodlums. You recognise that you should be punished for such conduct as that?'

Lloyd and Hugh said nothing. The headmaster seemed to them to have exhausted all the words that ever were.

'Lie over the table, Evans.'

Hugh did as he was told. He grasped the further edge of the table. The table was long. His toes were two or three inches from the floor. He had a pain in his stomach where the table's sharp edge was beginning to press into it. He kept his eyes on the fireplace.

The headmaster put his hand behind the bureau. He

pulled out a walking stick, thick, brown, made of cherry wood, with the handle at right angles to the stem. Hugh felt it crash down on the bottom of his spine. He turned his head round, surprised, one hand releasing its grasp on the table. He had it in his mind to slide down from the table and demand an explanation. He saw the headmaster raise himself on his toes and the stick in the air, in preparation for the second stroke. There was something sick, frightened and undecided about the man's expression.

Lloyd was leaning forward, interestedly. The dancing dust from Hugh's trousers, mounting into the sunbeams had caught his fancy. He crinkled his eyes every time the stick sank into Hugh's flesh. He was wondering how much it pained. His hand still held the little mirror George had given to him. The headmaster paused after the third stroke. Hugh did not stir. He was chewing his thoughts thirty-two times each. He heard the headmaster talking to him, gaspily. The small exertion of three strokes had winded him.

'This may seem … very stupid … to you, Evans. But … you've got … got to be taught … You've got to remember what I said … words … words … quite futile'.

Came three more strokes. Hugh heard himself being told to get down. He had stared so hard at the fire his gaze had become clenched and rigid: the red coals seemed to have entered his brain. His brain seemed to be on fire. The ache around his legs was fierce. He had a feeling he'd like to sing so loud he'd smash his ear-drums, then strangle somebody.

He left the room quickly without closing the door. He stood by the bell-rope in the hall, waiting for Lloyd. He was taking too intense an interest in what he felt to be aware of how long he stood there. It crossed his mind that he might tug the bell-rope, bring the boys out of their classrooms and start a riot. That would not be easy.

Getting some of those boys to see that it was raining or not raining was next door to impossible. Getting them to take political action along a given line would be holding out both hands to disaster.

Hugh pressed his bruised buttocks against the distempered walls. He knew that that increased the pain. He hoped that by bringing the pain to absolute fullness it might take his place altogether and exist as a separate thing in which he would have to take only a dry, nodding interest, the sort of interest he took in the books he had to read as part of the examination course.

He looked across to the class-room on his left. Through the window he saw the senior English master, in light checks, reading aloud from a Shakespeare text, wearing on his face a blank, uninterested melancholy that didn't go well with his suit. The boys in front of him wore the same kind of expression, which didn't go well with the class-room. In the room on the left, the master of mathematics was having trouble. He had been scribbling some formulas on the black-board. He dusted the chalk from his shoulders. He was looking around the class for one face that might appear to suggest that he had not been wasting his time scribbling on the board.

The headmaster's door opened. Lloyd came into the hall, looking beaten about, pale and vindictive. He was rubbing his fingers together. His nostrils were shiny and distended. He stopped by the bookcase and groaned. He rested himself against the narrow ink-stained projection that separated the books that nobody wanted to read but did, from the books that nobody wanted to read and didn't. Lloyd lifted one leg slowly from the ground as if it was cramped. Hugh led the way across the hall towards their form room. Lloyd followed a yard behind, his shoulders stooped, mumbling at the back of his mouth the words of a song that had been popular up and down the valley five years before:

'They give us poxy wages,
And we live in dirty hovels,
But one day we'll beat their heads in,
With picks and bloody shovels.'

Hugh said 'Amen' and whistled the tune that fitted the words. One of the masters, a man in his middle twenties, with a belted coat and a moustache that struggled under the nose like an endurance race, crossed their path. He was new to the staff. He had come from a temporary post in one of the most refined and plague-producing High Schools in Wales. The proletarian manners of his new pupils pleased him not at all. He considered whistling in the main hall as an act of sedition. He snapped his fingers at Hugh. Hugh stopped the melody but continued to whistle in a monotone, just to show that he was not to be frightened into silence by any amount of finger-snapping from any manner of hairy lap-dog of a High School tyke.

The master was not quite sure of his ground with the older boys. He was waiting for his social philosophy to crystallise before trying to get any firm grip on them. He passed on, convinced that by reducing the whistling to a single tone note he had made some advance against the forces of that indiscipline which moved like a monster amongst that shabby mess of four hundred valley boys who attended the school. He passed on.

Hugh looked back at him. 'Nice man. He's prettier than we deserve. He doesn't like whistling. That's a new one. You could think there's somebody lying dead in this school, the way they try to make us act as if we were mourners.'

'There is somebody dead, Hugh.'

'Who?'

'I feel half dead. From the back, you look half dead. Between us we make a bloody good corpse. Take us away, O God!'

The form-room was empty, except for George. He was

waiting for them, sitting in his usual desk. He looked from Lloyd to Hugh, from Hugh to Lloyd, hoping that the movement of his head and the expression of concern and pity on his face would help him think of something to say that would comfort and inspire them at once. but George's mind was of the sort that could hope for years before the hope grew strong enough to fertilise his imagination and provide him with the words necessary for its expression. He remained dumb.

Hugh took up his usual place by the window, leaning against the sill, putting his teeth into the hanging cords. Lloyd got slowly down into the armchair, making a long noise that was half-groan, half-belch.

'That noise sounds pretty hollow, Lloydie.'

'Don't know whether it was my stomach or my soul. I'm not eating much breakfast these days.'

'Why not?'

'No time to catch the bus.'

'Make time. Get up earlier.'

'Don't be daft. There wouldn't be any breakfast if I did. It sounds better to say "No time" than "No food". We had a lot of mice in the house about a year ago. My mother said it was the food that attraced them. She got rid of the food. We haven't had any mice since. We haven't had any food either. But it's good to be rid of the mice. Christ! I feel as if I was in a fever or something. My head's thumping.'

'That bloody Turk! How many'd he give you, Lloydie? You look white as a sheet.'

'Wind me up in it and let me lie. Cover my limbs with the funeral sheet. Home is the hunter from the hills and the harlot in from the street asking for her sheet back. Why doesn't Epsom come in here a bit oftener. I make up poems for his benefit and he's always somewhere else when it starts to pour out ... You're right, Hugh. That headmaster's a bloody Turk.'

'How many'd he give you?'

'I counted twelve. I thought that would be the lot. I never thought a Christian would wallop you more times than were apostles. The number of apostles must be going up. After twelve I started wriggling off the table. I took out my handkerchief, p'raps it was to wipe my nose, p'raps it was to use it as a white flag of truce. It couldn't have been white enough, because as soon as I took it out of my pocket he gave me a hell of a homer across the shoulders and told me to lie still. Then came about nine or ten more, right flat across the arse like the first twelve.'

'Gee! Only six he gave me, and I feel as if I'd been run over by a train.'

'The train didn't run over me. It stayed in the same place and stamped on me.'

George kicked the wooden bar that ran beneath his desk. There were lines of anger and revolt stirring in the unhappy quietude of his face.

'It's too bad,' he said. 'It's too bad and it ought to be stopped. He's got no right to do that to you. We're not kids any more. We're almost grown up. I got a good mind to tell him. I'm leaving next week so he can't do anything to me, can he?'

Lloyd raised himself an inch or two from the seat of the chair. He twisted it around and faced George. He wiped around his mouth with his handkerchief.

'Don't bother. It doesn't amount to as much as you think. He'll get a lot more sleepless nights out of this than we will. Ever since he came here, he's been trying to get me and Hugh to go down on our bellies and kiss his feet. We can find better use for our bellies than that. He could find better use for his feet, too, but we can't expect him to think of it. We didn't pay any attention to him and that got under his shirt a bit. If he'd had any sense he wouldn't have paid any attention to us and let us go on in our own way. He knows we do our work. He told us so. But that wasn't enough for him. He wanted us to scratch his backside like Wilf does. We didn't, and he pays us out by letting us have it with a walking stick.'

'Well,' said George, 'that proves he's got a pretty mean mind.'

Hugh spat the sodden window cord from his mouth.

'Who said we needed proof of that, George? We've always known that. I've heard that he comes from a family as poor as any of ours. You'd think that would make him kind of friendly to us, wouldn't you? Instead of that, he tries to fool himself into thinking that his family was the richest and the strongest in the land. That's why he goes out of his way to treat Lloydie and me as if we were a couple of disobedient serfs.'

'He wants a school full of boys like Wilf. If he could get them, God help the school, but God wouldn't have to help, because he wouldn't find upwards of a dozen Wilfs in the whole valley, and he'd have to interfere with the drainage to find the other eleven. Never mind. Patience we need. Patience and a pint of raw emulsion to rub into the folds of my poor suffering arse. It feels like the Mount of Olives. Two months more and we'll be out of this place. We're ripe for a change. We've outgrown this school like an old coat. It gets smaller and peskier as we get bigger and healthier. I think the future is pretty promising.'

'Is it?'

'I think so.'

Hugh took a paperbound edition of gems from the French poets from his pocket. He opened the book in the middle section, where the gems of the Romantic period glistened. He picked the most baleful and apostrophic piece he could find. In two hundred lines and one hundred exclamation marks he had worked off some part of the hatred he felt against tyrants.

George unwrapped some cheese sandwiches from a

small sheet of tissue paper. He handed one to Lloyd and another to Hugh. The three of them ate quickly. The cheese was red, strong. The smell of it filled the room. Lloyd bent over and took the tissue paper from George's desk. He rolled it into a ball. He tossed it full-tilt into the portrait of Bishop Morgan.

* * *

The store that Herbert managed stood at the juncture of two streets. The two streets resembled each other not at all. One was long, uniform, squalid, inhabited by unemployed, or by people still working in the pits. The roadway was in a bad condition. The loose stones and treacherous furrows that tore the shoes of those that walked there were almost as plentiful as the swarm of children that played on the pavements.

The practice of scouring the portion of pavement in front of each doorway had been abandoned by nearly all the housewives in possession. They found that if their own children did not immediately remove the effects of the cleaning, somebody else's children would.

The other street was on a higher plane of income and architecture. Each house was fronted by a green patch. Laurels and fir trees were there in abundance. The houses obeyed no single pattern. They had not been thrown into position by a colliery company to accomodate a new influx of rural immigrants for work in the pits. They had, for the most part, been built separately to satisfy the demands of this or that bureaucrat, official or upper-rank artisan. There were one or two sun-blinds, vividly striped, covering doors and windows. There were one or two deck-chairs and flag-poles. Altogether, a satisfied, full-bellied and inconclusive sort of street.

Herbert's store was in a good position. It was alone in that district. All he had to do was steer a middle course between the inhabitants of the two streets, alienating no one and retaining the custom of all. Herbert did so, with a none the less strong bias towards the sun-blinds, fir trees and flag-poles. Herbert sent his carrier boy around to the mansions of the blessed to receive their orders and dispatched them promptly around by the side entrance.

Herbert had an idea of playing his cards as a merchant so well that one day, a day fixed somewhere in the future when Hugh would have landed himself a decent job and ceased to be a nuisance, he'd go and take his place among those blessed ones. It would be a good finish to a career full of cares and worry.

The shop was not a big one. It had been built on the site of two company houses where two unlucky families had lived for a space of ten years. They had been hit spinning every once in a while by some little thunder bolt of tragedy. Death in the pit for the older members. Street accidents and dirt-diseases for the younger with an impressive record of puerperal fever running through the female side of both family groups.

The houses had got a bad name. The agent responsible for the letting had tried to minimise the importance of this reputation, branding the black chronicle of deaths and disasters as rumours worked up by revolutionists to undermine the stability of the landlord class. But no new tenants could be found. Not that the spectacle of sudden death and suffering was strange to the inhabitants of the area. They were part and parcel of the local idiom. But no one relished the sight of disaster concentrated and served up in all its known forms.

The two houses were torn down. When the last wall had been smashed and made level with the ground, it seemed to those that lived near that an old cloud had broken into rain and given way to the sun.

The grocery store was two-windowed and broad of front. The window displays were neat but humdrum. On one side was dairy produce; on the other dry goods. The prices were higher than in most stores. That reflected the monopoly position. The window panes were well washed. The paintwork, red and yellow.

Inside the shop the atmosphere was close. The upper-most smell was bacon. The bacon sides hung on hooks from the ceiling. Some of them had hung there for a long time. Next in the order of pungency came cheese. Herbert didn't like the smell of cheese. He wished people would learn to do without it. Herbert stood behind the counter, fingering a large ball of twine, unused as yet. He had taken it from its paper wrapping only a few minutes before. The shop was empty. Not for long, though. Herbert was glad of the rest. Wednesday afternoons were always like that.

From twelve o'clock there had been a thin straggle of customers, mostly people on parish relief, people who took about an hour puzzling over every commodity in the shop, wondering how best to spend the five or six bob they allowed themselves for groceries, making constant maddening caterwauls about their poverty, poverty, poverty, that sickened Herbert and drove him to the edge of the sink.

He'd have given his right arm to have done once and for all with that class of customer. They dirtied his goods, they dirtied his shop and they dirtied him and bruised the natural dignity of his being, with their gutless, cringing, self-pitying pauperism. But they were customers. A customer must never be lost except by death, and even then life would immediately provide another to take his place. Herbert had the laws of economic development at his finger tips. That's why he scrubbed his finger tips so often. To get the dirt out.

There were so many people on the parish, people who got their thimbleful of relief on Wednesdays and got so flat broke on Saturdays that they spent Sunday staying away from chapel getting down on their knees in an attitude of prayer in front of the empty shelves of their pantries, and making vows never again to buy groceries but only luxuries that would confirm by their transience the necessity of self-slaughter and sweeten its execution. Those people had to be nursed every Wednesday back into a condition of normalcy.

Herbert tried hard with them. He'd tell them that always would he try to deal justly with them, to give them all the help he could, indefinite credit excepted, that being forbidden, not by himself, but by the company for which he worked. With each customer, he'd crown his solicitude with the expression of the belief that, soon, things would pick up. Fat pay packets would be the order of the day again, and for the first few weeks of the golden age people could eat the packets as they stood to get some flesh on their protruding bones as a basis for the glorious things to come.

There'd be new clothes for the kiddies, new kiddies for the mothers, and new mothers for the fathers. There'd be new furniture for the parlours and dancing on the green when they grew tired of fooling about on the furniture in the parlours. Herbert always spoke with authority to all his customers who earned less than two pounds a week. Always he tried to speak with as much accuracy and sincerity as possible, but if the customer's income was less than a pound a week, he didn't care whether what he said was true or not.

He referred to new schemes for using coal that were being discussed in the closets of the coalowners. Herbert genuinely thought that coalowners spent all their time in closets thinking out new uses for coal, much the same as the unemployed spend most of their time in closets thinking out new uses for coalowners. Herbert talked about the getting of oil from coal, the new employment of coal for making buttons, milk, lyrics. There was nothing that couldn't be made from coal. A few more years and they'd be making profits and fires from coal.

With some of his customers Herbert found this kind of talking uphill work. They had nothing left in their mind, no soil of gullibility or happiness in which he could plant the seed of any belief, any hope in the goodness of the future. They wore black blinkers, swore at the mention of coal or coalowners and told Herbert to get on with his own business and his bloody grocering. That sort of customer reminded him of Alf: disgruntled, bitter, brutish, always ready to draw back their lips and show unclean, discoloured teeth and snarl at the mere sight of humour or goodness.

Herbert looked around the shop. It was comfortably well-stocked. Next week there'd be stock-taking. He was looking forward to it. It wouldn't be difficult. He had a perfect knowledge of what was in the shop. But he was worried. Of late there had been some dark-faced circulars issued from the head office of the firm. Herbert knew that the total profits of the firm from all its branches in the valley had been falling for two years. He couldn't see how that could be helped. The whole area was going to the dogs. No shop could increase its profits. To keep them on an even keel would be possible only in a good neighbourhood.

But the head office of the firm was nowhere near the valley. The irreducible skeleton of profit-making was the main concern of the company's directors. The decaying flesh around the bones was an affair they willingly delegated to their underlings, Herbert among them. If the underlings could arrest the decay and bring back a look of prospering wholesomeness to a body doomed to die and quickly dying, so much the better. If not, so much the worse for the underlings.

Herbert had received two circular notes that week. In the first the writer dealt with the weaknesses of the credit

— 122 —

system which was left mainly to the discretion of the branch managers. Too much credit was being allowed. Much too much kindness was being shown. He saw full well, he said, the need for kindness. But he did not see the need for kindness disrupting the affairs of an entire company. Those who lagged behind in their payments were to be brought sharply into line. The worst offenders were to have their morality kicked into shape by a County Court summons. Those who owed only from three to five pounds were to have their credit stopped and themselves subjected to an ultimatum to wipe off their arrears within a given time.

Herbert had been going over his books. There were some bad cases. He proposed to deal with them immediately. Nearly all his customers in the poorer street owed him something. That was inevitable. Even if people were working, wages had sunk so low it was practically impossible for them to make a cash payment on everything they bought. Herbert knew that. He had decided to use discretion. An intensive campaign against defaulters in an area where occasional defaults had become as habitual as the breathing in of oxygen, would only drive his poorer customers away from his store down into the town where they would get their goods a penny or two cheaper.

Herbert thanked God for the blessed mansions that stretched away to the right of the store. There was the backbone of his custom. There were no snivels or snarls or whimpers from them. They wanted the best. He gave it to them. They paid for it, were willing to pay for it. He worshipped their payments, the fruit, as he saw it, of right thinking and clean living. They were the only solid patch on which he could rest the feet in all that swamp of impoverished living and early, ugly dying.

Herbert would have kissed their very flag-poles, so great was the love he felt for them. He would have cleaned their sun-blinds with his very blood. Such desires were not compounded simply of snobbery. Herbert had enough natural melancholy in him, not yet squeezed out by the tight collars he wore, to see that the sky above him was pretty black. Those people, with their assured incomes, their luxurious appurtenances and comfortable philosophies were the only fixed stars he could see in that sky. Therefore, he loved them.

The second circular was an intimation to branch managers that the salaries obtaining in the branch staffs of the firm were too high. They had to be reduced. Of course, if the head office wished to be ruthless they could take up the axe and start in on the wages of the managers, but as this might cramp initiative which was, in the phrase of the hand which had framed the circular, the only force capable of tempting depression out into the open and striking it down, the managers would be invited to see what economies they themselves could effect in the running expenses of each shop. Herbert had no intention of seeing his own wage reduced. He was looking around for the best means of carrying out the policy of the cheese-paring that had been advocated by his head office.

Herbert watched some flies that had settled on the sides of bacon. He shouted 'Dennis'. A slim, wakeful-looking lad of eighteen, with black hair slicked back from his forehead and his skin drawn tightly around his nose, stepped out from the warehouse behind the shop, where there were draughts, rats, flag-stones from which water oozed, sacks of potatoes and smells which belonged neither here nor there.

Dennis had been trying to track down those smells during the three months he had been working as Herbert's assistant. He had failed, and he had come to the conclusion that they were the echo of the history of those two houses that had stood on the corner before the shop had been built.

Herbert told him to fix a fly-paper from the iron bar on which the bacon was hooked. Dennis did so with a will. He was keen. If Herbert had asked him to smear himself with glue, hang himself from one of the hooks and do service as a fly-paper, he would have done so. In all things he admired Herbert. One day, by following in the master's footsteps, he himself would be a manager. Then he would really do things: dress like Herbert, act like Herbert, talk like Herbert.

Dennis got fifteen shillings a week as Herbert's assistant. He was cultivating dignity. He was thinking of having a parting in his hair, taking Herbert as his model. He believed himself to be as happy as he could be. He saw boys of his own age who earned more than he did, but, with the aid of dreams, he foresaw that the future might yield him greater riches and contentment than they would ever have.

He wasn't so badly off as it was. Ten shillings he gave to his mother, who didn't make much use of it, but that was her business. One shilling a week he put by to provide himself with clothes. If he had left it to his mother to provide him with clothes he'd have been going about in sacks or in his bare skin. There was no method about his mother. He knew Herbert had had trouble more than once making her pay for the groceries. That caused Dennis a great sadness. He looked upon it as he would a black patch on his white shop-coat. One and six a week he spent on his girl, who would have broken her faith for less than one and six. Three pence he dropped into the chapel collection box every Sunday evening. Herbert had advised him to become a steady and regular church member. He did so, but without much satisfaction, because every time the preacher mentioned God, Dennis thought of Herbert, so it was just the same as if he had spent every Sunday evening at work.

Herbert admitted to himself that Dennis was one of the

best assistants he had ever had. He thought Dennis should be having more than fifteen shillings a week. He was worth more. The boy would make a good manager. Herbert bit his lips, puzzled. His hand tightened around the ball of string. He was up against it. He wondered why it was that life always seemed to condemn him never to give expression to the generosity that he felt within himself. He liked Dennis and wanted to help him. But between the desire and the accomplishment was interposed that second circular that threatened a cut in his own wages if the total expenses of the branches were not cut to the very bone. He wanted to give Dennis more. That circular reminded him that the point was not how much more Dennis should be getting but how much less.

Dennis's wage would have to be reduced. Herbert couldn't see himself asking Dennis to take a reduction. To do that, he'd feel himself forced to explain to Dennis the policy of the company directors upon whose shoulders responsibility for all pain caused would have to rest.

Herbert placed dignity above food or rest. The only alternative was to tell Dennis nothing: just get rid of him. There were lots of boys leaving school who'd work just as hard and efficiently as Dennis for twelve shillings a week. They'd take twelve shillings a week gladly if the alternative was taking a course at one of the juvenile instruction centres where they endured a long series of headaches and received nothing in return.

Herbert made up his mind, dusting away all emotion primly from his thoughts. It would be simpler and less painful to let Dennis go and give him the chance of finding a job at the same rate of pay, or perhaps, even at a better rate, than to ask him to stay on and give the same quality of service as before for less wages. Let him go, and get his conscience to agree to a policy of silence and understanding that would enable him to feel well about the matter. The head office would be pleased. To have effected a reduction of three shillings in the wages of an assistant in less than a week after their first circular would make Herbert first favourite with the company. That thought cheered him up.

A woman came in and dropped down on one of the high-legged chairs near the door. She leaned on her left elbow against the counter. She wore a long grey coat and a wide brimmed hat in black straw. Her shoes were new, the polished surface covered over with a thin dust. There was a look of bleary merriment in her eyes. Under her eyes were dark-shaded puffs. Two or three times she put her hand to her mouth as her shoulders heaved and begged her own pardon. Her voice was husky, her speech slurred. She'd been drinking.

'Good day, Mrs Rees,' said Herbert.

Mrs Rees waved her hand at him. She looked across at Dennis. Dennis seemed embarrassed. He played with the handle of a sweeping brush that stood by his side. He took the brush and went off into the warehouse. Mrs Rees was his mother. Dennis was in process of outgrowing the age of sentimental indifference to the shortcomings of his parents.

Mrs Rees flung her hand down, as if dismissing Dennis from her life. Herbert recalled that Mrs Rees was the first person he'd have to deal with under Section 3 of the circular. She owed about four pounds. No more credit for Mrs Rees. She had swivelled her chair round to get a good view of all the articles on the shelves. She mumbled the name of this or that commodity, reading even the announcements of content or quality on the packages and tins. She hadn't bothered to make out a list of what she wanted. She was trying to remember, closing her eye and wrinkling her brow occasionally, as if she couldn't understand why she took the trouble to keep awake.

Herbert had heard patches of her story. Not from Dennis. He had never said a word to him about her. But people who came into the shop often paused to laugh a while at Mrs Rees. Her husband had worked with a firm of contractors. A fair job, as jobs went, with good enough money. They lived in a poky four-roomed house in one of the terraces, with no room to have a good bath or to take a deep breath. In the two houses on either side of them had lived Mr Rees's blood relations. To them he had been very loyal, working as he did with a firm of contractors who had neither honesty or subtlety, and who had outraged every one of man's moral concepts not less than twice a month.

Mr Rees felt the need to be loyal to something. He'd have been loyal to his wife, but she talked so much that every time he made a pompous and deliberate declaration of his loyalty, she always accused him of just saying something with an idea of keeping her quiet for a change.

Mrs Rees had never liked the idea of living in the terraces. She had been born there. She had sickened on the diet of dirt, squalor and noise. She had regarded marriage mainly as a means of revenging herself on the bed of her birth by moving out of the terraces. Instead marriage seemed to have caused her to sink more deeply into the terraces. She saw Mr Rees's blood relations as a strong fence that was building itself up around her, making her chances of escape smaller and more remote.

She demanded that as a builder his first duty was to build a house of his own. He explained that a builder made money because he owed no particular duty to anybody. She was obstinate. She made his life miserable. She led him around by the nose, showing him every aspect of the dinginess in which they lived. She organised violent campaigns of fainting and swearing to bring him around to her way of thinking. His blood relations stood by his side, organising counter-pressure. The terraces, they said, once they had claimed a man for their own, became part of his nervous system. Without them, the system went to bits, leaving the man a shivering wreck.

But she won. The marriage bed was a sector in which the blood relations could never trespass. It was there that he weakened. He agreed to sink his savings and a fixed part of his wage in buying the material necessary to build a bungalow. He could do the building himself. The savings went quickly. The site he had chosen was a patch of flat land high up on the mountain above the terraces. His friends told him that if they had known he was going to end by living among the crags, they'd have advised him to marry a goat.

Mrs Rees was happy. She could see the walls sprouting from the foundations. She got hold of an armful of furniture catalogues and knew their contents backwards. Mr Rees went pale at the sight of them. He saw in each catalogue a source of ruin. Mrs Rees was triumphant. She had the blood relations on the run. She was coming close to the moment when she would snap the bonds of family unity. The prospect of emancipation looked very sweet to her. She spent so much time poking her tongue at relations that the tip of it got quite cold, for there is very little heat in the winds that walk abroad in the higher streets of the terraces.

But Mr Rees was sick in the heart. Building materials are costly. The amount he spent on them each month didn't leave much out of his pay to buy food. Mrs Rees lived on visions and had no pity to spare for the emptiness of his stomach. His friends had found him sucking bits of plaster. They forecast death from petrified guts. The sooner the better answered Mr Rees. He had access to his employer's storeyard. What materials he couldn't buy he stole in considerable quantities. What materials he stole and didn't need he sold, and used the profits to buy himself a square meal once in a while, in this hotel or that.

The walls of the mountain house continued to grow. They reached six feet from the ground. Mr Rees's employers were a pair of razor-sharp North Welsh men who had graduated into the building trade from the undertaking business. Their last act in that profession had been to coffin and fasten the lid screws tightly down upon what was left of their professional morals. For their own larcenies they felt a religious adoration. For the larcenies of others, a devilish and destructive hatred. It came to their attention that Mr Rees was taking away from their yard enough stuff to build a chain of schools. They determined to be extra-specially devilish with him and to destroy him with real Flintshire thoroughness.

Mr Rees got wind of it. There are many winds in the terraces, albeit without warmth. He applied secretly to a committee set up by an amalgamation of religious bodies for permission and help to emigrate to Canada. The committee, being anxious to help the poor and oppressed, and being free from responsibilty for what happened to their clients after they got to Montreal, gave their permission.

Early one morning Mr Rees had gone up the mountain to take a last look at the half-finished house that had brought him so much grief and so much pain. In his hatred he tried to tear the walls down, but he had built them so strong and as he saw them still standing there was pride as well as anger in his eyes. He left without a word for Mrs Rees. She had applied to the Relieving Officer and relief had been granted. That had happened three years before. She still got her relief. She spoke to very few people, not even to Dennis. Twice a week, fair or rain, she walked from the terraces to where her half-materialised vision still stood to a height of six feet above the ground.

Every Wednesday she did just a little drinking. Some said she did some whoring round and about on Fridays and Saturdays, but that was said of all women in the district who had no husband and wore shoes that were less than a year old. It didn't much matter whether there was any truth in it or not, because Fridays and Saturdays are feast days in places where the weekly feast ends on a Monday, and in time of feastings only churls forget their bodies.

A rumour had come about that Mr Rees had been seen starving to death in a hayrick somewhere in Saskatchewan. But that sounded so much like the first line of a poem, most people believed that he must be doing very well for himself in Toronto. Mrs Rees didn't believe the rumour. She remembered her husband's appetite too well. He'd have eaten the hayrick before starting to starve.

Mrs Rees made a recital of all the things she needed. Herbert noted them down on a little pencil pad. It wasn't a long list. Half a dozen articles. No more. She told Herbert to give them to Dennis. He'd bring them home. She got off the chair carefully and made to go.

'Are you paying for them now, Mrs Rees?'

'Why should I?'

'It would be better if you would.'

' 'Course it would be better. Who's disputing it? It would be better if we didn't have to buy groceries. Put them down in the book. You've got it there somewhere. I left it with you last week.'

'I've just been looking at it. You owe four pounds.'

'That's the richest I've been for a long time. Go on, put it down in the book and stop bothering somebody.'

'I can't give you any more credit.'

'I've always done my best to pay.'

'I know that. This is a new rule.'

'Just brought in for my benefit, I know.'

'It's a new rule for everybody.'

'All right. Dennis works here, don't he? Take something out of his pay every week. That'll make it all right, won't it?'

'No. Dennis finishes here this week.'

'I can see it now. You're persecuting me. That's what it is. Persecuting me. Because my husband goes away and leaves me and ends up in a hayrick. You think you can do what you like with me. You can't, do you hear? You can't. Nobody's going to hurt me any more.'

Mrs Rees was boiling over. She flung herself against the counter. Herbert stepped back, but Mrs Rees's fingers were on his tie, mounting up until they got between his collar and his neck. His ears were buzzing. He felt Mrs Rees's hand come slapping hard on his face. He felt more comical than hurt. Crazy drunks ... He pulled her hand away. She slumped down on to the counter and started to weep on her sleeve. Herbert told her to get out. Without straightening herself she walked away.

Dennis was watching her from around the corner of the warehouse floor. Herbert felt sorry for Dennis. The boy was embarrassed. Herbert knew the torture of embarrassment by heart. The sight of Mrs Rees's bent back, capable of beautiful straightness in normal moods, the sight of her grey sleeve rising to wipe the tears away from her blank features filled him with a sense of radical dissatisfaction, a sense of fear that elements were combining in a conspiracy to lead his feet away from the hard solid foundation on which he loved to stand, and plunge them into the depths of the surrounding swamp which he detested with a passion that made spots dance before his eyes.

The buzzing of the flies grew louder. They were beginning to get caught on the fly-paper. Herbert was glad of that. He was in a mood sympathetic to the sight of slaughter and the sounds of desperation. Dennis came out into the shop. He was uneasy and fumbled with the ties of his apron.

'I'm awful sorry, Mr Evans.'

'It's not your fault, Dennis.'

'She's not always like that, Mr Evans. Sometimes she's all right and then we're all of us happy in the house together. Then she gets sort of lost again. She's had a lot to put up with they tell me. This won't make any difference, will it, Mr Evans? To me, I mean.'

'Perhaps it will, Dennis. I want you to finish on Saturday.'

'Christ.'

'Don't swear, Dennis.'

'Sorry, Mr Evans.'

'Let's leave it at that. You can go home now, if you like. I don't think I'll be needing you again today. And those goods your mother wanted. You can take them with you.'

Dennis muttered his thanks. Through the doorway he could see his mother making her way up the hill. He clenched his fists and pulled off his shop-coat petulantly.

'All her fault, the ... bitch, the bloody bitch.'

Herbert closed his eyes and seemed to be on the point of crossing himself, piously.

* * *

Alf and Bob collected their last pay packets from the colliery office. Hodges, the cashier's clerk, made a few comradely quips about their being on the peg. Alf told Bob to look carefully at his pay docket to make sure that the company weren't celebrating their parting by cheating them of a few bob.

'You don't think we'd do a thing like that, do you?' asked Hodges out of the side of his mouth.

' 'Course I do,' said Alf. 'wouldn't you?'

'Of course. One day I'll write a book covering all the forms of swindling that have been thought up and put into practice in this office. The book would be twice the size of the Bible and ten times as heavy on account of there being a hundred times the amount of truth in it.'

'You're a decent fellow, Hodges. I say that because it's most likely I'll never see you again. Most of the clerks in this office I'd like to see dropped down the pit-shaft.'

'The management wins their hearts when they are young. You can't blame them for being craps. And if they unite in a conspiracy to cheat you fellows by playing sharp tricks with your pay dockets you can't blame them for that either. The men are damn fools to let themselves be cheated. That's my way of looking at it.'

'It takes away a lot of fun when you stop blaming people for what they are.'

'Men are what they want to be. That's what you mean?'

'That's near enough. I've met two men so far who have been what they wanted to be. There was something wrong with both of them. They spent most of their time stopping other people from being what they wanted to be.'

'That's the way of it. A few get what they want. The rest of us chew damp rags to stop our dreams from rattling against our ribs.'

'Are you satisfied, Hodges?'

'What do you want to know for?'

'Oh, nothing much. I'm training to be a bloody nuisance asking other people questions they might not be able to answer offhand.'

'Am I satisfied? I don't know. I've seen the wages I've handled out of this window getting smaller bit by bit. That makes me feel bad. I'm a great believer in justice. I'd get along a lot faster in this world if I wasn't. They say I make a good clerk. I suppose being satisfied depends on a fellow's job.'

'What if you didn't have one?'

'I'd want to be the first of those clerks you feel like throwing down the pit-shaft.'

'Honest?'

'Honest.'

'Good enough.'

'In this job I've got you're surrounded by chaps who seems to be satisfied. At first you think you're different from them. That makes you feel good because they all look dead, dumb or constipated. But slowly you get to be like them, talk like them, think like them, and you don't rest until there isn't a point of difference between you and them. That's being satisfied.'

'Sounds kind of daft.'

'Being different is a risk.'

'What makes you so honest, Hodges?'

'What do you mean by honest?'

'You sound almost like one of us fellows.'

'It's only for a while. Tomorrow's my last day here. I finish. Then I go. I'm happy about it.'

'Where you going?'

'Cardiff. Shipping office. Same company. They've found work for all the office staff. I wish they showed as much consideration for you chaps. They don't waste much thought on you.'

'We'll find our own way out of the woods.'

'They're pretty dark woods, Evans. Lots of trees.'

'Nobody can see what you're doing in the dark. That's one good thing about it. So you're going in for shipping? This company owns a bit of everything, don't it?'

'They take in a lot of ground.'

'So long, Hodges. Bob here is going to show me a view from the top of the mountain that's supposed to be so good it stops a man being miserable. Can you imagine a view like that? No? Well, Bob knows one and he knows more about those mountains than he does about his own wife. Come on, Bob. So long, Hodges.'

They took a path that wound around the mountain. That mountain was the highest in the district. As they climbed they saw sections of different valleys coming into sight, each section a duplicate of the next. Their path got steeper as it approached the top. Twice on the journey

Bob had taken a rest, sitting on the grass bank, rubbing his fingers into his eyes. Alf, as usual, remained standing.

Alf was no great lover of walking. He was afraid that if once he sat down he'd take a long time getting to his feet again. He remembered a tale his father had told him about a retired world-weary miner who sat down so long and so fixedly on the slope of the mountain he had become part of it, and started a quarrel between two landlords who couldn't agree as to which of them the man belonged. Alf picked up some stones from the path and shied them, closing one eye, at a 'Trespassers' notice, thirty feet away. He hit it every time.

'I wish that notice was the fellow who put it there.'

'Why?'

'He'd be stoned to death by now. I'm a dead shot with these stones.'

'One day you'll get into trouble, Alf.'

'How?'

'Law's got to be respected.'

'Mountains ought to be respected, too. And one way of not respecting them is sticking up those notices about trespassing.'

'There you are. I still think you'll get into trouble some day, Alf. Keep a hand on yourself.'

'If I kept a hand on myself they'd probably put me in court for stealing. So what does it matter. Coming to think of it, you look as if you're in trouble yourself. What's the matter with you, Bob? You ill?'

'No. Didn't sleep much last night.'

'It was a poor night for sleeping. Too heavy.'

'It was Annie, the girl next door. She kept me awake.'

'Trying to make love to you?'

'How could she do that? There was a wall between us.'

'That wouldn't stop Annie. She's bitten her way through worse things than walls.'

'She was screaming all night. Not loud screaming,

quiet, like she was crying for something.'

'What if everybody who wants things they can't get around here started to cry for them as soon as the sun set? There'd be a hell of a noise. Nobody'd ever go to sleep. But only Annie does it. She's supposed to be a half-wit. She's free to make as much noise as she likes if she thinks she's only getting half as much of a thing as she wants. We're normal. We got to bite our lips and look as if we're doing all right.'

'Annie's a nuisance.'

'Get twelve people to sign a paper that she's keeping them awake and they'll have to keep her quiet. If that doesn't do the trick, sign a few more papers. That's bound to send you to sleep.'

'I'm the only one she keeps awake. Lily and Roger sleep like logs.'

'How long has she been crying like that?'

'A couple of nights now.'

'Give her what she wants.'

'What's that?'

'A man.'

'You mean I ought to satisfy her?'

'It's you are losing sleep, not me.'

'No bloody fear. I wouldn't touch it.'

'That's the point. Was a time when Annie had so many men waiting their turn she looked like the Labour Exchange. Morals gets better as trade gets worse. It's dangerous to fool with Annie now. A chap would get a few months if he tried it. The law protects Annie and she shows her gratitude by going crazier than ever. So, until trade gets better and morals go to blazes again, Annie's going to get the hunger out of her system by screaming and you'll have to spend the nights reading if you can't sleep. It's a good chance for you to get educated.'

Alf pulled Bob to his feet. They proceeded with the walk. A low, roughly built wall ran along the mountain's breast. The mountains all around were cut into pieces by those endless walls, intersecting each other like the veins on a hand. Alf put his foot into a hole in the wall and pulled himself over. Bob tapped him on the leg.

'Wait a minute, Alf. You're not supposed to climb over that wall. There's a gate a quarter of a mile along.'

'A gate? Look here, Bob. Do you realise that if this wall wasn't here we wouldn't have to climb over it.'

'That doesn't make sense.'

'Neither does the wall. Come on.'

They both climbed over. There was a man standing in the field, ten yards in front of them. His clothes were strong and well worn. His mouth gaped. He held a stick in his hand. He switched it about, knocking the heads off mountain-flax which grew profusely in the field. Bob stepped behind Alf. He was uncomfortable. No more so than the farmer who didn't know what to say.

'Who's this chap,' asked Alf, half turning his head towards Bob.

'That's Rufus. He's the farmer. He owns this mountain.'

'The whole mountain?'

'I think so.'

'What's he like?'

'Funny. He gets moods.'

'That's what comes of owning mountains. Why don't he own something he can carry about.' Alf greeted the farmer with a salute. 'Hullo, Rufus. Nice day for walking. We're taking a short cut to that gap between those two hills over there. Do you mind?'

Rufus pointed his stick at them, holding it out with the full length of his arm. The stick trembled. Rufus was excited, but still silent.

'What's he doing?' asked Alf, 'measuring us or telling us to get out?' He raised his voice. 'How about it, Rufus?'

'Get out,' shouted Rufus, in a voice that sounded

unused, 'get out, or you'll be taking a short cut all right: to court.'

'That's no way to talk.'

'I'll talk any way I like. This is my field. I got the deeds. Prove to me that I haven't got the deeds and I'll talk different. But till then, you just take my word for it and get out.'

'We're not doing any damage. God damn! You could swear we were runnning you out of house and home.'

'You'd do that if you had the chance.'

'You know we won't have a chance. So why worry?'

'Get back over that wall. And that's another thing. Don't let me catch you climbing over one of my walls again. What do you think I build them for?'

'I don't know. What for?'

'To keep my cows from straying.'

'As long as we don't teach your cows to climb, you're all right. Walls, fences, notices. You fellows that own things spoil everything that's worthwhile in this world. Everything. Do you hear me, Rufus? It's you ought to be in jail, not the trespassers. You ought to be in jail a year for every foot of wall you've ever built.'

'Do you want to see my deeds?'

'I don't want to see any part of you.'

'Get back over that wall, or I'll use the gun on you.'

'I knew it would come to that. Start to talk to you fellows and you go and fetch your guns. You're savages. You need missionaries as well as manure on these farms up here. Come on, Bob. He can't frighten me. There's a path through this field. He can't stop us.'

Bob pulled Alf by the arm. His voice was an anxious whisper as he talked hurriedly to Alf.

'Come back, Alf. Rufus is a funny man. Mad as hell when the mood takes him. He'll take us to court or something. How'd you like a ten bob fine? Ten bob out of our last pay. Just think of it. Come on, Alf. 'Tisn't worth it. I'll show you that view some other time.'

'That's one way of looking at it. No view's worth ten bob. But I can't abear seeing Rufus looking so pleased with himself.'

When Alf turned round Bob was already dropping to the other side of the wall. Alf followed him. He sat for a moment on the wall top. He repeated the salute.

'Rufus, make this wall a foot higher, and you can keep yourself as well as the cows in. I'd hate to see you walking about in the valley.'

Rufus threw his stick violently in Alf's direction. Alf dropped on to Bob's side.

'All right, Bob. Let's go down the same way we came. What's the matter with you? You treat these bloody landlords as if they were gods. They're as dumb as the fields they own. Tread on them.'

'I don't know, Alf. When I start on a walk, I got a notion that I won't be turned back by anybody, that I'll tell them to go to hell. But once I see them I turn cold, and all I can think about is getting away without a squabble.'

'And you a nature-lover. You must have been frightened by a landlord when you was a kid.'

'Must have been.'

Alf picked a reed and started to chew it.'

'Bob, there's a net being woven around here.'

'A net? I don't see it.'

'I see it. It's closing in around us.'

'Take that reed out of your mouth. I might be able to follow you.'

Alf spat the reed out.

'I was thinking. There was that chap who was talking to us on the square that morning you went down the street to fetch bacon. He was saying that twenty years ago you only had to open your mouth to get a job around here. Today they are taking our jobs away from us as fast as they can. That's one side of it. Here's the other. You talk to any of the old chaps about here and they'll tell you that when they were young they could walk anywhere they pleased on these mountains, and there wasn't anybody to tell them they were trespassing. Is it the same now? Oh, no. They take our paths away from us. We waste hours walking around walls that should never have been built, like we waste hours down there in the valley crying over derelict pit-shafts that should never have been sunk. It's some sort of plot, don't you think so?'

'Oh aye. Some sort of plot. This path's too steep. I'm slipping on these stones. It's shaking my guts out.'

'Might as well get rid of your guts. Now's as good as any other time.'

Part Two

1931

'There are knives in this wind.'

'It's sharp. It's nearly killing me.'

'Draw your muffler tighter round your neck.'

'I tell you I'm freezing. You ask me to choke. It can't go any tighter.'

'It's a hell of a day.'

Bob and Alf got to the top of the incline. The iron track flattened out. Walking became a little easier. Climbing up the incline they had been bent double to keep their faces from meeting the wind. Now they straightened out. They walked slowly in the direction of the highest tip which ran in a sharp ridge on their right. At the end of the ridge, further than they could see through the cold wet air, was the crane that lifted the full trams over the slope, tipping them. Both Bob and Alf had sacks wrapped up underneath their arms. Bob shook his out and wound it loosely round his neck. He looked colder than ice and more miserable than sin.

'That was a fine idea you had, Alf.'

'What idea?'

'Coming up this tip to pick coal on a day like this.'

'We had to start sometime.'

'Why start at all? It looks to me like one sure way of making life worse than it is already.'

'I never thought I'd come up here. But I had a talk with Herbert. He thinks that since this new government cut the dole by ten per cent and my dole came down to fifteen and twopence that it would help to balance the budget if I came up on the tip and picked what coal we need instead of paying the coal-merchant two bob a bag for it.'

'I didn't think you ever agreed with Herbert.'

'Mostly I don't. I'd rather pull his ears off than agree with him. The less we get on the dole the more we got to do to justify our being alive. Anyway, two bob a bag's too much to pay for coal. And what coal! That coal merchant's a bloody crook. Half the stuff he sells never saw the inside of a pit. He must be digging it out of his teeth every time he finishes a meal.'

'He doesn't look as if he ever finishes a meal. He looks half-starved.'

'He's saving up to buy himself a chapel.'

'God! Winter's a hell of a time. I wish I'd said no when you asked me to come up and pick coal with you.'

'Look, Bob! You are not chained to me. You can go back down if you like.'

'No. That's all right, Alf. I'm not used to the cold, that's all. I'll get used to it by and by, or it'll get used to me or something.'

'Act as if you were dead. It'll just sniff at you and leave you alone.'

'Is that right?'

'No.'

'Still I'm glad I came with you, even though you might have to carry me home in a sack.'

'Make up your mind. First you're sorry then you're glad. Which are you?'

'Glad. Sticking weather like this on top of a tip will make Lily think twice before she tells me I'm only half the man that Roger is.'

'Don't let her bully you, Bob. If I were you I'd try a few

tricks with her. Women like Lily poison this place. Leave her one day. That'll teach her to realise what a good fellow you are. Leave her. Live on the mountain for a couple of weeks. Then, when the tent collapses, or the grass gets wet or the food runs short, come back suddenly. Either she'll welcome you back with open arms and tell Roger to go to hell, or she'll arrange for you to live permanently on the mountain. You can't lose either way ... But serious now, Bob. You are twice the man that Roger is.'

'You think so Alf?'

'I do, and that doesn't make you good enough to boast about. I see Roger looking middling prosperous these days. Has he got a new job?'

'No. He's still on the dole, but he's got a part-time job canvassing for a washing-machine company. He's on commission. He makes about thirty bob a week on it. Not so bad for spare-time work, is it?'

'How does he manage it? He's got the luck of the gods that Roger.'

'He pushed himself forward and he puts four spoonfuls of sugar in every cup of tea he drinks. He says that gives him energy to go on.'

'And he puts four spoonfuls of the constitution into every breath he breathes. That gives him energy, too. If we could hide the sugar and the constitution we'd have Roger by the seat of his pants. He wouldn't be able to move.'

'He says he's got to have energy to go on.'

'Where's he going on to?'

'To a good job. He reckons that all the pits in these valleys could close down and there'd still be room for a man of talent.'

' 'Course there would. Somebody's sure to get a job counting the number of pits that have closed down, just to make sure they are all there and the kids haven't taken any home to play with.'

'Roger's been pretty good to Lily.'

'Lily hasn't done so bad by Roger.'

'Last week he bought her a new dress. It fights her tight around the body. It's got lilacs printed on it.'

'Doesn't that make you feel nasty?'

'No. I like to see Lily looking nice.'

'She looks all right when she's dressed up. Trouble is she always seems to be dressed up. How much work does she do about the house?'

'Not much. She's still pretty busy with that charity scheme.'

'Distributing those old clothes?'

'We get some pretty ragged-looking kids coming to the house asking for help.'

'And there are probably many more ragged-looking kids who come as far as your door wanting to ask for a new shirt or a new pair of trousers and hop it before they can ask, because they can't swallow their pride for long enough to ask ... Well, here's the tip. Here's where we pick our coal, if there's any to be picked.'

'Are we allowed to fill our bags here?'

'Who's to stop us?'

'This tip's private.'

'Who owns it?'

'Hasketh. He's the landlord of this mountain. I was told he had the sole right to pick coal from this tip.'

'Who gives him the right, God?'

'The colliery company.'

'Same thing by a different marriage. Well, no Hasketh or army of Haskeths is going to stop us picking a bagful of coal after climbing all that distance for it.'

Twenty or so men were standing on the slope of the tip with sacks in their hands. Some stood quite near to the top. The majority stood in the middle, three or four taking their positions near the bottom. As Alf and Bob looked up, the cranes were swinging the full trams out into the air. Each load as it left the tram came down in a black violent torrent. The load was made up of coal, dirt, dust and stones. Some of the stones were heavy. They hurtled down the slope, causing the men either to lie flat and let them pass over their bodies, or skip out of the way. Alf put his elbow into Bob's side.

'How often do those stones kill anybody? They travel down at about sixty miles an hour.'

'They say it's easy enough to dodge them.'

'You make it sound like a game. And if you don't dodge them, you're liable to get one through the stomach or walk home without a leg.'

'They had a bad accident up here about a week back.'

'I had a feeling there might have been. There's something in the air.'

'A tram broke loose from the crane.'

'God help! That's worse than those stones.'

'It broke a fellow's back.'

'Is he dead?'

'Not yet. They are waiting for him to die. He's got a house full of kids.'

'Will he get any compensation for that?'

'How can he? He was up here at his own risk. He wasn't working for the colliery company.'

'That's the first time I realised there were blessings attached to working for a colliery company. D'you say that chap had a house full of kids.'

'Six or seven.'

'Poor little devils. They are due for a great start in life. They'll probably have reason to be grateful to somebody … It seems we did the right thing to come up here. We were getting a lot too happy down there at home. A bellyful of this ought to make sensible people out of us again. Where shall we stand to do our picking?'

'The bottom looks safest to me.'

'That's where the stones are travelling fastest.'

'There's a better chance to dodge.'

'Trust you to think of that. Come on then.'

They watched two more trams being emptied. Not much coal dribbled down to where they were standing. The three intermediate belts of pickers had large competent hands. Alf noticed how intensely their eyes were concentrated on every object that rolled down the tip, distinguishing the coal from the slack, ever ready to lurch sideways out of the path of a fast-travelling stone. Alf threw his sack down and looked in his pocket for a cigarette.

'Those boys up there know all about this job. They are experts. All we are getting down here is experience. At this rate we'll get a sackful by next summer.'

'We'll have to get up higher.'

They were starting to climb when a man started to signal to them from the top of the tip. He was standing near the crane, a man of noticeable breadth and height.

'He's trying to tell us something,' said Bob.

'We can't give him any attention until we've picked our coal. Here's a lump. A beauty. The first bit I've seen since I've been up here.'

'That bloke's signalling again. He's shouting as well.'

'The wind's blowing the wrong way for us to hear what he's saying. Either we go up to where he is or he comes down us. I don't like the look of the climb. He'll have to come down to us. Keep your mind on your work, Bob. They're just going to tip a new load.'

They heard the tram jolt on the crane's arm. They saw the tram's door swung open. The load came down with a roar. A cloud of dust blotted the top row of pickers from view. A large piece of coal came rolling down in Bob's direction. He made ready to plunge sidewards to grab hold of it. It was intercepted by a lad of sixteen who was standing three or four feet above Alf. The boy's sack was a quarter full. In the intervals between each tipping he leaned on it and sang an interminable medley of love

— 148 —

songs, slipping from one song to another with a skill which suggested he might have heard the medley on a gramophone record.

Some of the songs Alf sang with him, others Alf didn't know and let the boy sing solo. The boy put his shoulders back to sing high notes. He had the outline of a good tenor voice. At moments he interrupted the singing to spit and clear the dirt away from his throat. He wore a suit that had once been light-coloured. It was made in a cheap material that looked like sack cloth. It hung away from his body as though it were going to fall off. His hair was blond and streaked with darker patches.

Alf had five bits of coal in his bag. Bob had three. The rain still drizzled. The sky was getting heavier. It looked as if the rain was going to come down in torrents.

'I don't think we'll be able to stay up here much longer. There's going to be a storm,' said Alf.

'I think so, too. There's that big chap coming down to talk to us.'

Alf looked up. The man who had been standing by the crane was racing down the tip towards them. As he came clsoer they noticed that his face was a lot cleaner than the other men's, his clothes better. He had the bearing of a naturally-born mining official. Big shoulders, big voice, big face, eyes diluted by beer, and bags in abundance. He came to a stop just above Alf and pointed his finger at him.

'Are you blind, chum?'

'No. I see all right,' said Alf.

'Are you deaf?'

'You know I'm not.'

'You act as if you was both. For the last ten minutes I've been telling you to get off this tip.'

'We are just picking coal.'

'That's it. You're not supposed to.'

'The tip's free, isn't it?'

'It belongs to Hasketh.'

'Are you Hasketh?'

'I'm his agent and I got orders to take your names and addresses?'

'Why bother? You know they won't be the right ones.'

'No tricks like that. This is a serious offence. You were stealing.'

'Stealing? This is a rubbish tip! You can't steal from a rubbish tip.'

'It belongs to Hasketh. All coal tipped on it belongs to Hasketh.'

'And on the seventh day there was light. What about these other fellows. They are picking coal, too.'

'They work for Hasketh. The coal they pick he sells.'

'What are we supposed to do now?'

'Either you tip that coal back where you had it or you pay me sixpence a piece for every bag you pick.'

'You mean we pay sixpence for the pleasure of standing here in the bitter cold, dodging those bloody stones and picking a sackful of coal.'

'That's Mr Hasketh's orders.'

'Has it ever struck Mr Hasketh that the few sixpences people have got are usually spent on food. If it hasn't something else ought to strike Mr Hasketh, something hard, and on the back of his head.'

'Shut your mouth. Mr Hasketh is a bigger man than all you bedbugs put together. Only Mr Hasketh could have thought of making a small fortune out of a rubbish heap.'

'Now somebody ought to think about making a small dungheap out of Mr Hasketh. What if we say we haven't got sixpence and we'd still like to pick a sackful?'

'You pick six sackfuls for Mr Hasketh and you're allowed to pick a seventh for yourself.'

'You are joking.'

'Don't tell me I'm joking, they are the rules.'

'God of mercy! Do you hear that, Bob? You pick six

bags at the rate of a penny a bag and then you're allowed to pick one for yourself. Are any of those fellows up there doing that?'

'Some of them.'

'The dull devils.'

'The tip is only free to pickers on Monday, Wednesday and Thursday, and then only after half-past two. This is Tuesday and it isn't half-past two.'

'They stop tipping at half-past two don't they?'

'That's right, and when the tipping stops, it isn't much my men leave over for anybody else to pick. Make up your minds. Are you going to pay the sixpence or will you pick six bags?'

'I wouldn't mind ramming six bags up Mr Hasketh's date. As for picking them for him at a penny a time and see him making a profit of a bob on every bag, I'd rather die, if it's all the same to you.'

'It's all the same to me.'

'I could have guessed that by the look of you. But I'll tell you what I'll do. We've walked a pretty long way up here. It's a lousy day for walking. We are wet through already and liable to get wetter. We don't want to go home empty handed. We got kids who haven't seen a fire for weeks. Let's pick a bagful and we'll pay you the sixpence next time we come up.'

'Fair enough. You look honest. I shouldn't do this by right. Mr Hasketh wouldn't like it, but it's your kids I'm thinking of. This is bad weather for them to be without coal.'

The agent made his way back up to the crane.

'He's not such a bad chap,' said Bob.

'He's got no eye for faces. He thinks we are honest.'

'Are we going to pay the tanner?'

' 'Course we are not. We'll find ourselves another tip. We'll never be rich ourselves. I don't see why we should slog to make Hasketh rich.'

The young blonde-haired tenor in front had turned round. He was smiling at them. He asked Alf what the agent had said. Alf said, 'Nothing much. Nothing very much.' The boy came down a step to hear what Alf was saying. A tram dangled from the crane. Alf shouted to the boy to keep his eyes in front of him. There were stones coming down.

The boy smiled, still more broadly. He turned round to face the tip again, just in time to have one of the biggest stones smash into his left leg. He went down with a scream. Alf and Bob dragged him towards the bottom of the tip. Alf stepped over him, to get in the way of any further stones that might roll down in their direction. The boy had fainted. There was a blank undernourished pallor about his face. His leg was badly twisted and bleeding. Bob raised the boy's trousers. He was trying to stop the flow of blood with his handkerchief. Alf bawled up to the other pickers, 'Hey you up there! Come down and give us a hand. This kid's hurt.'

Most of the men heard, but not one came down. They stayed where they were. They saw what had happened and resumed their work, concentrating as hypnotically as before on the task of gathering into their hands and sacks as many as possible of the bits of coal that rolled down to the tip's side. Alf shouted again: 'Can't you chaps hear me? This boy's hurt. Come down here some of you! For Christ's sake!'

No one came. Alf's anger came close to choking him.

The boy opened his eyes and started to groan and swear in turns. He had fallen on to his side when the stone hit him. One side of his face was smeared with damp dust. The other side of his face was deathly white.

'We better get him home,' said Bob.

'Where does he live?'

'I don't know.'

'We'll have to wait to find that out.'

'We might make him some kind of stretcher.'

'Out of what?'

'Some sacking and two bits of stick.'

'We wouldn't find stick strong enough. Not up here anyway. We could ask Mr Hasketh for a lend of a stretcher, but he'd probably sue us for disturbing his peace of mind. Whatever sticks you'd find around here wouldn't be strong enough for the job. He's a pretty big kid. Look at him. Bigger than you or me. His leg's in a mess. If that bleeding would stop it would be better. If we did fix up some kind of rough stretcher he'd break through it. We don't want to go out of our way to give him two broken legs instead of one … I wish those twits up there would put a stop to their picking and give us a hand. What's about the time?'

'Half-past two near enough.'

'They must be just about finishing.'

They heard the agent blow his whistle. Some of the men came down the tip carrying full sacks which they deposited in a heap on the side of a rough track. One of them, an oldish man with a limp, came towards them, wiping his face with a piece of old rag which left his face no cleaner and no dirtier than it had been before.

'Why didn't you come down when I shouted?' asked Alf.

The man kept on wiping his face, staring without interest at the boy's leg and at the boy's face.

'It wasn't our fault,' he said. His voice was low and submissive. He appeared to take no relish in talking.

'We got to fill a certain number of bags or we wouldn't get paid, so we couldn't stop.'

'That makes good Christians out of you. You couldn't stop, be damned. 'Course you could have stopped.'

'We got to fill a certain number of sacks or we wouldn't get paid. You heard me saying that.'

'How much do you get?'

'Ten to fifteen bob a week.'

'Hasketh gets his slaves on the cheap.'

'The money comes in handy, and it's work, isn't it?'

'It's work all right. Come on, let's get this boy down. Do you know where he lives?'

'Next door to me.'

'Bob and me'll carry him the best we can. You show us the way and pick us the easiest path, for Christ's sake. We don't want to shake him about more than we can help.'

The man with a limp led them down into a little valley. The path they took led them into swamps. They sank into them over their boots. They stumbled over hard, rushy little hillocks. Every time they stumbled the boy squealed, the old man told the boy to sing and forget about the pain. The boy didn't sing. Alf hummed, thinking that might make things easier. He was walking in front. The rain, heavier now, was beating into his face, rolling in streams down his cheeks, soaking through his muffler and drenching his shirt. He swore at swamps, rushes and hillocks. They passed a large house standing amongst trees to their left. He turned his head and asked the old man:

'Who lives there, mate?'

'Hasketh.'

'I hope he gets something he'll never get cured of.'

'He's got it.'

'Thank the Lord. How much longer have we got to go before we get this boy home?'

'Two or three minutes. It's that little street down at the bottom of this valley.'

'What's his name?'

'Wilkins. The Wilkinses are an unlucky family, always have been.'

'What's unlucky about them?'

'Tom Wilkins, that's the father, was in an explosion just after this boy was born. They never found his body. Dai

— 154 —

Wilkins, that's the boy's brother, he's in jail.'

'What for?'

'Hasketh cheated him. Said the boy hadn't filled as many bags as he said he had. Dai put Hasketh on his back and the judge put Dai in jail. Three months.'

The street came into view. The man pointed to one of the end houses.

'That's the house there. See where that shirt is hanging on the line. The number is fourteen, but we call it thirteen. That's because the postman never calls and the Wilkinses never get no luck.'

They entered the house by the back way. There was a short cobbled path running between two tiny plots of garden. Then eight steep steps down on to the back pavement. They had to be careful coming down the steps. Alf almost slipped. The flat paving was covered over with rain water that came down in a stream from the garden. Alf saw that the sink was clogged. Two bowls and a tin tub hung from the white washed walls of the back pavement. Their soaked shoes trailed through the rain water as they carried the boy slowly towards the kitchen door.

'This place is like a swimming bath,' said Bob. He was gasping and unsteady. The boy was heavy and the journey down had tired him.

'That's what comes of building bad houses on good hills.'

Mrs Wilkins was standing by the fire when they got into the kitchen. Bob and Alf stood by the door. They continued to hold the boy between them. They were waiting for the woman to tell them where to put him. Alf noticed that she seemed to look at the boy with the same lack of interest and curiosity as he had seen on the face of the man with the limp. He had the feeling that in the street where Mrs Wilkins lived calamities were not uncommon. Mrs Wilkins looked towards the man who had led them down.

'What's the matter now, Amos,' she asked.

'A stone hit him. It isn't bad.'

'It don't ever stop, do it? Always something happening to somebody. I'm thankful I've only got two boys. If I had more something would happen to them too. I'm thankful. I'm very thankful.'

She turned round to a saucepan of broth that was simmering on the fire. She drew the lid of it back to rest on the handle. Steam rose, tarnishing the brilliant brass work around the fireplace.

Put him on the sofa in the parlour, Amos. Show them the sofa. I'll ask Mrs Jenkins to go and fetch the doctor.'

Mrs Wilkins went out on to the back pavement and stood calling for Mrs Jenkins. Amos opened the door that led into the parlour. They followed him. The room was dark. The blinds on the windows were drawn. Amos warned them to be careful and not to fall over anything.

'The sofa's by here, right under the window. Can you see it? Not much light in here.'

'You better put that blind up, Amos.'

'Perhaps Mrs Wilkins won't like me to.'

'If the doctor's coming in here he'll need light, won't he?'

Amos pulled up the blind. Mrs Wilkins came in and stood by them. In the light that came in through the window Alf looked at her face. Her skin was yellow. The wrinkles around her mouth seemed almost bottomless. Her hands fidgeted on her stomach. Her whole bearing had been manufactured by successive phases of being in pain and feeling lost.

'Nothing much more we can do,' said Alf. 'So long now.'

'Thank you very much,' said Mrs Wilkins, as if she was wondering at the same time what she was thanking them for.

Alf waved his hand at the boy on the sofa. The boy's

face was turned towards the clump of mouldy, untidy-looking ferns in a flowerpot on the window sill. 'So long,' said Alf.

They made their way home along the main road that ran along the lowest spur of the mountain. There were houses on both sides of them, built on the stock and dreary mould common to the whole valley. A few people stood on their doorsteps giving a casual examination to whoever passed.

A tramcar came lumbering along, splashing water like a ship, tossing and rolling like a ship. Two children standing in a passage way looked into each other's eyes and sang in full voice the last few bars of a chorus for children. They stopped singing and cheered the tramcar until it turned the corner out of sight.

'What's there to cheer about a tramcar?' asked Bob, looking more puzzled than he usually did.

'The tramcar makes a noise.'

'So do the kids.'

'They don't make money out of it, though. There's nothing in their lives worth cheering about, so they just cheer to convince themselves they're still outside the cemetery. If their old man walked out on to the street in his woollen pants they'd cheer him, too. It's a habit, that's all.'

'I'm tired.'

'So am I. We've had a profitable day, Bob. We've had our first taste of ambulance work and I don't like the taste of it. We didn't get any coal. We haven't even got the sacks we started out with.'

'Our reward will be in heaven.'

'That's what I'm afraid of.'

'What are you doing tonight?'

'Nothing.'

'Come over our house after tea. I'll be in by myself.'

'Right.'

'How's Hugh getting on in college?'

'Fine. I got a letter from him last Monday.'

They did what remained of the journey in silence. Above the hills the darkness was already forming.

* * *

When Alf got over to Bob's house, Bob was still in that tub in front of the fire, bathing himself, enjoying the heat of the fire on his wet limbs. Lily was sitting by the table finishing her tea. Her beauty was graduating into the broad indelicate stage. She was wearing the lilac dress given to her by Roger. She cut a slice of banana and made a pâté of it with her knife on a piece of bread and butter she held in her hand. She told Alf to find himself a chair. She turned towards Bob.

'When this bright bugger gets himself dry and puts the bath out of the way, we'll have some room to move.'

'All right, all right,' said Bob. 'You can't hurry a thing like bathing. Remember old man Saunders, remember what happened to him.'

'I don't know him. What did he do?'

'He was too mean to use a towel on himself after he bathed. He always puts his shirt on straight. But the rheumatism got him. He stiffened up soon enough.'

'The rheumatics will never get you, Bob. They'll pass you by thinking you've got them already. In the bath or out of it you're always the same, slow as a slug and twice as useless.'

'I'm satisfied.'

Alf heard the chain of the closet outside being pulled. The door opened and Roger stepped in. He was younger than Bob, older than Alf and stronger than either of them. His shoulders were massive. The rest of his body was imperfect. One of his legs was lame. One of his eyes blinked perpetually. He spoke as if he were reading a will.

His hair was parted close to the middle. It gave a simple, open expression to his face that was out of tune with the cunning one felt to be a part of the man. The skin of his face was raw after a recent shave.

He looked at himself in the mirror that was hanging from a wall between the window and the door. He picked up a box of talcum powder that stood on a shelf built above the mirror and patted some on to his sore cheeks. He wore a brown suit in which the creases of brand-newness still persisted. The jacket of the suit was single-breasted with square cut bottoms.

Lily pushed a cup of tea over to the side of the table where Roger was standing. He watched himself drinking it in the mirror. Inwardly Alf described Roger as a cross between a peacock, a crap and a bloody nuisance.

'Bob says you were on the tip today,' said Roger.

'We were up there for a bit,' answered Alf.

'Get anything?'

'The startings of a cold in the head. We carried a kid home who was hurt by a stone.'

'Some chaps can't look after themselves.'

'You are not one of those, are you, Roger?'

'No fear. I've always looked after Number One.'

'What does it feel like?'

'Haven't you ever tried it?'

'Not as I can remember. I always get my numbers mixed. Never was no good at figures.'

'Well. Take it from me, Alf, my boy. It feels fine to be able to look after yourself. You'll never catch me larking about on tips wasting my time. Ever since I had my accident I haven't done anything for nothing.'

'A lot of us never get the chance to do anything, pay or no pay.'

'You never look. Would you have thought of canvassing for a washing-machine company?'

'No. Don't suppose I would have. We don't do any

washing in the house. When our clothes get dirty we make wine out of them.'

Roger laughed. He laughed at any jest whether it came from his critics or anyone else. He considered it a principle to encourage humour. There were inarticulate clerks at the Labour Exchange who thought they were masters at conversation after a talk with Roger.

'What tip were you on?' he asked.

'Hasketh's. At least he says he owns it.'

'Now, there's a fine man for you.'

'What's fine about him?'

'Nobody pulls the wool over his eyes.'

'When they do they should pull it so tight his eyes will pop out.'

'Get away. You are just jealous. He started from nothing and I guarantee he'll leave fifty or a hundred thousand when he dies.'

'Bastards or pounds?'

'Pounds, you fool. And he started from nothing.'

'That's true if you call being left a whole mountain by your father nothing. Where do you start from, Roger?'

'Nothing.'

'And you hope to end up like Hasketh.'

'I live in hope and keep my bowels open.'

Roger got his hat and brushed around the rim with a corner of the tablecloth. He had told Lily to hurry. He got Lily's coat, a thick red coat, with a collar that looked like a cat. She put it on, finished her sandwich, washed it down with a gulp of tea, wiped around her mouth with a tie that was hanging from the back of a chair. Bob asked her where they were going. She looked doubtful as to whether she'd tell him or not. Roger explained for her.

'There's some sort of do on at the British Legion. Men and women's branches, mixed meeting. They are picking the treasurers for next year's outing fund. Most likely they'll pick me and Lily. They couldn't do better, could they Lil? We like being treasurers, us two.'

Lily smiled awkwardly at Alf, seeming to hope from the expression on her face that he wouldn't draw any wrong conclusions from Roger's tone. Alf smiled back, suggesting by the shape of his mouth that he was drawing all the wrong conclusions that he could. Roger went off into the passage way. Lily followed, turning back before reaching the door.

'While I remember, Bob,' she said. 'If any kids call with vouchers from school asking to be fitted out with a suit or something, tell them there's nothing here for them. If they can't come when I'm in, they can go around with their backsides sticking out and welcome. There's not many clothes left from the last consignment, and I've already picked out the kids who are to have those.'

'All right. You always seem to have them picked out.'

'That's my business.'

Alf heard the front door slam behind them. He moved nearer the fire.

'Oh. She's an active woman, is Lily,' said Bob, with a half tone of admiration on his face.

'She certainly leads a full life. Full of what I won't say until my own conscience is clear. I don't like the way she talks, Bob. Does she talk any better in her sleep?'

'I don't know.'

'I thought you said you was a light sleeper.'

'I am, but I don't sleep with her. We got three bedrooms.'

'You mean two bedrooms and a lodger. Does he sleep with her?'

'I don't know and I don't care. What do you ask me things like that for? There's times when you are as bad as that bloody Roger himself. Why don't you leave me alone?'

'I'm sorry, Bob. I didn't think you worried about it.'

'A chap's got the right to worry over what he likes.'

— 161 —

'Aye, aye. Of course, Bob. I never thought … '

'Never mind. I shouldn't ought to have started shouting like that. Daft of me. Only sometimes I feel that people are taking advantage of me, that's all, and I don't like it.'

'You remember what I said you ought to do with Roger.'

'No.'

'Strangle him out of the way.'

'I couldn't do that.'

'His chest isn't always expanding. You'd be doing the whole place a good turn.'

'I haven't got the right to do a thing like that.'

'We've got the right to do any damn thing we like. This is the land of the free.'

There was a knock at the front door.

'Answer it, Alf. I can't walk through the passage without any clothes on.'

Alf opened the door. A boy of eleven or twelve stood there, with a sheet of newspaper over his head keeping off the rain. He held a piece of white paper in his hand. He handed it up to Alf without a word. Alf read it: 'Please fit bearer with a new trousers and a pair of shoes. He is a very necessitous case.' There followed a signature which was illegible.

'Who gave you this?' said Alf.

'The master in school, Sir.'

'He says you want some clothes.'

'Yes, Sir.'

Alf looked at the boy's clothes and boots. They looked as if somebody had been going at them with a sharp knife.

'The master's right, boyo. You are certainly necessitous. Step in here for a minute out of the rain. Where do you live?'

'Up the top terrace.'

'That's the wrong place to live for a start.'

'Uh?'

'Nothing. Talking to myself.'

'Oh!'

Alf opened the door of the front room where Lily kept the clothes she was suppose to distribute as local official of the Old Clothes Charity Scheme. On the table in the centre of the room there were twelve boys' suits, second-hand, and half a dozen pairs of shoes, new. Bob called in from the kitchen.

'What are you doing in there, Alf?'

'Working my way up to being JP,' muttered Alf to himself. Bob repeated his question. 'Just looking around,' answered Alf.

'Don't touch those clothes.'

'I wouldn't touch them if I was paid to. It's the shoddiest stuff I've ever seen.'

'They serve the purpose.'

'That's the point. They don't serve any purpose. These kids need the best. They never get it.'

'They don't have to pay for them.'

'Why should they?'

'If that's a kid at the door, tell him to go away for God's sake. Lily'll be tamping if you go fooling about giving clothes away.'

'Let her tamp. We fear no evil.'

Alf went out to the passage way where the boy was waiting staring about him ashamedly and grasping his sheet of newspaper under his arm.

'You got any pals, boyo,' Alf asked him.

'I got a lot of pals.'

'How many?'

'Seven or eight, easy.'

'Do they want clothes?'

'Most of them got holes.'

'Bring them here as soon as you can.'

'All of us?'

'As many as you can find.'

The boy ran off. Alf joined Bob in the kitchen. Bob was fastening his braces. He asked Alf to help him out with the bath before he sat down. They carried it out through the door.

'Don't bother about tipping it down the sink. Just let it go down the steps. The rain-water'll wash the soap suds away.'

Bob put the bath away in a little wooden shelter on top of steps. The shelter was full of that dull, sickening, damp-rotten smell that ran through the whole block of the company houses like a theme-song.

'What's that shelter for, Bob?'

'It's handy when it rains.'

'Where do you shelter from the smell in the shelter. It's enough to knock a chap over.'

'It's always been there. It must be something in the stones.'

'Or it's the way a place smells when you pay too much rent on it.'

'All the houses smell like that.'

'They all pay too much rent. Ten bob a week for cribs like these is robbery.'

Bob put his bare feet on the fender and started to cut his toe-nails with his finger-nails.

'What new method of cutting nails is that, Bob?'

'Lily's got the scissors. She carries them about with her. She says she's looking forward to the day when they'll come in handy.'

'The same reason as she got for carrying Roger about with her. She's looking forward for the day when he'll come in handy.'

Alf picked up the evening paper. The headline was a loud cheer for the country's impending prosperity. Alf glanced at it and threw it down.

'Lies and Rubbish, Limited. There was a time when I could read one of these things through. Births, marriages, deaths, racing tips and all. Now I can't even look at them without feeling as if I've eaten something bad.'

'You are getting too moody.'

'I'm getting too wise.'

'What's the cure?'

'Wrap a shroud around my head to stop me thinking.'

There was another knock at the door. Bob started to pull his stockings on hurriedly.

' 'S alright, Bob, I'll answer it,' said Alf, going to the door. There were eight or nine boys between the ages of ten and twelve waiting outside. In front of them stood the boy who had come before. Alf told them to come in. They followed him into the front room. Alf could hear Bob stumbling about trying to get his boots on, and asking in a shout what the hell was going on in there.

Alf took up his stand near the table. He told the boys to get themselves marshalled in a straight line and march past him slowly. He warned them to pick their feet up as they walked, and not to drag the mats up as they passed. To each of the nine he gave a suit. To the first six he gave a pair of boots each, to each of the three who got no boots he gave an extra suit.

'You can see if they fit when you get home, and if they don't fit don't go blaming me. Cut them up into floor cloths. Sell them or put them aside until you grow into them. Come back next week and we might have some moth balls for you.'

The boys made for the door. When they got there they found Bob standing fullstretch blocking up the opening. He looked angry.

'What in the name of Jesus are you doing, Alf?'

'Trying to feel like somebody important.'

'You can't do this.'

'It's done already. Let the kids go.'

'What'll Lily say?'

'She'll have plenty to say.'

'It's I'll have to listen to it.'

'Act as if you can't hear.'

'I've tried that once before. It only made her worse.'

'She can't get worse. She starts at the bottom.'

'For God's sake Alf. Listen to reason. Take the clothes back. You heard what she said before she went out. She's got the kids picked out who are going to get these clothes.'

'Kids whose parents can afford to slip her a couple of bob. I know Lily's games. Look at these kids here, Bob. Look at them.'

'I'm looking.'

'Do they look poor?'

'Poor as hell.'

'Do they look ragged?'

'Ragged as hell.'

'Do they need new clothes?'

'Aye. 'Course they do.'

'Well I'm giving them clothes. What's wrong with that?'

'Nothing, Alf. Nothing.'

'All right then. Let them go. We'll spend the rest of the night feeling proud of ourselves.'

Bob stepped back into the kitchen. Alf closed the front door after the boys. He got back to his chair in front of the fire. The fire was piled up and hot. Bob gazed at it glumly.

Alf put his feet out on top of the black-leaded oven. He felt contented and sensual. His thoughts were light blue like a heat haze. He wished he had gone along to see Gwyneth. At the back of his mind, coaxed out of its hole by the heat, was an idea of regret that Gwyneth meant so

— 166 —

much to him. She had never given him all he wanted. From the women he had known before he had met Gwyneth, he had taken what he wanted by the mouthful and the armful, and never felt any sense of gratitude from what he got.

Gwyneth had kept him dangling. He always had a feeling that she'd like to tear all her clothes off and go mad, just as much as he did. He could tell that by her eyes. They burnt and seemed to keep on burning deep down inside her, until he felt after looking at them for a couple of minutes that if he touched her stomach he'd find it hot; hot just like this fire that was scorching the leg of his trousers. But Gwyneth kept him dangling.

She had notions about purity that made Alf squirm. Notions about going down the aisle in white. Alf hated aisles as much as he hated the colour white. He had the warm gospel of happiness on his lips, and there were times when Gwyneth froze it into long icicles that sank into his flesh like knitting needles. But he liked Gwyneth. She was the only woman he could stand to hear talk like that from. He groaned and thrust his hand down into his trousers. He could have slobbered over the body of any woman, even Annie, Annie who lived next door, whose eyes were too stupid almost to look at, whose face and body were out of gear.

They sat for an hour without lighting the gas. Alf thought of the things that pleased him that he didn't have, Bob of the things he had that didn't please him …

'I'm going over, Bob. I'm tired.'

'Aye. Best thing I could do is go to bed.'

'If you're thinking about those clothes, tell them I did it before you could stop me, and if Lily wants to chew my ears off, I'll be waiting for her. Send her over.'

It was still raining when Alf got outside. He waited on Bob's doorstep while a bus passed. The road was narrow. The bus filled it, splashing the pavement with the water it churned up from the pot-holes. Half-way across the road Alf heard someone calling. He looked around. Annie's father, Mr Taylor, was beckoning to him. Alf walked back to hear what he had to say.

Mr Taylor was standing in the full light of the lamppost. He was wearing a navy blue suit of ancient cut but worn so little the material still looked new. There were numberless buttons on the coat and waistcoat. Both were unbuttoned and Alf didn't blame him for baulking that job. Mr Taylor's boots were heavy and unlaced. Their soles were half an inch thick, and the uppers were lustreless with the preserving greases that had been rubbed into them. Mr Taylor's boots were like himself. With careful handling both looked as if they might see the century out. He wore no collar but made up for this with a flat-crowned bowler that gave him a pressed and mournful appearance. His face had been fixed into lines of immovable contentment by the mechanical piety he had cultivated in his thirty years of chapel-going.

He had finished work at the pit a week after Alf. A year later he had forfeited his unemployment benefit for not genuinely seeking work. His Christian training had debarred him from saying lies fast enough to suit the local unemployment authorities. When he applied for parish relief the Relieving Officer had warned him that before relief could be granted, Mr Taylor would have to subsist on the one hundred and fifty pounds he had put away in a savings bank. Mr Taylor had said he'd rather starve.

The grocer, whose philanthropies had been so many pints of life-blood to the town so that his normal activities could take away all the life-blood at a later date, found Mr Taylor a job as a handy man in the grounds of his mansion. There Mr Taylor had stayed, straightening the back of every flower in his care and keeping his own back persistently bent lest the grocer should think he lacked in servility.

Mr Taylor shook Alf by the hand. Alf sensed patronage in his gesture. He had observed that men in jobs, even in such a lousy little underpaid job as Mr Taylor's, were falling into this patronising attitude towards men who drew the dole. It angered him and made his throat feel like a kettle on the boil, ready to shoot scalding steam into the faces of those whose actions towards him seemed to smack of pity or contempt.

'Good evening, Alfred,' said Mr Taylor. He had heard two thousand different preachers in his time, and had learnt the art of speaking in instalments from every one of them.

'Hullo, Mr Taylor.'

'I was wondering if you would do me a favour?'

'Anything, Mr Taylor. Anything. I got lots of time to do favours.'

'I'm getting a load of coal tomorrow. I'm getting it by the ton. It's much cheaper when you get it like that, if you understand.'

'If you can afford it, it's all right.'

'Whether you can afford the pounds depends on whether you are able to save the pennies. Do you save the pennies, Alfred?'

'Not that you'd notice it.'

'That's a pity. I believe in thrift for young people.'

'That's a true word, Mr Taylor. All us young people need now is something to be thrifty with. What about this load of coal?'

'The men tip it in the back lane. They come early in the morning. I'd put it into the coal-shed myself, but I'll be busy in the mansion until the evening.'

'You want me to put it in for you?'

'If you'd be so kind.'

'I'll be kind. What time shall I come over?'

'Nine or ten .'

'Right. The load'll be in the shed by ten o'clock.'

'There'll be a reward for you, Alfred.'

'I was hoping so.'

' 'Tisn't often those without work have the opportunity to earn a little extra.'

'Not often.'

'I feel it is my duty to do all I can for young men who can't find work.'

'That's a fine faith, Mr Taylor. It ought to be made public.'

Alf shook the rain from his shoes. He couldn't decide whether the wet feeling at the bottom of his feet was the rain coming in or his self-respect going out. The look of beaming complacency on Mr Taylor's face was getting more and more intense with every second that passed. Alf felt that a few minutes more of Mr Taylor's neat and tidy saintliness and he'd have to rub his forehead against the cold, streaming corrugation of the lamp-standard to save himself from vomiting.

From one of the upstairs rooms in Mr Taylor's house came a formless moaning sound. Alf heard Mrs Taylor call out in a voice that sounded like finger nails being scratched over a blackboard, 'Quiet, Annie.' The noise stopped. Annie was quiet.

'Good night, Mr Taylor.'

The house was empty when Alf got in. It was one of Herbert's busy nights. He wouldn't be in till late. Alf turned on the light. The food was still on the table from tea-time. Alf made some toast and ate it standing up. Moving around the table with long dancing strides, he took some of the sting from his restlessness. Some of the butter from the toast ran onto his fingers. He considered himself lucky to be unemployed and still have butter to eat. He licked the butter from his fingers. It seemed to him that toast was the only thing he had eaten for years and years. It was easy to make and cheap.

Alf thought it would be better if Hugh was still there.

He missed Hugh more than he liked to say. He turned the wireless on. There was a religious service coming from somewhere. The minister or vicar, or whoever it was, was well under way with a sermon that kept referring to peace as if it was something well outside the scope of human power ever to obtain.

Alf stood with his head on one side trying to chew loud enough not to hear what the man was saying. He changed the station. He landed in the middle of an Italian opera. Alf didn't know the music, but there were a few people singing and what they sang sounded full of unreasonable love and unreasonable hatred. That's what he liked.

He heard steps coming up the stone passage way at the side of the house. They were too light and hurried to be Herbert's. He felt almost certain it was Lily. Without knowing why, but feeling sure that he was doing the very best thing he stood in front of the mirror and brushed the grease from around his mouth with a tea towel which he picked up from the armchair.

Lily it was. She did not stop by the door. She came straight in to the kitchen as if it were her own. She had taken off her hat and coat. Her big body was almost bulging the lilac pattern off her dress. She was short of breath as if she had run from her own house and up the steps that fronted Alf's. Alf guessed from the look in her eyes and mouth that she had already come pretty near to talking her head off. Her breasts looked hard as flint. It struck Alf that she might have been rubbing her eyes in them to make them blaze as they did. Lily's anger was a wonderful thing. Those people in the district who were timorous and subservient as well as chronically poor went in dread of it. Lily was, with or with out her plastering of painted lilacs, a very wonderful woman.

Alf found himself wishing that she had come as a lover and not as a quarrelsome neighbour. Large, strong and mordant as his desires were, she seemed larger, stronger

— 171 —

and even more liable than his own lust to bite the corners off him. At that moment he would have betrayed Bob with a smile. In all likelihood Bob would have smiled with him. Lily looked ripe and ready to be taken any time of the day, any day of the week. If Roger could do it, so could he. The practice of breath-control hadn't made a superman out of Roger.

'Have a sit down. Lily. You're out of puff. Been running? Take this chair here. It's so hard it'll make you glad to get back home.'

'I wouldn't sit down in this house, not if I was busting.'

'Please yourself.'

'Bob just told me what you did with those clothes.'

'You want me to go over the story again?'

'I know it off by heart already. Bob said it three times. Three times he said the same story, so it must be true.'

'Bob couldn't say lies if he wanted to. You are lucky to have a husband like that, Lil.'

'Shut up. I know that you've been trying to poison Bob against me.'

'You poisoned him against himself. If it hadn't been for the poison I gave him he'd have been in the County Asylum by now.'

'That's where he belongs, mixing up with chaps like you.'

'What's wrong with me?'

'You've got a dirty mind and you're a thief.'

'I got a dirty mind; sure enough, but I'm no thief. I never got the chance to steal anything.'

'So what you did with those clothes in my front room wasn't stealing, was it?'

'Do you think it was?'

'They were my clothes, in my front room.'

'Those clothes belonged to the people who needed them. They were no more yours than mine.'

'I suppose the people in charge of the charity scheme

picked you to distribute the clothes?'

'I'm too honest for the job. Why did they pick you anyway?'

'Because they know that I got the cause of the suffering kiddies at heart.'

'Lily, when you talk like that you make me sick. I'm no Women's Branch of the Legion. You can say the truth to me.'

'You make me sick. Alf Evans, and that's the truth.'

'We make each other sick. We ought to get married and start a plague ... The suffering kiddies! I like that, Lil. As long as there are people like you, who'll stand up with tears in their eyes and say they got the cause of the suffering kiddies at heart, it's a safe bet the kiddies are going to keep on suffering for a hell of a time.'

'Since this charity started the kids about here have been a bit better dressed, haven't they?'

'The kids I see look just the same.'

'They are the people who are too proud to apply for help.'

'They are the salt of the earth.'

'The scum of the gutter I call them.'

'Salt just the same, though. They smell like something else. But one thing I will say, Lily. You are looking a good bit better dressed, since you started having a finger in the charity pie. There's that dress you got on now. It makes you look like the queen in a flower show.'

'Roger gave me this for my birthday.'

'What charity is he running?'

'Roger's a man. He stands on his own feet.'

'Because he buys you a dress ... That's the best of living in a place where there's a lot of unemployed. Spend ten bob on a woman and you become something like a sultan.'

'Would you spend ten bob on me?'

'Would that make you like me?'

'I'd be grateful.'

'Christ! It's easier than I thought. Lily, if you knew the thoughts that are passing through my head you'd throw something at me.'

'I could throw something at you without knowing your thoughts.'

' 'Course you could but you'd miss half the pleasure. No, Lily, I wouldn't spend ten bob on you.'

'Perhaps you don't think I'm worth it.'

'I haven't got ten bob and I don't want to be a sultan.'

'You prefer to lie flat on your stomach and grouse.'

'That's one way of keeping out of sight.'

'Another way is to go to jail.'

'Who's talking of jail?'

'I am.'

'Who's going there?'

'You are.'

'What for, for Christ's sake?'

'Taking those clothes.'

'Still on about that? And I thought we was going to be friendly.'

'We are too poor to be friendly. Come and see me when I'm about sixty. I might be in need of somebody to talk to then, but not till then.'

'I'll be willing to wait. Roger might have let his chest down by then. It'll be nice seeing that chap looking normal and less like a battleship.'

'One day you'll be sorry you ever said these things about Roger.'

'One day I'll be sorry I ever was born, but I'll wake up the morning after. That's the damnable part of it. What are you going to do about those clothes?'

'Report you or get you to pay for them.'

'I wouldn't pay and I don't think you'll report me.'

'Why not? Think I'm afraid? I'm not. When anybody swindles me I get my own back.'

'By swindling someone else. You'd better not report

me, Lily. I could make a good speech about the way you handle this second hand clothes charity scheme.'

'A speech? How much do you know?'

'Those clothes are supposed to get into the homes of the unemployed, is that right?'

'They do. That's what the charity is for.'

'And you never made anything out of it for yourself?'

'I don't get paid, if that's what you mean.'

'You've never accepted sixpences and shillings from people whose kids have come to you for clothes?'

'No.'

'You're a liar.'

'Well, what if I have? The people who organise these charities at the top they make plenty out of the unemployed, they get good screws. I do my bit and I'm entitled to a share.'

'That's right, Lily. Sting them for all they are worth. If they are daft enough to pay you blood money, it just shows that being unemployed has made them softer in the head than when they were working.'

'But you can't prove that I ever made anything out of it.'

'No? What about all those clothes you've taken down to the rag market and sold to the second-hand dealer with a stall close to the door? That's a funny way of distributing clothes among the needy.'

'Who told you about that?'

'Bob.'

'He tells you everything doesn't he?'

'He's my friend.'

'He's a pest.'

'Shove something in his mouth and your secrets will be safe.'

'He's almost as much of a pest as you are. I was planning to make five or six bob on those clothes you gave away tonight.'

'Is there anything you wouldn't do for five or six bob, Lily?'

'Nothing that I can think of.'

'That's a hell of a state for anybody to be in. If I was an Apostolic like that bloke next door I'd try to save your soul. I'd go out on the nearest street corner and bawl my guts out telling people about all the stinking rotten things you do with that charity that's supposed to help them.'

'Why don't you?'

'I'm too lazy. What could I tell people about the wickedness of man or woman that they don't know already? The tale is told a million times a week. Nobody gets any better and nobody gets any worse. If we all went out preaching about the wickedness of dogs or horses or cats, they might get interested enough in the business to hang you and Roger outright for making such a ramp out of this charity business.'

'You'd like that wouldn't you, Alf?'

'I'd provide most of the rope and all the cheers.'

'You're a funny fellow. Alf.'

'But don't you worry. I told you I'm lazy. As far as I'm concerned you can keep on being dishonest until the day you die or people wake up. Good luck to you. Good luck to them! 'Cause I think we are all damned in some fashion or another. There was a time when I had a lot of energy. That was in the good days when the corn was ripe, when there was plenty to do and plenty to earn. If I saw anything mean it turned my stomach like the sight of a dead sheep. I wouldn't sleep until I kicked it out of the way. But I'm slipping now. This being out of work for a long spell is worse than I imagined. If I see a dead sheep these days I poke it with my finger to see if it's fit for eating. I'm going all to the devil. And the things and people around me are going to the devil faster than I am. I sit back and watch them.'

'You can't watch me. I'm not going to the devil.'

'Yes you are, Lily. You ought to be glad of it. He'll give you a dress made out of real lilacs. That'll make you smell good as well as look good.'

'Have you got a regular girl, Alf?'

'Aye. Why?'

'God help her.'

'That's what I was thinking. Good night, Lily.'

Alf listened to Lily's feet rattling down the passage way and on the steps. The opera on the wireless still continued. The tenor and soprano were proceeding with a love duet. Alf thought they were carrying harmony a bit too far. He felt glad Lily had gone. Talking had dried up most of the lust in him. He wondered how the boy with the injured leg was feeling, and whether Mrs Wilkins looked much yellower in the light of gas than in the light of day. He switched the wireless off and went to bed.

* * *

Alf was half way through putting Mrs Taylor's load of coal into the shed. He had carried in all the bigger lumps. His back was aching, but not much. His hands were sore. He had opened the skin on his right palm, but it had stopped bleeding. He was shovelling the smaller coal into two buckets that Mrs Taylor had entreated him to use very gently and very carefully. Mrs Taylor's life, small, drab and unmanured, centred around things like the state of her buckets. If she found them bruised, dented or stained, she'd grieve for many days.

Alf shovelled the coal in carelessly. He didn't believe that buckets should be allowed to play a part in any person's life. It was still raining. He was wearing a mac that Hugh had left last time he was home. On his head was a cloth cap turned back to front. He had swivelled it around when the raindrops began to collect on the peak and drop before his eyes. That had annoyed him. He felt more industrious when he had nothing to overshadow his eyes.

Mrs Taylor was in the back bedroom, cleaning. At intervals she leaned out, shaking the fluff and dirt from the head of her mop or beating a yellow duster against the wall of the house as if she was signalling for help to someone standing on the mountain. Every time she leaned out she looked down at the buckets and asked Alf to remember what she had said about treating them with proper respect. Alf told her that if the buckets were his own children, he wouldn't be treating them more gently. He whistled his satisfaction when Mrs Taylor closed the window and went off into another bedroom. He had long ago come to the conclusion that Mrs Taylor had a stomach full of crab apples that twisted her life into all shapes except the right one.

Alf saw Mr Rees, the old age pensioner who lived next door to the Taylors, coming down the steps of his house with a cardboard box full of ashes and old papers. His face, as always, was merry-looking and red. Alf thought he saw the beginnings of sadness in the droop of the old man's mouth, but that might have been due to the rain. Mr Rees was all wrapped up. He seemed to be wearing every garment he possessed. He looked twice his usual size. He walked slowly as if each of his limbs was being held back separately. He put his ashes out into the back lane. His voice quavered badly as he said 'Good Morning' to Alf.

'Hullo, Mr Rees,' said Alf. 'How are things with you?'

'Not bad, boy. Not so bad.'

'You don't sound as if they are so good.'

'It's the weather. We old people feel it worse than you.'

'You're looking all dressed up.'

'I'm wearing everything I've got.'

'Waste not, want not. I thought you looked a bit bulky.

— 178 —

You are walking about like a bear.'

'It's cold in the house.'

'Haven't you got fire?'

'Not today. We are waiting a bit before we buy more coal. Coal's dear and the pension isn't much. Sarah I'm thinking of more than myself. She's poorly.'

'Borrow some coal. If Mrs Rees is poorly she'll freeze to death without a fire.'

'I asked some of the neighbours to let me have a bucketful till ours came. Some of them said they didn't believe we'd ever pay it back, others seemed to be as short of coal as we are.'

'Mr Taylor isn't short. Look, he's got a fresh load here.'

'I couldn't think of asking Mr Taylor.'

'What's wrong with it.'

'You know how he is. He says that if he can mange, other people ought to.'

'No wonder that man sings his hymns so sweet. Ask me for a couple of buckets of Mr Taylor's coal. I'm not religious, so I don't mind pinching a bit off Taylor to keep you warm.'

'I couldn't do that.'

'You are not doing it. It's me. Go back into the house. You're getting wet. Where's your coal-shed?'

'Just round by the back door.'

'Right'o. So long now. Tell Mrs Rees not to worry too much about the winter. Winter's just another dirty trick they play on us to see if we are really made of flesh and blood after all. Tell her I'm going to see her about again strong and well.'

'I don't know how to thank you.'

'Go on. Remember how you used to give me toffees in paper when I used to go to chapel as a kid.'

'Aye. I remember well.'

'Those toffees were the only reason I ever had for going

to chapel. Think of that. If it hadn't been for you the chances are that I'd never have gone to chapel at all.'

Mr Rees made his way up the steps back into his house. Alf looked up at the bedroom window from which Mrs Taylor had been shaking her dusters. He couldn't see her there. He called 'Mrs Taylor', not too loudly. No answer came. Mrs Taylor was busy in the front bedroom. She was throwing her whole weight and zeal into the job of polishing a walnut dressing table.

Alf called her name again. There was no answer. He filled the two buckets and slipped them into Mr Rees's shed. He repeated the journey, then carried what was left into Taylor's shed. He had an idea that Taylor's eyes had been so sharpened by years of counting the collection in chapel he might notice there was some of the coal missing.

Alf was not disturbed by what Taylor might say. He didn't like Taylor nor any of Taylor's back-bent toadying breed. Alf leaned against the shed, not bothering to take shelter. The work had warmed him, he felt the rain cool. He recalled that this was the third good turn he had done in twenty-four hours. It worried him. Nobody ever seemed to give him credit for being able to do good turns, and he got no satisfaction from doing them. They seemed to leave the total mass of poverty so little diminished. He didn't see that he had ever been treated well enough to justify his ever being kind. Kicking people in the face was more in his line. He thought of Mrs Taylor's face and wondered what it would be like kicked. Hard in the middle.

He felt a deep desire to hurt Mr Taylor, to lay strong, merciless hands upon him and see the smug, happy, little man squirm and yelp and confess himself as capable of desperate misery as those irreligious wretches for whom he wept every Sunday evening with all the waterworks of his piety. Alf walked up into the Taylor's kitchen. Right

— 180 —

oppposite the door, the first thing he laid his eyes on was the photograph of Mr Taylor, much enlarged, and crystal clear in every respectable detail. The photograph did nothing to lessen the nasty taste in Alf's mouth. Mrs Taylor was still upstairs. Alf stepped in from the doorway and looked around the kitchen.

Annie was curled up on the sofa behind the table. Her lower lip hung down like torn wallpaper from a damp wall. Alf thought she must be grieving for a moment for those children she had had, which Mr Taylor had exiled to his sister's farm in Carmarthenshire. Annie's eyebrows were black with no space between them. She had a girl's weekly paper in her hand. She was turning the pages over, looking at the illustrations, looking at them as though they were reflections of herself and many miles away.

She was talking to herself without much rhyme or reason. She kept curling and uncurling her legs on the sofa. She was dressed in black. Dressing Annie in black was Mrs Taylor's way of apologising on behalf of the whole family for Annie's lapses in the past. Keeping Annie a prisoner in the house was Mrs Taylor's way of forestalling any lapses by Annie in the future. Alf could guess how much of a Calvary Annie had been to Mrs Taylor. He felt grateful to her for the damage her idiocy had caused.

When Annie saw him she jumped up, looking excited. She came from behind the table, dragging her hand along the oilcloth covered surface of the table, tipping a full just-opened tin of condensed milk. She stood by his side, laughing. He looked at her seriously. He could feel the seriousness in his own expression. It affected him like an ill-fitting hat. It made him feel like a probationary officer, passing juvenile deliquents under his view in the Thursday morning court, with a reformatory staring out of each eye.

He stopped looking serious and laughed back at Annie.

She ran her right hand over her breasts, pulling her dress down, wiping away from her fingers the condensed milk that had stuck to them when she upset the tin. She came very close to Alf. He wondered if there was anything except a curse a man could say to Annie without sounding a fool. He said nothing. He knew he wasn't a fool.

She started to unbutton his mac. He pushed her away.

She sat down on the sofa and cried. He heard the tempo and passion of her sobs becoming higher. He took another look at Mr Taylor's photograph. He felt again the full flavour of his hatred for that man with his philosophy made from the powdered leaves of desires hung up from the ceiling to starve and dry.

He made up his mind to do full justice by Annie and treat it as an act of social vengeance on the head of Mr Taylor. He pulled the table quietly away from the sofa. He beckoned her to move up and give him room. Alf was an expansive lover. Annie stopped her tears and gave herself to him, thanking him with three or four minutes of low, faint whimpering, coming from some place within her body that Alf could not fathom.

He got up quickly, as if wanting to run away from himself. He had decided from the beginning that the event was going to make him feel a bit sick. He bore with the feeling as best he could. He buttoned his coat, stood at the bottom of the stairs and shouted up to Mrs Taylor that the load was in the shed and his job was finished.

Annie was leaning forward with her elbows on the table, watching everything he did as if expecting him to come back to her. He kept his eyes away from Annie. Mrs Taylor came down, carrying a handbag the size of a shopping basket. She opened the bag and sunk her head in it. Alf thought that with a few straws in her hair she'd look like a horse with its feed. She gave him a shilling. He took it in his hand and gave it back to her.

'Isn't that enough?'

Mrs Taylor's voice always went into a worse screech than usual when she came across something she couldn't quite understand. It went through Alf like the tiny teeth of a fretsaw.

'It's enough, all right. Today I'm working for nothing, that's all. It helps to make a man feel better than he really is.'

'You're daft, mun.'

'Nobody's denying that, Mrs Taylor. Use the shilling to buy Annie a bagful of sweets.'

'We never buy Annie anything like that.'

'Start now. It's not a sweet life. That's why people eat toffee. So long.'

He pulled his cap the right way around and left them, Mrs Taylor put the shilling back into her bag, peering into it once more as if expecting to see further miracles in its depth.

* * *

Alf slipped half a dozen potatoes into the saucepan. The potatoes were perfectly clean and as near white as they could be. Alf had scraped them first and scrubbed them after. He himself was not particular about the state of the potatoes when he ate them. But Herbert always pouted if he found any blemishes on his vegetables. Alf humoured Herbert on as many points as possible. When Hugh was not there, Alf and Herbert were never far from each others' throats. They tried to make things as easy as possible. They treated each other with respect, which worked itself out in the form of carefully sustained and indifferent silences.

Alf kicked the fire down with his heel and put the potatoes on the boil. He knew exactly how long they would take to boil. He had become expert in the simpler forms of cookery. Herbert had asked him to try his hand at making cake. Alf had answered that he'd rather try his hand at murder, with Herbert as the object of the first lesson. Herbert had left it at that, contenting himself with the loaves of yellow cake he had brought home from the shop.

Alf lit a cigarette end that he had found on the mantelshelf. He settled down in a chair and took Hugh's last letter from his pocket. The notepaper on which the letter was written was thick-lined and inexpensive. It was folded up and bulky. The outer pages were stained with the dirt from Alf's pocket. He straightened the letter out and started to read.

Dear Alf,

This is our favourite time of day. About nine in the evening. Just about the time when we used to come out of the pictures and go for a walk around the back streets before going home for supper. I've been around this college place a good few times looking for back streets that might resemble ours, in the hope of finding people that might smell of humanity, but I haven't found any. I've never seen a place where people smile so much as they do here. They smile at me, they smile at themselves, at the weather, at every damn thing you can think of. One day they'll tell me what makes them so happy. I see no reason for it.

Being born where we were born, in the valley, must have an effect on our eyes. I confess myself to be in a fog as far as these people here are concerned. Maybe they've always had more than enough food, and always a penful of fat porkers to throw the surplus to. They'd better watch out. Some time in the future their contentment will lead them to its logical conclusion, and they'll feed themselves to the pigs. And as far as I can see no higher use could be found for them. We feed pigs with acorns. If we eat acorns it stops up our bowels, and that's the effect these people have on me. They try their best to make me feel at ease and sociable, but I don't see the joke of living as clearly as they seem to. My face remains as cheerful as a heavy mist on the mountains when the night's coming down. Because I look surly, they think me ill-mannered. Because they look tickled to death, I think them crazy. So we are quits ...

Our kind are the poor people. Among them we were moulded, to them we belong. There are poor people here. I've sought them out, looking for comfort and comradeship. Some hope! They are like seaside donkeys with all the lights beaten out of them, full of awe and worship for the wealth and leisure they see straddled on top of them. Miserable, worthless people. Fit to be swept into the sink and forgotten. Some of them crawl like worms. Chop them with a knife in an effort to make them spring from the dirt and the parts keep on crawling. They made me discover something about poverty that I didn't know before. Our own valley folk are poor, but they are poor only in necessities. In all else they are richer than the gods themselves. Why people who are richer than the gods should have to go so often through a few days of every week without enough food is something I'll leave you to find out. I won't try it. The land around here is much too flat and swampy for me to think very much. Mountains are the only place to think. You can have your thoughts on one mountain and beyond that there can be another where you can forget what you've been thinking about.

As I sit here, the valley seems thousands of miles away from me. Every inch of the distance is a thorn in my flesh.

Beneath my window a group of fellows are singing. They bring back to my mind those nights during the big strikes, when the boys used to sit around on the mountains harmonising till the light came up. *That* was singing.

These chaps come up here clenching their teeth with the desire to have as good a time as possible before the day of leaving college brands them as old and serious citizens pledged by all the vows that stupidity and cowardice can think of to earn, procreate and never do one single thing that will cause a ripple in the waters of social security.

Have you ever heard an idea that was more on the slant than that one? These boys here are fed from babyhood on the notion that their elders have life properly in hand, have surveyed and analysed all its recourses and possibilities and planned out the whole of existence like a race which is to be run in given stages, with a bullet in the back as the reward for anyone found deviating, even by an inch, from the decisions of the Executive Committee. The result of this is that these chaps are never anything else but babies. They drink beer, but they do it in just the same way as they drink milk from their mothers' breasts, with just the desire to fill their bellies and to prove that they exist. They kick their footballs and row their boats with the same babyish pride in being able to move about and feel the muscles of their bodies that drove them to walk for the first time round the walls of their nurseries. They go to their debating clubs and literary societies. I've watched them and listened to them. Do you know what they sound like? You remember those little infants they used to put to stand in the pulpit in chapel anniversaries to prattle off a couple of verses from the Bible. That's what they sound like.

Usually I stand apart from them. They understand my desires as little as I sympathise with theirs. Some of them look at me as if I was some new form of manure. But I've got the drop on them. I know that they are manure, and not even in a nice form. Right or wrong, I feel I stand as far above them as Moses above the Israelites. It's ten to one that I am as wrong as Moses was, but that's the way I feel. They are happier than I am and I envy them for it. They know all about their lives, because there's so little to know. They know where they are going, and they are training their bodies and minds in the best way they know how, to go there. I haven't got that certainty. That's because I've lived in the valley. There life contains so little and that little can be so easily kicked away, we don't attach too great a value to it. Always at the back of our minds there's an idea that tomorrow or the day after tomorrow there'll come a blow-up so terrrific that even if we survive we'll be faced with a task that's harder even than dying in the form of starting our lives all over again from scratch, perhaps without the gifts, the materials, or the desires we had before.

I have no clear idea of what I want to become. Blessed

was the day when I could say outright that I wanted to be a missionary, and have people laugh at me because I looked less like a missionary than the people the missionaries go to work on. Sometimes I get the urge to jack the whole thing in, come back to the valley for good and justify myself by putting on a pair of heavy-nailed boots and kicking the entrails out of everybody who is sufficiently a fool or a swine to sprinkle the holy waters of approval over this corrupt stew of ignorance, poverty and wretchedness that passes for a civilised community in the eyes of those who benefit from it.

But slowly, I may be changing my mind about that. In the valleys you see just one side of it. You see the large majority oppressed and conscious of oppression, primed with anger and ready for revolt. Living among such people gives you an optimistic faith that social change as sudden and violent as a lightning stroke, as sweet as the cessation of pain, is a daily possibility, waiting only for the right degree of crisis and desperation and the right incidence of trained, resolute leaders. But where I am now, I see another side of the question, a side that is darker and more depressing.

Here we have people who are satisfied and stable, not hungry and afraid. The highest thrill most of them get is taking magnesia because they are dyspeptic. The world where people drink spirits of ammonia because they are starving is more than a closed book to them. They look at it as a horrible mystery, to remain in ignorance of which they would sacrifice three-quarters of their earthly goods. They not only like things the way they are, they consider it criminal that an alternative arrangement of things has been spoken of in whispers by their pale-faced brothers of the pits, foundries and fields.

When I came here first I tried to explain to them about the valleys I came from. I told them exactly why we thought that bailiffs, policemen and preachers were basic elements of that ceaseless, maddening oppression that makes such a sordid, miserable mess of nine out of every ten lives that see the light between the hills of a mining valley. I thought they'd understand. That understanding is part of the intelligence with which we are born and it stays with us until we go to earth, unless in the meantime the zeal of our parents turns us into a bailiff, a policeman or a preacher. But these people didn't understand. They thought I was being smart and witty. They looked pleased at having discovered a fresh talent. They told me they'd have me back to tea again when the weather was not so sultry.

As far as I can see at present, these people are the real strength of society. We protest with words. They would answer back with forms of violence that we would never dream of. Even when our hatred of unemployment, want, insecurity and avoidable disease is at its angriest and most violent, we have doubts about how far our anger and violence can go, and how best to direct them. These people have no doubts. Their cause, in their eyes, is sacredly, unquestionably just, and exclusive of all fears and hesitations. Having no doubts, they have rid themselves of the most damnable hindrance know to human activity. It makes them invincibly strong. There is something serene in the completeness of their armoury. It makes me afraid and draws my horns in. It brings me up to the conclusion that I had best look after myself and those who are closest to me, and let the rest of the world go to the hell where it rightly belongs.

I'll go through with this business of a college training never mind how much it hurts. At the end of it I'm almost certain to get a good job. Just think what that'll mean! It'll be a form of vengeance on the poverty that rocked us as children. It'll give Herbert the idea that he had created a masterpiece in the spectacle of my life entering slowly and proudly into the paths of worldly success. I can subsidise you and Gwyneth in a great campaign of making up for all the happiness you are losing during these frozen years. Then she can spend all her time getting back the health which working in that shop has taken away from her.

I'm sorry to hear you say she's getting to look worse. It makes me sick to think of it. It's like standing still waiting for the time to cover you. There's so little we can do. We might try screaming, but that's too much like being religious about it. It almost finishes the job of convincing me that this selfish worship of narrow, personal desires is better than the dangerous and possibly useless pursuit of social justice.

I wish Lloyd was up here with me. Between him and me we'd have this place walking around in circles. But he always was an obstinate mule. He picked a college that nobody else had thought about. He reckons the headmaster hadn't even heard about it. That's why he went there. I got a letter from his last week. He'd just been to a lecture on the white slave traffic, given by a woman who looked as if she knew the business back and front. Lloyd was taken up by the idea. He tells me that as soon as he's finished, he's going to start a chain of brothels up and down South Wales. They'll bring in enough money for him to buy the navy and convert it into a wholesale fish and chip range, and he'll also use them to infect every member of the enemy class with syphillis. Some of Lloyd's ideas ought to be marketed. That would get rid of the market.

Herbert's letter makes good reading. He tells me he's been trying to persuade you to go to London to tease a job out of Uncle Henry. He sounds hurt because you told him to mind his own business. Herbert understands nothing about other people's minds. That's what makes him so happy. If he did he'd worry himself to death trying to decide whether he was understanding the right things. He says the managing directors of the firm are very pleased with the way he's running the shop. He appears to have got the wages of the assistants down to the lowest level in the history of the firm, and now all the assistants in the other branches are getting their wages trimmed in honour of Herbert's business genius.

If you ask me, we'd be doing the world a favour if we dropped Herbert in the river one night and saw that he stayed there. He gave me a full description of that posh dinner he went to a month or so ago. Bank managers, pit managers, cinema managers. He sang hymns to them all. He says that the dinner was the happiest three hours of his life. But if I remember Herbert properly, his whole life has been a succession of happy three hours fooling about in functions like that. He was willing to bet me that the company of such men as these mixed managers, with their obvious air of assurance and power, would transform my outlook completely. I wouldn't be surprised. Transforming someone's outlook is only one of the effects that death has ... Herbert will prosper as long as pettiness and cruelty are sponsored as virtues by the whole of society.

My scholarship money comes next week. I'll send you on as much as I can spare. It comes from the government so have no scruples about taking it. What they take from you in the form of a ten per cent cut on the dole, I'll make up to you in this form. If they only knew how they were being swindled they'd hold a special all-night sitting to save the state from ruin. So long, Alf.

Always your brother, Hugh.

Part Three
Midwinter, 1935

Hugh threw the pen away from him and sprawled over the table, burying his face in the litter of application forms and testimonials that spread over the table's surface. He raised his head and stared and stared at them. He had the notion that they were coming to meet him like an ocean of seaweed, getting in his nose, his eyes, his ears, his hair. He looked down at the half-copied testimonial that lay under his hand. He had long ago outgrown the necessity of looking at the original. The words looked like empty barren lies, like a childhood prayer in the mind of a man who had just thrown the faith of his fathers down the drain.

Hugh Evans. That was right. Applying interminably for jobs that seemed to have evaporated from the face of the earth hadn't altered that. Evans was the name of his father. Hugh was his own Christian name. Hugh Evans. That was right. Maybe if he altered it, it would charge his application with a new significance in the eyes of the Education Boards, or whatever sponge-brained lackeys had the giving of the jobs for which he applied. Hugh Evans BA: fine official sounding talk! Hugh thought of a news item he had considered sending in to the national press. 'Youth has been discovered in this mining valley who is not a BA. This individual has been taken into custody and closely questioned.'

Hugh went on reading the testimonial. 'Studied at this college.' It was good of them to admit that. There seemed to be a lot of doubt about it in people's minds. 'He bears a very excellent character.' That was merely a recognition of the fact that they had at times been conscious of his being alive. They might just as well have said that he bears hair on certain parts of his body. They wanted to make quite certain that a man wanted a job. They made him write the fact down in ink on an endless stream of forms, so deadly monotonous in their shape, their place-proud clerkly formulas, that they'd end up driving a man mad and giving him the lunatic strength necessary to send him out into the streets screaming, 'I don't want a job. I don't want a job. I don't want a job.' Then the authorities, good men who believe anything they hear three times, could shrug their shoulders, glance at each other with professional understanding based on two chapters from a bad book on child psychology and say 'He doesn't want a job.' They will then order the candidate to be impounded along with dogs who have lost their reason and their jobs, and forthwith to be destroyed, either by putting gas in his stomach, or strychnine on his tongue, or by making him eat raw all the certificates and diplomas he had ever won on his way through school and college ...

'What experience of teaching have you?'

Hugh looked at the top of the form. It was an application for an educational post in one of the British Protectorates. He felt that his chances for such a job were slim. It would be reserved for one or other member of the public school pack of baying imperialist hounds. He answered the question carefully, in the roundest handwriting he could make his pen accomplish. 'Twenty-two years of being taught. Take it or leave it.'

He enclosed the forms and testimonials in envelopes. There'd be two and six needed for stamps. He'd have to wait for Herbert to come back. Herbert said that if Hugh stopped applying for jobs, the post office would have to start selling fruit as a sideline to keep up its profits. Hugh didn't deny that. If he had a job, at least he'd be able to buy some fruit. That was more than he could do in his present state. He shredded some cigarette ends into a pipe and lit it. The smoke left a taste of old death in his mouth, but buying cigarettes was getting more and more difficult. His pocket money went on stamps. Herbert would not tolerate even one single penny going on things that did not help forward the search for a job. Herbert had asked him to submit himself to a programme of disciplinary vigilance. Hugh had submitted, committing himself only to a promise that as soon as his difficulties were over he would clench his fists and cut some of the complacency from Herbert's face.

Alf came down from the backyard, whistling. He had grown much thinner. The straight, deep furrows that ran down his cheeks gave an expression of increased hardness to his face. The casual humour that had once been in his eyes and around his mouth had gone. In his hand he held a cartoon he had cut out from that morning's newspaper. He found a pin and stuck it to the wall. He stood back to look at it.

'What are you going to do with that?' Hugh asked him.

'Frame it, if I can find some wood.'

'What's it about?'

'Can't you see?'

'My eyes are going all to hell. I can't see anything but forms, testimonials and positions vacant.'

'Are they getting you down?'

'Driving me scatty.'

'This cartoon'll have the same effect on Herbert.'

'It's the drawing of fellows marching. Is that right?'

'Hunger Marchers on the road to London.'

'Herbert won't eat his meals with that hanging on the

walls.'

'That's what I'm hoping. He doesn't believe there are people in this valley living so close to starvation it would come to them if they whistled. If he goes off his meals it might rub his nose into the truth.'

'He's never forgiven you for going on that Hunger March last spring.'

'I'd never have forgiven myself if I hadn't gone. The only thing I am sorry about is Bob. I should never have persuaded him to come on the march. He wasn't strong enough, but he had the spirit. I think he'd have gone even if I hadn't influenced him. Bob was all right.'

'He might have died because it was time for him to die. It happens like that with some people.'

'That's daft talk, Hugh. Daft talk. It's never time for anybody to die unless they've had everything from life that life can give them, unless they are so happy they are afraid there can't be any more happiness, only less. Does that go for Bob? What happiness did he know? Lily made him unhappy. She acted the wife with Roger and all she could spare for Bob was the hope that he'd be sensible and die out of the way. If only there was a law stopping men from loving women the way Bob loved that goddamn Lily, the sun would shine oftener in these parts. But the only laws we've got are moonshine.'

'Moonshine is right. They get deeper under the skin than any other kind of shine.'

'I always told him he ought to strangle Roger. It always worried him because his arms never seemed strong enough. He was hoping that a few weeks on the march to London would make him stronger than Roger and he'd be able to get on with the job. But heaven protects the wicked. Roger's still walking about. Large as life and twice as rotten. Singing praises to the constitution. Seeking adoption as an Independent Councillor, pledged to fight the Communists tooth and nail, fixing the price

— 194 —

lists already for the jobs he's going to sell when he gets elected, and so used to sleeping with Lily without a marriage certificate pinned to the pillow he's still doing it and she's still a widow. The world should have gone out of its way to preserve Bob like it preserves gold, so that he could have been cleaned and trained for the job of doing justice on that king-louse Roger. But Bob never came back from London and God Almighty only knows what damage that Roger was saving up to do on the world before that big chest of his goes down for the last time. When it does we'll dance on it, to make sure it never rises again.'

'You waste a lot of time hating Roger, Alf. He's just another odd crap among a million. Why bother about him?'

'This valley's got a dirty side. A side that's sore and festering. We can love it all we like, but it would be childish to turn a blind eye to that side. Roger is it. He'd betray all the comrades that ever were for a good word from a magistrate. He's something like Herbert, but more of a rat, more harmful ten times. There aren't many people I like. I never tell them I like them. I show it by hating the people who hurt them. Roger hurt Bob and I hate Roger. It's a funny thing, Hugh. There was no limit to the way I liked Bob, but I never told him with my tongue that I liked him at all. Now I wish I had told him. It must be rotten to die with a feeling that you've never meant the slightest thing in anybody's life but your own. Those walks me and Bob used to take over the mountain, I'd have gone stone-hatch without them. He kept on talking about the mountain the day before he died.'

'You were with him all the time?'

'All the time. He was feeling pretty bad when we reached London. Some Welsh people who used to live in the valley took him in. I knew he wasn't going to last very long. You want better treatment than we get on the dole to resist pneumonia.'

'And his dying won't stop the Means Test coming in. That Unemployment Act is going to operate in full force. They'll have to take the unemployed in hand if they want to keep this land a rich man's paradise.'

'I suppose they will. Sometimes I go cold and shivery inside wondering what's to become of this valley, wondering what's going to become of us.'

'That's the question, Alf. What's to become of us?'

'Can you answer it?'

'Not quite. I still have some hope left. Not much though. And that's wearing thin. When it's all gone I'll report back for instructions.'

'The valley won't get any help from the outside. Like a big fat, brainless cow, it's given all its wealth away, and all it can give now are the tiniest dribblings of milk. From now on all the valley'll get will be kicks and worse kicks. It'll have to find its own way out of the mess. There's no fear of us going so stupid we'll start taking the kicks for granted. Nobody kicks us and gets off scot free.'

'But we can't wait around here all our lives, waiting for people to wake up. We might grow old and still find ourselves waiting. We've got lives to live. Or so the story book tells us. Are you still fixed in your idea of never leaving the valley?'

'Having Bob at hand made it bearable. Now he's gone I might find it easier to get out.'

'What about Gwyneth?'

'She doesn't count any more, she's going to die.'

'What do you say?'

'I said she's going to die.'

'Christ! You say that as if you're talking about the weather.'

'I wish I was. I wish to God I was. But it's Gwyneth I'm talking about. Have you seen her?'

'No.'

'See her. And if the sight of her makes you feel bad, just

think how I feel when I look at her. I was the one who was going to marry her once upon a time, and give her all the happiness she could stand. No wonder she laughs at me sometimes, though she don't laugh now as often as she used to. But she sees the joke as well as I do. And what a joke it is! It ought to be on the back of every matchbox in the country, just to prove what a heaven on earth we live in. Five years ago I said I'd take her out of the shop because it was killing her. She's still there and every day she's finding it harder to walk there and stay there till closing time. She can hardly move. She can hardly ever sleep in the night ... I've treated her so kind and gentle I might have been her father. Why the hell didn't we go at it in the beginning like a pair of cats on the tiles, and tell the world to go to the devil? At least that way we'd have had some satisfaction. But we thought things would work out all right in the end. They are working out, I'm damned. They are working out fine. Gwyneth made me promise never to go the limit with her until we were properly married. That's one promise I kept and I can't give you reasons because I don't know any.

'Five years ago I knew what I wanted and had the guts to take it. I can't do that any more. I'm almost afraid to be myself in case people will think I'm acting under false pretences. If that's any consolation to the people who close down the pits they are welcome to it. They are making greenfly out of us. Either they squirt powder over us that puts paid to our acount or we get together and blight their roses. Five years ... ! For all that time Gwyneth kept herself clean as far as I was concerned. That might not mean very much to you. But here's the cream of it. Twice she'd had to sleep with that sandy-haired ram Owens, to keep her job. She doesn't think I know. But a fellow can feel things like that even if he doesn't hear about them.'

'It's hellish, Alf. That's the only word for it. And I was

the bright bastard who was going to get himself a good job and put you and Gwyneth on easy street.'

'That's not your fault, Hugh. You look as if you are going to start crying over all those envelopes. This is the way things are. If you don't like them, beat them into another shape.'

'They beat us into other shapes. Why doesn't Gwyneth go away?'

'She'll have to. To a sanatorium or somewhere. She might be doing it years too late, but it'll be a relief for her to get away from her old man. He walks about like something they've just dug up from wet soil. He's a madman. Every time he sees me he whispers in my ear, "She's sinking, Alf. Every day she's sinking. Just like her mother. Lower, lower every day she's sinking." As if I didn't know that.'

'She might get well.'

'She won't. I'm telling you she won't.'

'That sounds pretty cruel, Alf. You make it sound as if you don't want her to get well.'

'It isn't that. God help! If any amount of my blood could help her, she could have it. But haven't you ever had the feeling that you want to see a thing through to the end. Sitting in the pictures, you don't come out half-way, do you? Even if it's a bad picture you sit it out. That's how I feel about Gwyneth. Our lives are spoiled. Nothing will ever make up for what's happened to us. When Gwyneth dies it will be the finishing touch. That's what I want to see.'

* * *

The sub-editor of the *Clarioneer* was a stout man in the doldrums and the fifties. He sat at his desk, his chin in his hands, his brows contracted in a dreamy frown, that made him look as if the same thought had been worrying him for many years. He stared at Hugh as if he couldn't fit him in with the rest of the office. Hugh waited for the sub-editor to start talking. It was like waiting for a concert to begin.

'Working for the press, Mr Evans, is a great responsibility and a great opportunity. You are never to be forgetful of that. A great opportunity. Were you conscious of that when you applied for the position of local correspondent of our paper?'

'I was conscious of the fact that it might provide me with pocket money. That was all. I'm fully qualified to teach, Mr Anderson. I don't see that you are doing me any great favour by giving me this job. In different circumstances I might be earning a good wage. But I'm not. So the less we talk about responsibilities and opportunities the better.'

'Do you realise who you are talking to, young man?'

'I don't see that it matters.'

'I don't suppose it does. I like talent. Never had much myself. My father gave me this job. I inherited his pipes as well. But you seem to forget you're asking me for a job.'

'If it was a decent job, I'd adopt a praying attitude never fear. But for the chance to do scab labour at a few bob a week I don't see why I should.'

'You are not a Bolshevik, are you, Mr Evans?'

'I don't see that that's got anything to do with it.'

'This paper has got a long-standing reputation for fairness and independence.'

'You mean it circulates among a lot of people who don't do very much thinking as a rule.'

'Very respectable people and very old-fashioned.'

'Nobody more to the left than a Lib-Lab and nobody more to the right than a corpse.'

'I don't quite follow what you mean by that, but I wouldn't doubt but that you are right. See that your copy sticks to facts and that the facts don't amount to very much. Most of our readers believe that everything in the garden is lovely.'

'They are lucky to have gardens.'

'They are saving people. You don't have to comment on mining valley life. That's done by our editor.'

'Where does he live?'

'Cardiff.'

'What does he know of mining valley life, living in Cardiff?'

'That's the beauty of it. He doesn't know anything about it. That's talent, being able to write five hundred words a week on something you know nothing of.'

'Seem to be pretty widespread.'

'Our editor has a conservative bias. He owns the paper as well as edits it.'

'That's a talent in itself.'

'The most important branch of your work will be reporting funerals.'

'Funerals?'

'Our subscribers take a great interest in death.'

'They're probably all dying on their feet.'

'And the most important part of reporting a funeral is to get the relatives to have a two-and-sixpenny acknowledgement printed in the paper. Unless they give the acknowledgment we don't print the report. That's fair enough, isn't it?'

'Is it? It sounds pretty measly to me. Do you mean that I've got to go around drumming bereaved people for half a crown just to get their names in the paper? Why don't you print news? Stuff that really matters.'

'You are twenty-five years too young, Mr Evans. The stuff that really matters is not news. Anybody can find that. What matters is profit. We specialise in funerals because funerals bring in money to the paper, and the money they bring in we use to pay our local correspondents. Don't forget the rates. For the acknowledgment, two and six. For every wreath mentioned, threepence.'

'Wreaths too? This is a better organised business than coal. The people here are too poor to be levied like that.'

'Don't be too sensitive on that score. You young men have a weakness for overplaying the theme of poverty. Even the poorest have themselves insured. Every death means ten to twenty pounds in insurance: and because they like to have their names in print. That's the proudest moment in their lives for some of them.'

'Doesn't say much for the rest of their lives, does it?'

'And don't forget, Mr Evans. Don't be scrupulous about charging the full rates. If they don't pay you, neither do we. Of course, for your other copy you get the ordinary rate of two and three a column. But you pay yourself on funerals. Anything you make on funerals in excess of what you make on ordinary copy comes back to the office.'

'How much did you say I'd make per column?'

'Two and three.'

'The fellow who did the job before me got three bob. You haven't shortened the columns, have you?'

'No. They are the same length. But we are reducing the rate all the same. Your predecessor had a wife and child to keep. You have no such burdens.'

'That's as dirty a way of exploiting the unemployed as I've heard, Mr Anderson, and the only people in the country today who don't seem to be exploiting the unemployed are the unemployed. Two and three! That's slave labour.'

'Going to refuse the job?'

'Not me. I need the money more than I need my principles. But promise me one thing.'

'Within reason.'

'In case I never find such a job as I was trained for and might have to stay on this game for a while, will you raise the rate back to three bob when I get myself a wife and kid?'

'Of course. Of course. Good day, Mr Evans.'

* * *

Hugh's eyes closed, his head dropped over the notebook he held in his hand. He always felt tired when he sat in a strange kitchen. This was the tenth strange kitchen he had sat in that week, taking down the details of dead men's lives, the names of mourners, bearers, officiating preachers, graveyards and the relatives who had donated floral tributes.

But not a cent had he collected so far. The deaths he had reported all came from the lowest economic stratum of the working class, which took in nearly the whole of the working class. The relatives had smothered him with all the facts he had needed, but not one of them, so far, had seen eye to eye with him on the need for a printed acknowledgment in the paper.

Hugh had already spent some time thinking out the excuses he was going to give to Anderson. Anderson had been talking a lot of poppycock about that insurance. Six out of the ten families had no insurance. The other four had found plenty of vital necessities on which to spend the money. Hugh's conscience on the subject of squeezing money out of such people was as tender as a bruised eye.

He listened to the talk of the half dozen women who were sitting around him in the kitchen. One of them, the first woman he had ever seen starting to lose her hair, had known his mother and hadn't seen him since he was a small boy. She kept pointing her finger at him solemnly, overcome by the discovery she had made about his origin. Every time Hugh looked at her he felt as if he were being charged with a crime. He didn't like it. He tried to keep his attention fixed on the widow, who would have sat up straight, stopped crying and answered his questions if it hadn't been for the two women who sat on each side of her, holding her head down, commanding her to cry her eyes out for the good of her soul and the soul of Jabez, the departed, and telling her not to try answering questions, not in her state.

He tried to get some information about what Jabez, the dead man, had done to amuse himself during the fifty-four years he had waited to die. He sang in seven male-voice parties, said one of the women, who sat in a corner picking the almonds from a piece of cake and putting them in the pocket of her pinafore, keeping them safe, as she explained, for our little Winifred, who do find almonds very easeful for her little bowels. Hugh wished he had a foot of Winifred's little bowels handy to wrap around the neck of those two nuisances who were acting as bodyguards to the widow. He turned to the woman in the corner.

'Jabez must have been fond of singing?'

'Oh he was,' said the woman. struggling up eagerly, only to be forced back into her sorrowing position by the bodyguard.

'Seven is a lot of male-voice parties for one man to sing in. How did he manage it? He must have been throwing his voice.'

'No,' said the woman with the almonds. 'Jabe was a good second tenor, but there was some pieces where he couldn't stay in tune for the life of him. And when Jabez went out of tune he didn't make no bones about it. He'd bring the whole choir to a standstill, so out he'd have to go.'

'I can't put that in the paper.'

'Why not then?'

'It wouldn't be fair to Jabez.'

'He'd have liked to have seen it in the paper.'

'I bet he would have. But he won't, will he?'

'That's very true.'

Hugh ran his eye up and down the notebook. He

seemed to have all the facts he needed. He looked at each of the women in turn. They stared back at him, wondering what more he wanted. He addressed the bowed head of the woman, hoping that the hands of her protectors were not blocking her ears.

'I've got ten wreaths mentioned here. That'll come to two and six.'

The widow's head sprang up. This time with no resistance from the women on each side of her.

'How do you make that out?' she asked.

'Ten wreaths. Threepence each.'

'But I didn't want wreaths. Jabez didn't either. They just came.'

'But putting the list in the paper is a good way of thanking the people who sent them.'

'I don't want to thank them. I didn't want them. Jabez would have enjoyed the look and the smell of them when he was living and nobody sent any.'

'That was an oversight, Mrs James. I got a list down here. If it's printed it'll have to be paid for.'

'How can you ask me for money I can't pay?'

'Don't get worked up, Mrs James. You can't dislike the idea more than I do. It's just part of this job. If you can't afford to acknowledge the floral tributes, I'll scratch the list off.'

'That's right. Scratch it off. And you'll put the rest in the paper, won't you?'

'Mr Anderson willing, it shall be printed in full. Don't mind if I look a bit down in the mouth. I get paid according to what I can make on these funerals. This is the tenth funeral this week where I haven't made anything. If it gets any worse I'll have to go around stopping people dying, just to keep my job. That would annoy a lot of innocent people who really want to die; but, as I say, things are looking pretty slack.'

'I'd like to help you so much, Mr Evans. But we've got

to be so careful about how we spend our money these days. My sister Salina here, she lives with us. She's on the parish relief. She wouldn't like to be seen spending money on anything but food and rent, in case the Relieving Officer will bring her to book for making the wrong use of the money. The Relieving Officer's a very strict man. If he saw them wreaths in the paper, he'd think Salina had been frittering away her relief.'

'Tell Salina to remember that the money she gets on the parish doesn't come from the Relieving Officer. The storks bring it. And if he gets strict again, tell her to blow in his eye. That's the best way of bringing all local officials round to reason. I'll be going now. There's one favour you could do me before I go. Do you know any more deaths around here?'

'There's Mrs Beatty's little baby. Buried yesterday.'

'Who's Mrs Beatty?'

'Her husband is an engineer. Good job he got. You ought to do something there. They live in that nice little street at the end of this road, number sixty.'

'Sounds like the end of the drought. I'll go there.'

* * *

Hugh had a surprise when Mrs Beatty opened the door to him. She was small, plump, intelligent, not as grief-stricken as he had expected. He couldn't associate her with the idea of a dead baby. She reminded him of a baby, as alive a baby as he had ever seen. Her voice when she spoke appealed to him. Her body when it moved appealed to him. Even without the anguish he had culled from reporting unprofitable funerals he felt he could have followed Mrs Beatty into the everlasting. He followed her into the front room of her house where there was a large fire burning. The room was richly furnished and very large. It looked like the threshold of the everlasting.

Hugh tightened his fingers on the notebook in his macintosh to tear his mind away from the dreams it was feeding on. In this room could be found a measure of peace and security. She beckoned Hugh to take a chair. He took one near the fire and wished straight away that he had chosen one nearer the middle of the room. He felt too warm already.

Mrs Beatty sat opposite. She looked at him thoroughly from his shoes to his hair. He was glad that both his shoes and hair were black. He didn't want any particular part of himself to be prominent in the eyes of Mrs Beatty. He liked the way her dress hung from her shoulders. He stated his business.

'You've got a very nice face,' she said.

'I don't think so.' He wondered if there was anything wrong with Mrs Beatty.

'I'm looking at it.'

'Have it your own way.'

'You are a student, aren't you?'

'I was. I'm now returning to ignorance as fast as I can.'

'You are not satisfied, are you?'

'Why should I be? This job I'm doing would embitter the saints. It isn't dignified, it isn't decent. Sitting in front of you, I'd like to be both.'

'This valley's the wrong place to be sensitive.'

'It's the right place, but the wrong age.'

'Stop fidgeting. Still, it's nice to see someone who's on edge.'

'It might look interesting. It feels hellish. I'm sorry I ever came here to bother you. Why should we sit here and talk about a funeral you want to try and forget as fast as you can? I'll wait a few years, see if I can sweat this penury out of my system, then come back and we'll talk about something that's really interesting, something that'll do me justice and not make me feel like a belly-crawling tout.'

'No need to embarass yourself. You get paid for having a report of the funeral, don't you?'

'A little.'

'Here it is. "First, and most likely, last child of Mrs Beatty, buried January 3rd, age three months. There were expressions of grief from the mother, but not any signs of grief or interest from the father, who, as an official of the coal combine, working anything from twelve to fifteen hours a day, doesn't find much room in his life for trifles like loving and dying." Will that do?'

'I'd like to see that printed in full.'

'Why?'

'It was very moving.'

'I've been in this house a year and a half. Since I've been here I've had lots of chances to make moving speeches into the empty air.'

'I'd like to listen to you.'

'That's good. The sound of my voice makes my husband sick!'

'What's the matter with him?'

'He doesn't get the chance to have anything the matter with him. He's hardly ever here. He lives in the pit for the pit. It isn't a baby he wanted. It was a new patent coal-cutter, and he'd have expected me to suckle it even if it had torn my flesh to ribbons. It's funny the number of things that can make an idiot out of a man.'

'Idiocy has always been a byproduct of coal.'

'Are you a native of this place?'

'Since birth.'

'You know all about it?'

'I've made notes in the margins.'

'I'm not a native. My marriage brought me here, and since marriage I've been looking for whatever will take me away.'

'You are less contented than I am.'

'I could show you new forms of misery, if that's what

— 207 —

you mean. I've got quite a collection.'

'I'm always willing to learn.'

'Teaching you would be an experience.'

'Try it any time you like. My ears are always open. My nights are always free.'

'You say you know this valley. Is there any happiness here at all?'

'There was some when the druids used to cut people's hearts out. That was the quick way of dying. It pleased people whose lives must have been spent looking at the crops lying together under trees. Since the druids we've been given slow ways of dying. The biggest part of the people around here don't get enough to live on. They can't very well be happy, can they?'

'No. And what about me?'

'You are a different case. I always thought that people in the valley who had more than enough money were bound to be happy. If you are right, even that's a myth.'

'Mr Beatty doesn't think so. He claims to be happy.'

'He's a beacon light. He ought to be preserved.'

'He will be. He'll never do anything that'll make him different from what he is now.'

Hugh stood up. His tongue was finding it harder all the time looking for the right thing to say. There was something over and above spontaneity about Mrs Beatty. He thought she might be a little touched. Her eyes were bright and fixed, her body bending towards him.

'Well, thank you very much, Mrs Beatty. Talking to you has been all right. Any time you want to know more about the valley, I'll tell you what you want to know and more.'

'What if I wanted to know more about you?'

'Count me in with the valley. If the crisis deepens I'm likely to become one of its permanent landmarks.'

Mrs Beatty took a purse from the arm of the chair on which she was sitting. When she opened it Hugh saw it was full of silver. He had a feeling in his mouth and stomach that he remembered having felt as a child whenever he saw something he wanted very much. The feeling surprised him. He had never imagined that infantile greed had persisted in him.

'How much do I owe you?'

Hugh waved his hand. 'Don't bother, Mrs Beatty, please don't bother. Allow me the privilege of leaving without the taint of beggary on my head.'

He had spots in front of his eyes as he said that. He knew that he'd have prostrated himself in all his nakedness in front of her, and allowed her to stamp on his bare flesh trumpeting her domination over him in return for just one half of the money she held in that purse.

'Don't be childish,' she said. 'Here's five shillings.'

'That'll be a help. You'll find the report in the paper.'

'I won't read it.'

'Then I won't write it. Take the money back. I'm learning to be an honest tradesman.'

'You need it, don't you?'

'God only knows. It's manna from heaven.'

'Eat it till you feel you've had enough.'

'It makes me feel like a prostitute.'

'Wait till you've felt like one for as long as I have, then you can grumble.'

'All right. I'll take it. We are not encouraged to have much pride.'

'Do you think you'd be happy if you had enough money?'

'Happier than I am now?'

'Would you take it off me?'

'That would be a daft thing for you to do.'

'My husband earns good money. The company he works for doesn't give him enough time to spend it or to see how it's spent. I'd like to help you. I'd like to help you very much. I'd like to talk to you often. I'd like to know any man who is more intelligent than the things that happen to him.'

'That's me all the way. I think you're right, Mrs Beatty. A minute ago I had a feeling that I was playing around on the verge of a great sin. That shows how raw and sensitive my skin is, doesn't it? The feeling didn't last for long, but it sort of paralysed me while it did. It sprang from my Methodist parentage. My father and forefathers have been strict Nonconformists since the days of the great Revival. They'd look with horror at what we are talking about now. They were good people, or they wouldn't have been revived. All they knew about was the need for food and sleep. They knew nothing about unemployment, the sort I know of. They never guessed that there'd come a day when one of their sons would inherit the intellectual possessions of the ruling sect, have his mind overburdened with the most exotic intellectual dainties and then find himself thrust into all the damnable bitterness of penniless pauperdom, ruining his palate and taste for living by chewing the cold ashes of other people's bereavements.

'They couldn't have know very much about unhappiness either, not the sort we know. If a man provided a woman with a bed, pillow and sufficient income, they never considered that woman's right to change her affection, even if it had never been born. That sounds pretty sloppy to us, doesn't it? It is sloppy. I've got a brother. He's loved a woman for a long time. But all that time he's never had the chance to provide her with any part of what she needs. She's dying on her feet, and everything they ever planned is dying with her. That's only a little, little tragedy. Just one of the invisible corpuscles in the life-blood of this valley. Our moralists could stuff a hundred of such tragedies into their inside pockets and feel no heavier for them. Which means that to talk about right or wrong any more in this matter of men loving women and women loving men is just acting the goat. It's right to love when you can afford it and it's wrong not to love when you can't afford it.

'You say your husband makes good money. I make none. So you want to use part of the money he makes to help me? That's a good principle. Even the government says that's a good principle. This Means Test they're introducing says that those that have should help those that have not in order that the comfortable should have the opportunity of dragging out of the closet those love-thy-neighbour ideals that have been going to rust ever since people started living in streets among too many neighbours. But because we adopt those ideals because you give me money, because we'd see each other in dark lanes and be good friends and I'd give you as much worshipful affection as I have at my disposal in return for your kindness, these governing saints would have us shipped, for applying their own family Means Test on a non-family basis.

'Let them kick. Every kick they give loosens the foundations on which their precious society rests. It's we who are important, not they. They think in terms of institutions. We think in terms of men and women, because we have to spend time being frightened and trembling, seeing so little that is desirable or secure, having so little strength to secure what we desire. Worshipful affection! That's the slogan. That's what you can take from me. That's what I can give to you. And gladly. I'll take pride in it. More pride than I take in adjusting my own petty fortunes in the midst of unfortunates. Is it a bargain?'

'A good bargain. Never had a better.'

'When shall I see you again?'

'This evening.'

'I'll make it a place where it's dark. Is that right?'

'That's the only reason there is for darkness. Do you know many places where it's dark?'

'Like pitch. I know them all. I know places where not even the great power himself could plant a lamppost. Do you know that place by the brook where two lanes meet?'

'Where people have thrown a lot of empty tins?'

'Forget the tins. The shadows cover the lot. I'll be on that spot at half-past seven.'

'Till half-past seven.'

'Goodbye.'

Hugh walked home. In one leg he felt exalted. In the other he was lame, so lame, he found it hard to walk.

* * *

Hugh put the finishing touches to an article he was writing with the special consent of Mr Anderson. He had explained to Anderson that this article would make the paper sell faster than any amount of funeral acknow-ledgments. Anderson had told him that he had better be right about that, because judging by the number of acknowledgments Hugh had got for the paper, the lowest on record, the paper pretty soon wouldn't be selling at all.

Hugh had got the idea for his article a few days before. One of the local tradesmen had approached him and offered him ten shillings, plus a drink, for writing a column in the *Clarioneer* on the financial misdeeds of socialist councillors in local administrative bodies. Hugh had asked him why, with ninety per cent of the national press peddling a wagon-load of dirt daily about the financial misdeeds of socialists, he should go infecting the *Clarioneer*, the lowest and least important rung of British journalism, with the same phobia. The only decent thing about the *Clarioneer* was that it hadn't yet taken up with that line.

The tradesman said that they were anxious in the Chamber of Trade to get plenty of printed material to back up their campaign in the forthcoming election in which the Independents were going to work a cleaner politics slogan alongside the subordinate slogan that cleanliness is next to godliness, which was certain to bring a one hundred per cent religious vote.

Hugh had accepted the offer. He had written down all the quotations he had to hand on the subject of wanton extravagance, political illiteracy and blindness, pointing the barrel of each quotation at the head of the socialists. He finished the article with the sentence: 'It is impossible for the Independents to corrupt local politics, since it is known that, as merchants, or some other form of earthworm, they exhaust in their professional lives their entire capacity for being corrupt.' Hugh promised himself that if the drowsy Anderson allowed that sentence to be printed, he'd hand the ten shillings back to the tradesman. If not, not.

As he sealed the article down in its envelope, he heard Alf washing himself vigorously under the tap outside. He got up and fetched a towel from the airing cupboard and threw it at Alf as he came in.

'Where are you going, Alf?'

'Things are moving.'

'I see them looking still as usual.'

'Don't you believe it, boyo.'

'There's a rumpus blowing up. A hell of a rumpus.'

'What over? The new Unemployment Regulations?'

'What better reason for a rumpus than those bloody things? They've got people in a panic all of a sudden. Only now they are realising what the Means Test and the Labour Camps might mean to them. The march we made to London didn't wake them up. But now they feel the boot getting pretty near to the backside. They are waking up all right now. There's a meeting tonight.'

'I'll come with you. I wouldn't miss the sight of this valley shaking off its twilight sleep for anything. Where's the meeting?'

'In the vestry, up the road here.'

'Come on then.'

There was a thin dribble of people making their way towards the vestry when they got out on to the road. The night was frosty and clear. The mountains were distinct. The electric pylons that ran across them to other valleys stood out as plainly as fingers from a hand. Hugh noticed them mechanically. He felt he could look at the mountains now with less lyrical concentration than before. Not long ago they had been in his mind like consoling mothers at whose breasts he could suck with abiding content. Mrs Beatty had removed the mountains from his mind and taken their place. She was in his imagination, deep-rooted as the oldest, greatest tree, the source of all fertility and consolation, consolation in terms of copper, silver, kisses and caresses.

Hugh looked about the vestry. It had altered since those days, during the first part of his life, when he had taken his place on the little stage, with thirty or forty other choristers and sung the spots off hardy annual religious cantatas. In those days, when a good profit had been guaranteed for any performance, good or bad, that was sponsored by the chapel, the vestry had been prim, well upholstered, and meticulously cleaned. Now there was the smell and look of decay and palls of light-weary dust was on every object that met Hugh's eyes. Only one of the three available lights was burning. That was in the middle of the vestry. Hugh and Alf sat beneath it to avoid the shadows that came down like night on the extremes of the hall.

Alf was speaking to a man who sat behind them. The man was telling Alf of a case in his street where a young fellow in work had had the wind up at the prospect of

— 214 —

having to support his workless father under the new Act. He had shifted the old man's bed out on to the road and told him that he could sleep there if he liked. Hugh wasn't listening. He was lost in a sentimental maze of thrown-back thoughts. He was sorry when Alf nudged him back into full consciousness.

'Did you hear what that fellow was saying?'

'No. I was thinking about this vestry.'

'Over a million people stand to get half-strangled by the Unemployment Board and you sit there thinking about the vestry. That's very progressive.'

'The place here looks all gone to seed. What's come over it?'

'What do you think?'

'Palsy's my guess.'

'Nothing so easy or sure as that. The chapel this vestry belongs to gets about ten or twenty members in on a Sunday night. The absent members are either dead, too naked to leave the house or gone over to other creeds. They take a maximum collection of about three bob.'

'That's not enough to start them singing the right hymns.'

'They don't try to any more. They wait for it to work its way up from the cellar.'

'Three bob? How do they pay the preacher?'

'Are you expecting me to say that he's paid by weekly miracles?'

'No. How do they pay him?'

'He goes around on house-to-house collections, getting subscriptions from past or absent members.'

'Is it come so low, O Zeus?'

'You should keep your eyes on the ground. That's the only way of finding out what goes on here. The general scale is so low if you keep your eyes straight in front of you, you'll miss everything.'

'That might be the best thing you could do.'

'Rubbish. You're a student. You've been trained. It's up to you to find out everything about this valley, explain it, make it clear. Us chaps who've lived here all our lives, we only know bits and pieces of it. What we want is a clear picture of the whole damned thing. Then we can look at it. If we like it we'll hang it up on the wall and keep it for our kids to see. If it's all to hell, either we'll burn it or kick it to pieces.'

'I don't quite see that that will do much good.'

'Some day you will. What's the matter with you, Hugh? I've noticed you lately. You've been looking as pleased as a rent collector. Have you had a woman or something?'

'Mm.'

'Is she all right?'

'Perfect.'

'How old? Where from? What does she look like?'

'Twenty-seven. Short. Dark.'

'Single?'

'Married.'

'Watch your step.'

'I didn't think you'd talk like that.'

'Watch your step. Wiser chaps than you have caught a packet that way.'

'Oh, but she's fine.'

'The finer they are the bigger the packet.'

'Oh hell, look Alf. Let me tell you about her.'

'We won't talk about her.'

'Why not? I won't say her name, but she's a fit topic for talk.'

'We won't talk about her. If we do, I'll start giving advice. That'll be the end of you. It will most likely send you straight to jail.'

'I'd like your advice, Alf.'

'Well, you won't get any. Ask Herbert for his. It'll get you to heaven double quick.'

'All right, we'll drop it. What was that fellow behind

here talking about?'

'Chap in his street put his father out on the road. He was afraid he'd have to keep him under the new Regulations.'

'There you have a good fairy tale in the bud. It makes you stop short when you come across things of that sort happening under your nose.'

'That's what we've got noses for, to smell them out and stop them happening. We can afford to call this chap a cold-hearted runt. We are safe. We haven't got a father to put out, and we haven't got a spare bed to give him even if we did. It was thoughtful of that chap to put the old man's bed out on the road as well. It shows he wasn't the boy for half measures. He went the whole hog, and that just about sums him up. He's the whole hog and the back half of a second hog, thrown in to powder the first hog's face. I've always said they ought to put roofs over the streets around here. They might do that now, with a couple of thousand people camping out on the gutters, and it would encourage people in jobs to have no scruples about throwing their dependents out on their backsides when the going gets too rough.'

'It's savage. It's as bad as war.'

'Worse. The people who get ground down in wars get sung over and remembered. The state buries them after they are dead. We are not dead yet and the state's trying to bury us already. That's an example of speed-up for you … Of course it's savage. But if you told that chap who put his father out that he was savage, he'd probably break your nose for you, and I wouldn't blame him. He wouldn't know what you meant. When I think of all the people I knew in the good days who were as gentle and merry as they make them, and now, after a few years of feeling the pinch from tip to toe, they are gone hard as flint and miserable as sin. It makes me break out into a sweat.'

'They force their poverty down our throats, change us, ruin us, until all the goodness that was in us runs out into our socks. They make laws to keep us poor for ever more. We obey the laws, and there's nothing so mean that we won't do to avoid the laws coming down on us and crushing the life out of us. That's what makes us savage. And when we protest, they say that savages don't deserve any better treatment than they are getting already. That gag is older than the hills.'

'You never run short of black paint, do you, Alf?'

'They make me a special maintenance grant of two bob a week to keep me supplied. That's not paint, brother, that's facts, what I've seen and felt myself.'

'How many of the others feel like you?'

'There's not many of them that don't feel. They put up with the same things as I do. The way they feel must be the same. I'm no lone survivor of the great frost.'

'Thousands of unemployed have lost their feeling. You can't deny that, Alf. I've seen them. They are like the living dead.'

'So have I. I've come across plenty. They see the prospect of starving, but not the need to struggle against it. And they sink faster than the sun. They get to be so much like cats and dogs they lock themselves out at night.'

Hugh stood up in his seat and looked around the vestry. The benches were all full. There were a lot of young fellows standing against the walls. They were worried, anxious, puzzled. Some whispered, others laughed. The larger part looked depressed and kept silent.

Three men stood up from the front bench and went on to the stage. The first was a man in his thirties. He wore a dark suit, with a white collar that fitted him loosely, black tie with a large knot. His face was worn down, hard and far-seeing. He sat down on one of the three chairs grouped around the table on the stage. He took some hand-written notes from his pocket and bent over them. He tapped a cigarette on the surface of the table.

'Who is he?' asked Hugh.

'Howells, organiser of the unemployed.'

'He looks pretty strong.'

'He can go on for ever. Never seen such a man. Reads all night, talks and organises all day.'

'What's his pay?'

'Nothing.'

'He does all this work for the love of it?'

'Love, my eye. He hates unemployment.'

'His health looks as if it might have been pretty rough.'

'He's had a bad time.'

'Jail?'

'That and his family life. His wife doesn't encourage him very much.'

'What's the matter with wives in this world, anyway?'

'Married. That's their big difficulty.'

The next man to take his place on the stage was old, scarcely able to walk. He kept his hat on. He wore a heavy overcoat and a richly coloured scarf. He waved his stick to the audience as he sat down. His hair was white and well-washed. The kindliness of his face deepened as a thin round of clapping came up from the few benches in front.

'He's a popular figure,' said Hugh.

'He deserves to be. He's been a councillor for ten years.'

'Any use?'

'Hasn't opened his mouth on the council yet.'

'Perhaps he goes to the wrong place?'

'He goes to the council all right. He can't think. That's his sin. He doesn't know what life is all about. And the older he grows the truer that gets.'

'How does he manage to get elected?'

'He took part in a strike forty years ago. He's been opposing strikes ever since then, but all he's got to do is drag the memory of it out of the bag and he gets elected. The whiter his hair gets, the more votes he polls. He uses a pound of self-raising flour on every one of his curls before election time.'

'What's his name?'

'Bayne. Theo Bayne. Only time will clear us of blokes like Theo. He's got his roots pretty deep.'

The chairman, getting up from the chair in the middle of the platform, called for order. The chairman had no teeth and very little voice. He called three times for order, but the talk around the walls and along the benches in the back showed no signs of simmering down.

A man stood up from one of the front benches. He was bulky, serious and threatening. He roared for peace and quiet in a voice like a bull's, then resumed his seat, laughing so loudly that he drowned the talkers out of sight and the talking out of sound.

Howells on the platform beat impatiently on the floor with his foot. He pulled the chairman by the sleeve, beckoning him to sit down, and stood up himself. The chattering whispered away into silence. Howells began to speak. Hugh had settled down in his seat, expecting a tiresome preamble, full of allusions to the valley's fighting past. There was no preamble. Howells had a scientific knowledge of the Regulations. He had them at his fingers' ends, and he put his fingers around the audience's neck prior to pushing the Regulations down its throat.

He spoke tonelessly. He stripped the emotion from any anger he might have felt. He himself had thoroughly mastered the problems with which he dealt. He expected part of the same understanding from those who listened. Every phrase he used could be felt searching for absolute simplicity. Everyone in the vestry listened eagerly, with the exception of Mr Bayne, who played with his scarf and stared at the light.

Howells spoke for fifteen minutes. He analysed the purpose of the Act and made clear its workings. Hugh liked the way in which he showed how the slicing of seven shillings from a single man's allowance can lead, via destitution, fear and Labour Camps, to the launching of high scale war preparations. In his years of college he had heard nothing from the professional Nestors as scientifically clear or concise. It gave him a line he had never had before, on the exact nature of the political forces that were making for social change.

Howells interspersed his statement with douches of a bitter, brackish humour that caused no laughter, but only intensified the seriousness of those who listened. It struck Hugh that Howell's humour was nothing more than a sense of tragedy, having reached its full limit, converting itself into its opposite. When he taunted his listeners with their tendency to delay all measures of resistance against bad legislation until that legislation was already operating against them, the taunt seemed accidental. There was no trace of malice or superior knowledge in his face.

Hugh thought it strange that when Howells sat down, he made no reference to the way in which the Act was to be opposed. He had described the pit into which the unemployed were to be driven, but had suggested no way of climbing out of it. As Hugh listened to the conversation that began as soon as the speech had ended, he understood the value of the omission.

Howells was allowing the audience to do their own thinking. One man was suggesting a stay-out strike from the Labour Exchanges. Another went further and said they should dislocate the Exchanges by signing all wrong names on the register, then hanging the clerks by the thumbs to dry, after dipping them into a bathful of their own ink. This man, by the way he talked, served in the

— 221 —

Near East during the war years and was familiar with a dozen different ways of stringing a man so that his blood did tricks and his life died slowly. These methods he described with a morbid, rankling intensity of gesture and language that suggested a mental fixation.

Hugh wished the man would shut up and talk about something normal. An old fellow, sitting on Alf's right was thumping Alf on the leg, and saying that the only way to stop a government's water, if you didn't like that government or felt like a change from water, was to strike, strike, strike in ever-increasing circles. Alf was agreeing with him. Two young fellows at the back of the vestry called on Howells to tell them what was to be done.

The chairman was on his feet again. This time he got silence more quickly. He called on Mr Bayne. The men sitting around Hugh were leaning forward, their faces eager, some of them savage. Their tempers had been quickened. Howells had left them in mid-air. He had made their minds ready for struggle. The Act had been exposed as damnable and harmful. That was enough. Their minds were waiting now for the vital message that Howells had left undelivered, the message that would lay down for them on the iron tramlines of unmistakable class war, the methods of resistance and opposition they were to adopt.

Hugh watched the senile Bayne swaying about on his feet, poking his stomach out towards the audience as if inviting them to share in the blessings of his own well-fedness. He was buttoning and unbuttoning his overcoat as if tempting his listeners to envy the colour-splashed checks of his overcoat lining. He was playing with his thumbs, gazing at the queer tricks he played with them as if trying to put himself into a hypnotic sleep before starting to speak. He didn't seem to grasp the fact that eighty to a hundred people were waiting for him to start, the sanctimonious set of his face was bathing the audience in a glow of pious friendliness.

'What the hell is this chap's programme?' asked Hugh 'Is he going to sing, dance, pray or what?'

'The prayer will come later. He might keep us here for fifteen minutes like this with him looking paralysed and inviting us to share his thoughts.'

'He hasn't got any thoughts.'

'The audience'll take fifteen minutes finding out about that.'

'How does he get away with it? Why doesn't somebody tell him to go home. He's holding up history.'

'That's what men of Bayne's kidney are paid to do. He thinks we are enjoying this.'

The man in the front bench who had got up at the beginning of the meeting appealing for silence stood up again, looking more truculent than ever.

'Hey, Theo!' he said. 'What about it?'

The chairman came to the front of the stage.

'Sit down, Sam,' he said. 'We want to keep this meeting orderly. You've been shouting about the place like a ragman ever since I can remember. What good did it ever do you? I'd like to know.'

'It didn't do me any good at all,' said Sam.

'Then why do it, Sam bach? Sit down like a decent chap, will you?'

Sam looked around the vestry. He was asking all present to bear witness that the chairman was a clown.

'I'll tell you why I go about shouting like a ragman,' he said. ' 'Cause I go about looking like one. Look at this hole in my coat. Big enough to get a ten-year-old kid through. But I don't see Theo there looking like a ragman. He looks more like a Sunday School trip to Barry. We don't mind that. We gave up thinking of Theo as one of us a long time ago. But he's a councillor, he's supposed to give us advice. We want it now. Why in God's name don't he give it instead of standing there looking dressed up and swaying about on his legs like a balancing trick.'

Mr Bayne was just starting to come out of his trance. He looked upset. He frowned down on Sam.

'Who's making all this noise?' he asked.

'It isn't you,' said Sam. 'And that's what we are worried about. Why don't you say something?'

'I'll speak when I'm ready, Sam Llewellyn. No agitator is going to command me about.'

Howells looked up from his notes with a smile.

'Agitator!' said Sam, disgustedly. 'Agitator! Oh, my Christ! You are a soft one, Theo. Who's agitating? Who's commanding? Not me. We want you to talk. That's what you are here for. We want to listen. That's what we are here for. This isn't a seance, man. We are not spirits and we don't believe in them. But if there are such things, and we are cut down so bad on the dole that we'll starve to death, we'll come back to the cemetery and make a hell of a noise in your bedroom.'

'What about the noise you are making now?'

'I'm only practising.'

'Stop it then. I've got thirty years of service as a public man behind me. Who knows best, you or me?'

'The public knows best, and they'll never say in the open what they think about you, Theo.'

'You're trying to slander me, Sam Llewellyn. I see through your game, clear enough. You're trying to make me lose my seat in the next election, and give it to some hothead who'll bring disgrace to the borough. I appeal to you all who are here tonight to bear me out when I say that Sam Llewellyn has proved himself by his conduct to be in the pay of dark forces who are working against me and what I stand for.'

'Theo, you don't stand for anything except what you can make out of it. Being on the council has brought happy days to you. I won't tell you what it's brought to

— 224 —

us. We are still trying to wash it off. We've tried soap, lard and marge, but it seems to stick. And one more thing, you bloody old hypocrite.'

Sam was waving his arms in his anger.

'One more thing. You're a bit too fond of telling people who don't agree with you that they're in the pay of dark forces. The only dark forces around here are the pit companies and you. I haven't drawn pay from the pit for ten years. And all I ever got from you, Theo, was a kick in the arse when I was a kid, for treading on your allotments.'

'I stand for common sense.'

'Give us a little action as well. I've been living on common sense and cold cabbage for longer than I can remember.'

'Action. You want action? Let me tell you, Sam Llewellyn. Forty years ago ... '

'Forty years ago I had a grandfather. He'd have enjoyed listening to your memories, but he's been dead for thirty-five years, and he don't care any more whether he can hear or not. So change the tune, Theo. What about this new Unemployment Act?'

'I'll speak about what I like.'

'We give you votes to speak about what we don't like. This Act for instance.'

'Shut up.'

Sam sat down. Mr Bayne took a full minute to get composed. Sam had flurried him. His smile was slow in coming back, but once it got a footing, it came in full-bosomed like the tide.

'My friends. Tonight reminds me of a meeting I was present at thirty-four years ago. I look at things now, and I think of things as they were then and my how they've changed! They were the dark days, these are the bright. No dole then. Dole now. Nobody needs to starve in this old country. No pit-head baths in those days. It was a scrub in a tub in the kitchen for us when we were boys. None of that now. Even the humblest kitchen can be kept spick and span. When I have these thoughts, I ask myself, how has this change been brought about?'

Mr Bayne's tone was getting drearier and more soporific with every sentence he spoke. He had been known in the past to send himself to sleep with his own rhetorical questions. There was a stirring of feet from various parts of the vestry. Sam got up from his bench once more, and faced the audience.

'What about talking to us about the Unemployment Act, Theo?'

'I don't now anything about it,' said Mr Bayne. 'I've never been unemployed.'

'If you don't know anything about the Act and you don't care a damn about the unemployed, what are you doing here?'

'It's my duty to be here.'

'To keep an eye on things?'

'As a leader of the ward. I owe it to you to be here.'

'You don't owe it to us to waste our time.'

'I've got experience. You'd be wise to consult me, all of you.'

'You are helping us no end. Say the truth, Theo. You came here to keep an eye on what you call the hotheads. To see that we don't do anything disorderly. I never seen a man with such a mortal fear of riots as you, Theo. Your mother must have spent a lot of time walking about in big crowds just before you were born. If we decided to do anything rash to put our grievances right you'd run straight to the police station, wouldn't you, and start pulling the alarm. It's funny when a worker's leader of forty years ago ends up in his old age by being a police spy.'

'You're lying, Sam Llewellyn. You know me. I've always been honest with you.'

'You and the Inspector of Police are as thick as thieves. You know that.'

Theo waved his arms at the audience.

'Don't believe him, boys,' he said. 'He's lying. He's only trying to slander me, to make me lose my seat in the next election.'

'Look at him,' said Sam. 'Crying. All right, Theo. Calm down. You won't lose your seat. You can't. It's nailed to your backside. And if you do lose it, we'll buy you another.'

'I came here to help you. This is how you treat me. What they say is true. The more you do for the poor, the less they do for you.'

'Go easy with those proverbs, Theo. We don't like them. If you want to help, you're welcome. You've heard Howells there talk about the new Regulations. If they pass unopposed, this place will be more of a graveyard than it is now. The only use they'll have for councillors is to paint them white all over and stick them in the ground for tombstones. What do you suggest we do about it?'

'Be patient, boys. Be patient.'

'From the minimum wage strike onwards all we've ever had from you is talk about patience. Fold your arms, boys. Trust in the Lord, your leaders and your luck, and the sun will come out in no time at all. We've had no luck, Theo. And our leaders seem to have been hiding behind the same cloud as the sun. You might look like a silver lining yourself, but that's only because you sprinkle flour over the top of your head as if you're a piecrust. Patience might be all right for piecrusts, because they know that somebody's going to swallow them sooner or later. But nobody's going to swallow us. We've seen things getting worse since the '21, and there are still sheep like you who've got the stomach to preach that either they are better or they can't get any worse. We've had enough of it. They've driven us so far, but we won't be driven any further.'

'Don't be rash, boys,' shouted Theo. 'Don't do anything that's foolish. That'll only make them bring in worse regulations than these again. Don't lose your heads. Your leaders will reason it out with the people responsible. They are skilled negotiators. They'll get you better terms. They'll make things easier for you.'

'This isn't a trade union dispute, Theo. There are over two million people unemployed, and this Act will affect them in whatever part of the country they're in. This struggle we're facing now is bigger than any struggle that was in your life, Theo. We'll struggle in the way that looks most likely to get us back decent living conditions again.'

'There's no need for you to struggle, boys. You've got leaders. They are paid to do that. Don't you go starting any trouble. God knows we've had enough of that. Have a bit of patience. There'll be a deputation.'

'Where to?

'London. Where do you think?'

'It's here we live, not London. And we live here three hundred and sixty-five days a year. We don't even get the one day at the sea we used to have. It's here they are putting the offices of the Means Test. If you ask me, all that these deputations amount to is cheap trips to London for people who could afford to buy their own tickets, and while they are in London there's enough goin' on there to make them forget us.'

Most of the audience agreed with Sam. There was a lot of clapping and stamping. Mr Bayne got to his feet again. Somebody from the back shouted, 'Let Howells speak.' Howells stood up and held out both arms for silence.

'Friends,' His voice was more excited and more musical than when he had made his first statement. 'Sam here is right. The struggle against the Act, if it is to be strong enough to make the government surrender, must be conducted here, in the streets and houses of this valley. It is here the injustice has been committed. The protest cannot be expressed through a deputation of officials, who negotiate by habit and compromise by instinct.

'If they go to London, they'll allow themselves to be talked into taking no action until the Act has been given a fair trial. That must be avoided. We know in advance how this Act will affect us. We can truthfully call it vicious and brutal. It has been described in high circles as a measure that will benefit the unemployed. Lying, hypocritical rubbish, every word of it! The authors of it consider that any measure short of actually exterminating the unemployed is a measure benefiting us. We refuse to be starved out. We have the right to live. And every single man, woman and child who will be affected by this Act must demonstrate on the streets this coming Sunday to show that we are determined to claim that right.

'We'll have no well-paid official determining the amount on which we are to subsist. We'll have no inquisitionary pimps holding monthly, door-to-door inquests on our poverty. We know all about our poverty already. We don't need an army of Civil Service touts to remind us of its nature or its extent. We want work and decent leisure, not idleness and inquisitions. They can be provided. We want work and decent wages, not a pittance that has no fixed minimum. If the government devoted to the task of making us happy just one tenth of the attention they devote to making us miserable, there would be an end of poverty and suffering in these valleys.

'I have only to look at you to see that there isn't anybody in this vestry, with the possible exception of our friend, Mr Bayne, who is about to stamp off in a temper, who doesn't agree with me. We feel united now. Let us make a practical and enduring pact out of that unity. Let this coming Sunday see on the streets of our valleys such a demonstration of anger and protest that will eclipse in power and effectiveness all previous demonstrations. Forget your differences. Work to that one end. Whether you be Liberals, Socialists, Communists, Atheists or Christians, you must realise that there is only one way forward and we must travel it together. Your difference of creeds will be of no interest to the people who will administer the Means Test. For them you will be unemployed workers, a sore problem in their eyes, which must be dealt with, and deal with you they will, callously and quickly.

'From now until Sunday we have four days. We are not many more than eighty people in this vestry, and we've got to mobilise sixty to seventy thousand people from every part of this valley. It can be done. See that it is done. When the seventy thousand people are assembled in protest, we can soon work out the next step.'

The doors at the back of the vestry were thrown open. A cold draught came in. An elderly man sitting in front of Hugh, with his hands stuffed into a woollen cardigan and a pouting petrified look on his face, turned round with a yell and told those in the back to shut the door for God's sake, or with a draught like that on his legs he'd never be able to rise from his seat. The doors were not closed. Some of the men, who had stood through the meeting started to walk out. A small, lean, unshaven man, with a shock of black hair that grew over his head in the shape of an umbrella, came down the aisle.

'That's Charlie,' said Alf. 'Charlie the Apostolic who lives next door to us. What does he want?'

'He looks as if he's got a pocket full of healing balm.'

'He always looks like that. That smile struck him like a thunderbolt five years back and he hasn't been able to scrape it off yet. You wouldn't say he was half-dead, would you?'

'I wouldn't bother to say anything about Charlie. A man who goes crazy and still remains poor as well as out of the hatch, is beyond comment.'

'He's in a bad state. For a fellow who talks so much

about healing, I never saw anybody with such a stock of diseases as Charlie.'

'A word with you,' said Charlie, leaning over the platform and plucking the leg of Howell's trousers.

'Go ahead,' said Howells, pushing some documents into the inside pocket of his coat.

'And a word with you,' added Charlie, turning around to the audience. One or two nodded to show they were ready and willing for the word. Some others left their benches and made for the door.

'How much will I be getting under this new scheme?' Charlie asked Howells. He spoke slowly with a lot of deliberate eye-blinking, as if he were preparing a snare.

'What's the size of your family?'

'Myself, my wife, who is good; and my three children, who are healthy.'

'It'll depend on the exact age of your kids. But roughly you'll get about thirty-five bob.'

'Is that enough to live on?'

'If you got any respect for your wife and children, I'd say no, it isn't enough.'

'Am I complaining?'

'You'd be a fool not to.'

'Do I look angry? Do I look as if I'm out for revenge?'

'You look pretty pleased.'

'I'm happy.'

'I don't see why you should be.'

'I am because I tread material things beneath my feet, because there is a part of my life that cannot be touched by poverty or suffering.'

'In China they call that a pipe-dream, but here it's legal and you can't get prosecuted for it.'

'The devil speaks through you, Howells, and I cannot understand your drift. But there is a tremendous lot of unhappiness in your face. You'll never escape that or rid yourself of it. I pity you for that.'

'Don't pity me, Charlie. If you took that smile from your face you'd look half-crucified yourself.'

'Only half?'

'You're young yet.'

'Yes. Young. There is more happiness to come. Listen to me, Howells. You are eaten away by material things. You draw these men away from God by filling their minds with thoughts of food and conditions. They follow you now because they might get a little less to eat. You will tell them to agitate and perhaps they will get more to eat, but will they eat it?'

'Eating is like swimming. Once learnt, never forgotten.'

'They won't eat it. They'll drink it and become like beasts, like they was when there was no bad times here. Now they got to be sober, because they are too poor to get drunk. Thank God for unemployment. Thank God for poverty. If you cure them of poverty, Howells, you will be doing the devil's work. For you will be curing them also of virtue. Put plenty in their pockets, they will piss their substance against the wall and damnation will stalk through the valley once more.'

'Hasten the day. We'll throw flowers in its path.'

'You are an apostle of evil.'

'And you are a throwback to the Early Church Fathers. Look, Charlie. You can afford to be a swaggering martyr of the faith just now. You are not actually starving. If you ever do, come back to me. I'll tell you what you can do to get yourself out of the bog. You won't have to throw yourself down on your knees in front of me. I hate to see men losing their dignity as much as I hate to see them lose their wits.'

Howells gave a laugh and jumped down from the platform, breaking his jump by laying his hand on Charlie's shoulder. He laughed again and said: 'I am the father who forgives all and forgets all.' Howells had a curious sense of the comic. It broke out sharply and suddenly like a fire.

'I'd never go down on my knees before you,' said Charlie.

'I'd kick you in the stomach if you did.'

'That's it. Kick a man when he's down, that's just like you.'

'Have a purge, Charlie. There was a time when you could talk sense. But you're full to the eyes with dope.'

'There's a part of me that isn't touched by poverty or suffering. Wouldn't you like to be like that, Howells? Wouldn't it be better if all men were like that?'

'There are parts of this valley that are not touched by poverty or suffering.'

'Where are they?'

'In graveyards, you coot.'

'How can you joke about death? Your conscience must be sleeping very deep, Howells. That's because you are vain-glorious. You think you are making a big sacrifice for your fellow men by spending your time telling them how to make their bellies bigger. What about the sacrifice I make? Would you give a tenth of your dole and see your children getting less than they ought, just to keep the church of your belief in existence?'

'Do you do that?

'Every week. A tenth of my dole. And if my dole was cut down to a pound the church would still have a tenth of what I have.'

'You are a worse maniac than I thought. Because you like reading religious tracts, there's no need to penalise your kids.'

'Penalise my kids?'

'The money you give to your church should go to feed them.'

'They are healthy. As long as I remain true to my beliefs and to my church a power greater than you or I will keep them healthy.'

'I've seen your kids, Charlie. There's not one of them

that doesn't deserve a trip to the clinic.'

'I'll decide about that.'

'What part of the good book gives the cure for rickets, Charlie?'

'In goodness there's a cure for all things.'

'I hope so. For your sake. Judging by the way that youngest kid of yours is walking about, she'll need the best cure that goodness can give her. Her legs are twisted, Charlie. There might come a day when she won't be able to walk. You enjoy that spectacle. Seeing your kid looking dumb and helpless on a chair, at an age when she ought to be playing about the roads with other kids, getting her fill of pleasure and laughter before life starts closing in on her, and seeing her crippled would please you. You are that kind of blind idiot. You'd look at her with a holy flow of tears on your face and say that her afflictions are merely God's way of paying you out for some little bit of spiteful ramming you did in the days before you were reborn to the light.

'Rickets, Charlie, it's rickets. It hasn't got anything to do with heaven or hell, sin or goodness, except that those people who allow kids to develop rickets are committing a sin for which the punishment should be some form of hell on earth. Rickets come from lack of food. Your kids lack food more than they ought to, because you go handing three or four bob a week over to the Apostolic pastor, so that he can eat enough on earth to avoid rickets in the after life, or that somebody can decorate the walls of that tin shanty you call your church with some new season blooms.

'There are a thousand ways of sinning, Charlie. Fornicating, lying, stealing are only three of them; and the least important. Being stupid is another, and one of the most important. Being stupid in such a way as to leave lives of misery to your kids is another, and that's the most important. That's your sin Charlie. Take care of that youngest child of yours, or you'll be selling your collection of Bibles to buy her a bath chair.'

'I'm not frightened.'

'No, of course you're not. You get drunk lapping up your own miseries. You regard them as special signals of attention from on high. There's nothing you'd like better than a bad attack of leprosy. If you had that you'd be in direct line for the martyr's crown. They'd probably make you pastor of the church.'

'I get my share of bodily pain.'

'Do something about it. See a doctor.'

'I'm ready to die.'

'That's just as well. The rest of the world is getting ready to live.'

'As they lived in Sodom.'

'A combination of Sodom and socialism would suit me fine. Think it over, Charlie.'

Howells left Charlie with his head in his hands, thinking out some answer that would bury the argument once and for all. Hugh got his overcoat from the window sill where he had thrown it.

Charlie went on his way. He passed Alf and Hugh in the doorway. He quickened his step.

* * *

On their way down the hill the two brothers said very little. Alf dragged at a cigarette that had broken in his pocket. He held his fingers tightly over a puncture in the paper. Hugh had his hands stuck into his overcoat pockets.

'Impossible!' he said.

'What is?'

'Sixty or seventy thousand people on the streets on Sunday. Stupid optimism.'

'The streets are pretty long. There might be room for a couple of thousand more.'

'You've got too much faith in the valley dwellers.'

'It's you've lost touch. You don't know them like you used to.'

'They are not the same as they used to be. I remember a fire in their eyes, strong enough to drive the rainstorms from the pavement. Where is it gone? I see their bodies and their eyes looking as musty and as empty as rooms left idle for thirty or forty years. Poverty has killed them, but they are still standing. They still talk, move and make love the best they can. But the old militancy is dead. The brains of men and women don't produce militancy. It's the speed at which life is lived does that. When the coalowners made a riot out of profit-making, the workers lived in a riot of dissipation or revolt. When the oppressors slackened their tempo, so did the workers.'

'The oppression remains unchanged. It never slackens.'

'Changed in quality then. For so many people unemployment is the end of the world. Why should they struggle to change a world they think is going to end? It's a slow, grinding agony, Alf. First it drives you to thoughts of terrorism. But the oppression of the Labour Exchanges is so subtle, so persuasive, and man's got such an urge to be as the cattle are, that thought soon gives way to a quiet, starving surprised sort of tolerance, an existence that has no interest, no value, no responsibilities.

'When a coal boss closes a pit and tells his workers that they'll have to live on a lower level what he's telling them is that there's no level too low for them to live in. The very first moment a man became unemployed as a result of this God infernally crazy system, every Liberal lover of freedom and progress should have gone and made things easier for the Tories and hung himself on the nearest willow.

'For even ten men to be unemployed is a betrayal by those who order society of everything that humanity is supposed to stand for. We drink in the notion that humanity is supposed to stand for something at our mothers' breasts. But maybe our mothers' breasts are wrong, and humanity stands for nothing more than an incorporation into one iron ball of all these injustices that we consider opposed to humanity.

'These employers of labour, these Christian adventurers who came into these valleys and exploited men and mountains until they had enough wealth to put their lives right side up, then withdrew their godheads and their profits, abandoned pits until our lives are now upside down, where are they now, I wonder? The air might be cold and bitter for the poor bastards left holding the kitty. But their country and city homes are probably as warm as hell. Our throats might be dry. We might be moaning for beer we can't buy, we might be yearning for milk our mothers haven't got, but our late masters have a fine supply of rich red wine. Oh Christ, Alf, I'm talking myself to sleep. Perhaps that's what I was trying to do. It's a mess, a rotten hell of a mess. You've had it for five years, me for six months. Not much, not very much. Yet all the capitalists in all the world could toil at their ledgers for a hundred years and never get through enumerating all the kinds of pain those years and those months have brought us.

'When a man falls out of work, society should dedicate every dime of its surplus value to compensating him for that primal curse. Instead, society dedicates every ounce of its mental energy to persuade him that the curse is not a curse, but a normally unpleasant incident, that will become tolerable when life-conditions have become adjusted to it. Even you and I might get used to it. I'll wake up one morning, after spending a couple of years making a little loose change in the way of smaller scale post-graduate adulteries and I'll find myself looking like an eighty-year old peasant who had known only long hours of labour in the field, servile torpor in the church, without ever having felt one moment of either anger or revolt. That's a bonny prospect, I'll be damned.'

'An eighty-year old peasant. Our generation won't live that long, unless the government singles some of us out to keep alive by artificial means, to experiment with artificial means of starving us into subjection.'

'They might call in a witch from one of the Dominions and turn us all into sugar-beet.'

'They say the unemployed are red now.'

'That's a start. All we need now is roots.'

'That's all we need … Roots. That's what we haven't got.'

'You're right, Alf. We haven't got much contact with life, have we? We don't make much of a mark on life the way we are. When a man's without a job he's only half-born. If I'd known about this capitalist crisis twenty-two years ago I'd have jumped from my mother's womb after the first six months. The last three months were a dead loss. It was spent in taking a shape that no one would ever need and it was as dark as pitch in there.

'When society cannot use a man's capacity for being useful, it doesn't matter whether that man has the form of a man, a trolleybus, a jack-rabbit or the seat of a lavatory. Work is man. Man is work. Without work man is released from the responsibility of walking about looking as if he was made in God's image. Ask Charlie the Apostolic how many men who stand outside the Labour Exchange on a day of cold and rain present such an image as God would claim to be proud of. He'll give himself piles sitting down thinking out an answer to that one.

'The circle of God's images within society is getting narrower. Assuming, that is, that God would never face the public with a tail of dirty shirt sticking out of the seat of his trousers, with all the diseases of dirt, tedium and undernourishment sticking out a mile from the features of his face. As unemployment spreads, God's image will become more and more the exclusive property of the middle and upper classes. As the unemployed masses see that godliness is only another form of that jobliness which is denied them, the social and religious structure now standing are in for a walloping … What are you thinking about, Alf? You look like Elijah.'

'I was wondering how we'd be if we had never known this valley and everything that goes with it.'

'We are the valley. The valley is us. Nobody can alter us now, not even by Orders in Council. Either the world can like us or leave us, kiss us or kick us. We are here, fixed, unchangeable like those stars over the mountain there. The sum total of a dozen blind, lousy accidents, ranging from birth in the bosom of a still-enslaved proletariat to the greed and the business stupidity of a few coalowners.

'If we don't like ourselves, we can alter ourselves only by altering this valley. How? That's the question I stumble over in the dark. That's the question I've been trying like the devil to get away from me in the last few weeks. I doubt if it will ever change. In the days of wealth and plenty there was life enough in this valley, raw, real howling life to change not only the valley but the entire universe. The sun and stars could have been kicked out of their courses as easily as the money-grabbers and spell-weavers from their banks and temples. But the frost had killed that life. Ten years of unemployment for half the population and worsened conditions of labour for the other half, have proved that intelligence, energy and vision, are destructible, even if matter isn't.

'You've told me about demonstrations to the council. What did they demonstrate for? Extra relief. Thousands needed it, but only a few dozen were far enough away from snoring and animal hibernation to demonstrate. When people have learned to submit themselves to the rule of avoidable, unnecessary agony in that fashion they deserve to suffer. You think they'll create hell with these new Regulations. I don't think so.'

'I can almost hear them marching now. Ordinary poverty just injures poverty. This Means Test insults them. That might make a difference.'

'We've had religious revivalists insulting us for centuries. They have kidded us that we are the nation nearest in all the world to total damnation and most in need of redemption. We've certainly helped ourselves to redemption in bigger gulps than any other community. The religious revivals were a good basis for the Means Test. Our ancestors did so many damned silly things for the good of their souls there'll be some of their latter day descendants willing to take investigators and Labour Camps on the same basis. We might go to a Labour Camp and learn to be farmers. Our great-grandfather was a farmer. He took part in the Rebecca riots.'

'What grudge did Rebecca have?'

'That's just the name they gave the riots. Our great-grandfather wrapped a toll-gate round a bailiff's neck.'

'If the bailiff was anything like the brotherhood of bums we've got around here I bet he used it as a collar.'

'Wouldn't you like to be a farmer?'

'What the hell for? All the bloody seeds we ever planted never came to fruit. When I was a kid, I planted a handful of orange pips in the back garden. What came of it? The woman next door died of appendicitis and I was expecting orange trees. I planted a handful of dreams in Gwyneth. Same thing. No appendicitis this time. Dreams are soft and messy and they don't annoy the stomach like orange pips. But there's death mixed up in it and it's coming closer than that woman next door. This time it's Gwyneth.'

'Mm. The world's making a special job out of us two. They might pickle us and peddle us around under the noses of future generations to prove that bad as they may think things are for them things were a devil of a sight worse for us … Why shouldn't we go back to broad fields and empty valleys, anyway? Why should we stand still and see our lives taken away from us, dirtied and spoiled by a bunch of sanctimonious maniacs who are willing to sacrifice never-mind-how-many lives just in order to keep a few social relationships away from the cleaners. Why shouldn't we lead an exodus of all victims of the industrial revolution back to the pastures where they started.

'The Israelites did it, and they had steady jobs in Egypt, though nobody stamped their cards for it. Nobody needed a promised land more than we do. We could look for it. We could manure our fields with the distilled juices from the wrung withers of every politician who has ever given us lands of promise instead of promised lands, and we could use the priests to fetch us sweet water from the well when we are thirsty from singing and loving at night.'

. 'Better talk it over with Herbert. He knows a couple of priests.'

'Will he be in the house now?'

'Aye. This is his night for music and meditation.'

* * *

Herbert had an illustrated American magazine propped up against an eightpenny loaf. He was chuckling at a page of cartoons. Most of the jokes were maudlin and emasculate, but Herbert had been told that magazine caroonists were highly paid. He chuckled as a token of tribute to the scratchers and scribblers who had composed the page in front of him, and who were counted successful men on the strength of it.

Herbert had a newspaper folded over his lap to protect his trousers. There was a cheese sandwich on his plate, half-eaten. Herbert made a practice of leaving something half-eaten on his plate at every meal. That was his way of teaching moderation to his brothers. Alf made a parallel practice of always eating what Herbert had left behind, and saying 'waste not' as loudly as he could, in Herbert's ear.

The wireless in the kitchen was playing very softly. The music being played was droning, performed by orchestra and organ. Herbert was very fond of music. The only charge he had ever flung with any violence at the heads of his father and mother was that their religious sympathies had inhibited the use of any other music than hymns. He looked forward to an old age of leisure and material security in which twelve hours of every golden day would be spent in steeping himself in strange melodies. Herbert was tapping on his shoe with a pipe that was filled but not lit.

He looked up from his magazine as Alf and Hugh came in. He uttered a stupid-sounding greeting that was popular with the natives of the tennis court, and smiled broadly as if he wanted to bathe the whole kitchen in the white glow of his tooth enamel. He was in a mood to be sociable.

'Here's a man laughing,' said Alf, taking the loaf up and letting Herbert's magazine fall on the dirty plate.

'Be careful with that loaf,' said Herbert. His tone stung a little less than usual. He was prepared to make concessions if it meant being sociable.

'The loaf's to be eaten. It's not a book-rest.'

'Don't use that tone with me, Alf. For God's sake be a bit less like an animal and remember that you come from decent parents.'

'Chamber of Trade stuff again. You carry the torch. Use it to smoke your bacon. Don't hold it under my nose.'

'Shut up, Alf. You can't make me quarrel. You don't like me. I don't like you. I never found a reason and I won't waste time looking for it. I told our mother before she died that the three of us would live in peace here together. I've done my part. You know how you sneered at me, made fun of me and my friends, just because we try to make this valley look a bit better than it really is. You've even treated me as if I'm to blame for you not having a job.'

'You weren't to blame for that. I'm to blame. It's me who closed the pit down. It's me who invented the dole.'

Alf turned away from the table.

'How much do you want to eat, Hugh?'

'Two pieces,' said Hugh, moving his chair nearer to the wireless to listen to the music and to give himself an excuse for taking no part in the conversation. He had declared a truce with Herbert. He didn't want to see it broken. He wished Alf would shut up. He didn't feel ripe for hearing one of Herbert's homilies on a night so cold. Herbert's social morality was so white and frozen.

Alf poured out some tea. Herbert bent low over his magazine, his face muscles moving, waiting for the conversation to break out again. Alf sat down by the table.

'I hope you'll be very happy, Herb,' he said.

'That's a funny thing for you to say. Are you pulling my leg again?'

'No. I'm serious. Me and Hugh have been talking about life coming down the road. We decided that us two are damned. We'll always be in front of the wind and the wind will be strong. But we've got the satisfaction of knowing that you at least have got some contentment. It would be more than I could bear to see the three of us in the bog.'

'What bog?'

'You know. That sticky stuff.'

'Do you think I'll be happy?'

'You can't miss it.'

'If you had lived quiet, ordered lives ... '

'Quiet, Herb. I want this bread and butter to go down the right pipe.'

'We should have been better friends, Alf.'

'We don't touch at any point.'

'We could have made touching points.'

'That would have spoilt our original shapes. No! We live in a place that's bad for friendship. The valley has made you more of a shopkeeper than you ought to have been. Be glad we've never been anything more than bad friends. If we had tried to understand each other we'd have torn each others' throats out.'

'Things could have been different if we'd talked to each other like this for the last five years.'

'God help. This is just for a couple of minutes. I've got a feeling that life's coming to a head. It makes me feel brotherly. By the time I've finished this tea and bread and butter I'll be hating you again, and wanting to lock you in a matchbox because you're a smug louse.'

'There have been times when I should have kicked you out of the house.'

'Why didn't you?'

'We are brothers.'

'That's a hell of a lot. Blood's supposed to draw men together. It can't draw them together half as fast as the difference between a job and not having a job draws them apart. If you only knew it, Herb, we are worse enemies than jungle cats. Your life's turned out all right. Mine hasn't. We might live in the same house, but that little fact sends us to different ends of the earth. Every week you keep on drawing a decent wage makes a difference to your blood. Every week I draw the dole makes a difference to mine. We get further apart. The loving kindness of the whole Mothers' Union couldn't bring us together again. Shall I tell you why you've never tried to throw me out of this house?'

'Go on. Tell me. You know everything.'

'You weren't guided by brotherly love. Brotherly love was founded on equal labour in the fields. They've turned the fields over to the sheep and equal labour has gone by the board. I've stayed in this house because I've got as much right to be here as you. You've never had to support me, have you? Even the money I've spent on fags I've made up for by the coal I've brought from the tip.'

'That's true.'

'If my dole had been stopped, would you have supported me?'

'Not for a minute.'

'You'd have put me out on my backside?'

'I'd have considered doing that a good job of work.'

'Now you're talking like a business man. Brothers be damned! You might get a chance of putting me out pretty soon.'

'I know. I've read the Regulations.'

'You know you might be called on to support me?'

'Yes.'

'What were you going to do about it?'

'I was looking forward to the moment when I'd tell you that I'd sooner die than use any part of my wages to keep you alive.'

'The government will be glad to hear that. You wouldn't be sorry to see me go?'

'Glad. It would make things easier for me.'

'I'd never come back again, you know that.'

'I know you wouldn't. That's the best of a chap as pigheaded as you, Alf. You take your poverty so seriously. You take pleasure in making a clean break. I'd put you down as dead.'

'You might even get Hugh to acknowledge my passing in the *Clarioneer*.'

'Depends how I feel. No good wasting money on sentiment.'

'And if we pass one another on the road?'

'We might not, or we might not.'

'We might not. I'm sorry I can't wait long enough to give you the pleasure of telling me to go.'

'When are you going?'

'Now.'

'Tonight.'

'In about five minutes.'

'Don't be daft. You won't find lodgings at this time of night.'

'There are so many people worming their way from under threatened cuts, every house in the valley will be taking in lodgers till one o'clock in the morning.'

Hugh stood up, stooping to switch the wireless off.

'Don't go like this, Alf. Wait a bit. What if there isn't a cut? Wait just a bit. You're happier here than you'd be in any lodgings.'

'Don't bother, Hugh, for Christ's sake. I should have made this change a long time ago. I've only stayed here so long because I've got in Herbert's scalp. If I'd shifted when I first felt like it, he wouldn't be as bald as he is now. Look at his face, Hugh. He's frightened that I'll change my mind and decide to stay. I'm going. My life needs changing this way or that. There's no sort of change would do me any harm. It's only when life stands still and starts to fester that it poisons people.'

'Where are you going?'

'Gwyneth's. I'll live in sin for a while, and charge the dirt on my conscience down to the Means Test. At least that will glorify the last lap of Gwyneth's life. I'll coach her in a speech on unemployment that she'll be able to scream on the top of her voice on the day of judgment. Don't look so shocked, Herb. This girl I'm talking about is a girl that I've loved for a long time, in a very pure fashion, as you'd say. You can blame her for practically all the kicks I've given you. All the love that was in me, not much, it's true, I've given to her. That's why I've had so little to spare for you. When she dies I'll ask you to come and have a look at her. I'd rather you see her when she can't do any talking. You wouldn't like the way Gwyneth talks. Her tongue ripples like a fish. When you see her face it won't be very pretty, but the sight of it might give you some idea of what goes on in my head in those moods when you can't make me out. So long, Herb. So long, Hugh. You can bring my stuff over to Gwyneth's tomorrow.'

Alf left the house. Hugh and Herbert looked at each other in silence. Hugh wanted to talk, but couldn't find an idea that wouldn't burn on his tongue. Herbert said he'd like some music. Hugh switched the wireless on and turned it up to full volume. It was deafening, painful, but neither complained. Herbert looked through the pile of unstamped envelopes on the mantleshelf. He took a half-crown from his pocket. He told Hugh to buy the stamps in the morning. Hugh thanked him and walked out on to the pavement, where he stood still, running his hand over his mouth, cursing Alf for a fool, thinking of Gwyneth and pressing the memory of Mrs Beatty's plump, short body to his mind.

*　　*　　*

Alf ran up the steps of Gwyneth's house two at a time. He felt he was in a hurry to do something. The kitchen door was open. He walked in. He struck a match. There was a small dish of biscuits on the table. He took one and crunched it in his mouth. He wiped away the crumbs with his hand and began to walk upstairs. Each step gave a little under his feet. The landing at the top of the stairs was small. The doors of the three bedrooms were very close to one another.

He knocked on the door nearest him. Inside the room

a mattress creaked. Alf pushed the door open and walked in. In the dark he could see Gwyneth's nightdress rising white above the dark-coloured counterpane. The air in the room was close, unpleasant. He sat down on the bed close to Gwyneth. Her breathing was loud and hard. She took his hand.

'I'm glad you came, Alf.'

'You don't mind?'

'I said I was glad.'

'For once we'll do what we want to.'

'Light the candle.'

'We don't need light, and candles smell.'

'Going to stay here, Alf?'

'For as long as you want me.'

'I go to the hospital on Sunday.'

'Sunday? That's soon. Sooner than I thought.'

'The doctor told me.'

'He must be right. Sunday. That gives us four nights, Gwyneth. Four nights are something.'

'And all the nights after. I won't be away long, will I?'

'No, not for long. We'll take these four nights as a sample. We'll see if what's to come will be any better or any worse.'

Gwyneth leaned her head back on the blackpainted iron rail, rubbing her eyes.

'God!' she said, 'I'm tired. Not much sleep last night. Nor the night before. You should have been with me then. It won't be so bad tonight.'

'Not so bad, Gwyneth. Not so bad.'

He leaned over and kissed her. Her face was sweaty and cold. He lifted his legs on to the bed. He put his arms beneath her shoulders. The position was awkward but he wanted to make her warm, to feel that cold sweatiness leave her face. Gwyneth shifted down in the bed until her head rested on the pillow. At first she felt the heat of Alf's body oppressive. She stared up at his face and in a minute she found herself doing it as familiarly and without feeling as ever she had looked at the ceiling. The warmth of Alf ceased to oppress her. It covered her completely, like a loud, persuasive lullaby, telling her to rest.

She struggled against her sleepiness, increasing the tempo at which she ran her fingers over Alf's body. Alf found himself being tickled and wanted to laugh. He was glad when the movement of Gwyneth's fingers got slower. He wanted her to rest and let him master the ceremony. She lay still. He kissed her repeatedly. But there was no answer from her body. She had fallen asleep.

* * *

'See them,' said Alf, stretching out his hand towards the other side of the valley. Hugh followed Alf's fingers. Down the mountain road Alf was pointing at the thousands of men, women and children, with brass bands and banners, who were marching eight deep, well marshalled and singing.

Alf and Hugh were standing in the middle of their own contingent, the men and women of their own town who had joined in the demonstration. They were at a standstill, waiting for a line of cars to be shifted away. The policemen in charge of the traffic jam were doing their best to thicken the jam and increase the confusion, with an eye to delaying the progress of the demonstrators. The stewards left the body of the demonstration and got the motor cars disentangled. The motorists looked gratefully at them and restarted on their way.

The inspector in charge barked nastily at the chief steward, telling him that when the police wanted help they'd ask for it. The steward glanced at the officer with a stony contempt. He asked why the police never asked for help when they needed it so badly for twelve hours out of the twenty-four.'

The people in front of Hugh and Alf began to move. The brothers fell into step. That was not an easy job. Three of the four men in the rank in front of them walked with a limp. It was hard to say which leg they were going to put forward next. Hugh stopped for a moment and looked back. Their own contingent was six or seven thousand strong. It stretched too far back around too many corners to be seen as a whole. The contingent had two bands. The first was a colliery band and played the tune well. The other was a drum and fife combination, with the fifes too shrill and the drums too constant to be properly articulate. Neither of the bands could be heard from where Hugh and Alf were marching. The first was too far in front, the second was too far behind.

A young boy, the son of one of the limping men, walked by Alf's side playing a harmonica as broad as his face. The boy had a loose, undisciplined mouth and dribbled a good deal, but the music he produced was sprightly. He worked on three tunes: a Welsh folk song reset to a rhythm basis, a tune of the American Civil War and an anthem of the international class war. At interval's the boy's father turned round with a handkerchief in his hand and wiped the boy's mouth.

Hugh looked once more at the vast body of demonstrators who were advancing down the mountain road half a mile away. They were now approaching the bed of the valley, making for the point where their road converged with that along which Hugh's contingent were marching.

'It's significant,' he said. 'Watching this is like listening to great music, only greater, much greater. Wonderful people! When they can come onto the streets at a few days' notice with ranks as firm and as solid as these, there's nothing they can't achieve. I'll never forget this moment. Here is the final answer to all that goddamn poetic loneliness I've fed on like a swine ever since I grew to full height. Fifty thousand of the oppressed banding together against a common injury. Strong faces. Strong bodies marching. Strong voices singing. Strong wills. Strong arms to snatch us out of our dirty, brooding, fornicating little closets and plant us up on high, where the air is clear and worth drinking. From a point like this, life's immediate purposes seem so far away as to look like a straight, simple line without a twist or break in any part of it. I feel … I feel like an eagle.'

'Speak quieter. If the police hear you talking like that I'll spend tonight bailing you out.'

Silence, except for the sound of feet and the boy's harmonica. Hugh noticed that a lot of feet made sloppy sounds as they reached the floor, as if the soles were leaving the uppers. The sky was darkening for rain. Hugh could see no more than three or four men who had brought raincoats. He heard one man say he didn't care a damn if it did rain. The rain would make people think even more then they were thinking already, and their thoughts would flow with the rainwater into channels of active and desperate resistance. Alf looked gloomy, wrinkling his forehead and staring at the bobbing shoulders of one of the crippled men in front. Hugh thought he'd better talk to him.

'I thought Gwyneth was going away today.'

'She's leaving it till the middle of the week.'

They were passing the crossroads. The contingent Hugh had seen coming down the mountain road was halting, waiting to fall in behind. Hugh looked across at them. He saw a head leaning against one of the banner poles that looked very familiar to him, a head set far back on the shoulders, with shapeless, black curly hair. Hugh left the ranks. He told Alf he'd be back in a minute.

'Lloyd!' he shouted, and ran across the road towards the banner pole. Lloyd came to meet him. In the middle of the road they greeted each other. Lloyd was wearing a dark suit with a stiff collar. The collar made his face look more severe.

'Where've you been?' said Hugh. 'Haven't seen you for months. Learning to be a monk or something?'

'Learned that long ago and got so pure I started to rot.'

'What you been doing with yourself?'

'Just arsin' about. Nothing in particular.'

'Got a job yet?'

Lloyd put his head back and laughed.

'What's all the laughing about?' asked Hugh.

'You make the five thousandth person who's asked me that question. I haven't answered one of them. I'm keeping all in suspense. Their agony is the only satisfaction I get out of being without a job. No, I haven't got anything. My father and mother are worrying their guts out. I pity them. They build up a castle of hopes on me two miles high. Two more wasted miles I've never seen. The sappers are getting closer to the castle every day. A few more months and they'll be ready to blow it over the furthest star. Yes, Hugh, I pity my parents. They are the only people in the world I pity. For the rest I have a whip in one hand a bomb in the other. I'm their life's work. And look at me! I can't think of any job under the sun that I haven't applied for. I went round a dozen councillors trying to persuade them for a job as roadsweeper. They must have got the impression that the first thing I'd start sweeping into the drains would be the council itself, because I didn't get the job.'

'Something might come.'

'Think so?'

'I don't trust myself to think. Make it hope.'

'That's better. But I don't even hope. By the time society realises the need to absorb us unemployed graduates there'll be a new slump or a new war, and then we won't know which storm we were the orphans of. That headmaster of ours can celebrate the occasion by writing a new handbook of careers for the young and dedicate it to us. We were among the brightest children and it looks as if we are in for a lifetime's eclipse.'

'What's to do?'

'Here's the answer.'

'Where?'

'All around us. These thousands of people.'

'They can't give us jobs.'

'Who the hell wants them to give us jobs. There's something wrong with us blokes, Hugh. We get a couple of poxy, meaningless letters behind our names and we expect the sight of them to fool the world into giving us all we need. We believe that because we've built ourselves up into a position where we are ripe to leave the working classes, an overload of sensual and spiritual luxuries is going to fall in our laps as the world's reward to us for having uprooted all notions of revolt from our minds. It's got nothing to give except to those who already have more than plenty. So we've got to find out what we can give the world.'

'Free of charge?'

'All the best labour is voluntary, as the woman said.'

'The woman can keep on saying it. The only voluntary effort this world'll get out of me is a kick in the rectum.'

'That's my point. That's what I meant when I said the answer to our questions lies in this demonstration here. The world's got twisted guts. You admit that?'

'If I had done the twisting I wouldn't have made a better job out of it.'

'It can't digest us. These are the people who have got the strength and the will to straighten those guts. They suffer more than we do. We can give our lives to serving them. Helping them we help ourselves.'

'That means making a clean break with all the hopes and ambitions we've been fed on.'

'Fed on and poisoned on.'

'Poisoned is right. We'll need a long course of herbs to clear our blood.'

'I've been trying to make up my mind on this point for so long. I've had the notion of repaying the kindness of my father and mother crawling about in my brain like a beetle up till now. I might live till I'm sixty on the outer rim of their charity, preparing to do my duty by them. That's madness. The times are too urgent for moral musings. There's no room for doubt and no need for it. Yet our musings continue. Those college professors certainly did us a good turn when they taught us to propound unnecessary problems for our own delight. What we need is something to pitch us head first into the struggle without giving us time to think. Give us time to think and there's the old plague at work again and we're damned.'

'Who's going to do the pitching?'

'Any particular act of oppression will do it. We've been weaned away from the realities of class struggle. The moment we get back to them, our whole miasma of middle-class delusions about superior social status will evaporate and harden. I've gone out of my way trying to get a policeman to beat me up but they all avoid me as if I was one of their narks. Here's another thing. I went on a deputation to a Relieving Officer in our district, who was making himself a pest. He tried to put me out of his ofice. I decided to take the plunge by taking a swing at him. But one of the deputation who had some kind of pit-blindness mistook me for the RO and took a swing at me. He put me out. So as a revolutionary I'm still unbaptised and there are still echoes in my mind of all the speeches I've ever heard about nice, fat jobs waiting for us in the colonies if we only show initiative.'

'That collar you're wearing smells of initiative.'

'Do you like it?'

'How can I? It isn't true to form. The collars I

remember you wearing used to hang from your neck like saddles.'

'This is one of the old man's stock. He said he wouldn't allow me to go marching about the streets on Sunday with a soft collar. I'm glad I put it on now, though. It goes well as part of my uniform as a banner bearer. It keeps me upright. So even if the banners sags, I remain stiff and it's good as a tactic. People on the pavement who see me dressed like this think I represent solid backing for the march from the religious bodies.'

'There are some chapels on the march.'

'Some of them. They couldn't do otherwise. They were lagging centuries behind the community. There's more than one Christian today in this march performing his first Christian act by fighting for the unemployed.'

The end of Hugh's contingent came in sight. Lloyd got back to his banner poles. Hugh took his place right behind him. The band that stood at the head of Lloyd's contingent began to play. They swung into a march. Lloyd was shaking the pole about to get the banner straightened out.

'If the people can't see the slogan on the banner,' he said, 'I'm pulling my navel out of shape for nothing.'

They passed a grey, sad-looking chapel. The Sunday School children stood on the steps outside. They cheered, smiled and waved their handkerchiefs as each new banner and wave of marchers passed. Behind the children, four supervisory deacons stood in a line, watching over them, glancing hostilely at the demonstration. One of them, with a sick, chalky, labour-lined, visionary face was stretching out his hand and denouncing with a mouth made noisy with uncontrolled spittle, the military music and defiant banner slogans that were making a mock of the Sabbath. Lloyd waved at the chidren with his one free hand.

'Fall in, little comrades,' he shouted. 'This is for you as well as us.'

Some of the children came down from the steps and

started to march alongside the demonstration. The deacons rushed out and gathered them in again. The procession passed on. The children kept waving at Lloyd's banner which stood high above the heads of those who marched, until it went from sight.

They descended a steep hill. The first rain drops were already blowing casually into their faces. Hugh turned up the collar of his coat. Lloyd turned round and told him that if he got very wet he could have a yard off the banner to go home in.

They were now entering the town where the mass protest meeting was to be held. It was a lumpy, dingy, formless little town, with a main street of shops, as many closed down as not, with hillside terraces overhanging it. A few red flags hung from the windows. Lloyd pointed at a lean young man, with spectacles and bowler, who was walking along the pavement with a woman, grey-haired, tight-lipped and sullenly dignified with the dignity of fifty years of age, hanging on his arm.

'Know him?' asked Lloyd.

'It looks like Epsom.'

'Our school friend with a weakness for rhyming verse. D'you want to talk to him?'

'He can't tell us anything we don't know. But he looks as if he might be sympathetic.'

'All right. I'll call him.'

Lloyd shouted 'Hoy!' His voice rang like a bugle. It rose higher than the brass band. The people marching behind stopped to see what was happening. Epsom turned round and recognised Hugh. He took careful, courteous leave of the woman who hung on his arm. She stood still on the pavement, playing with a bunch of red cherries that hung from her broad-brimmed hat, and setting her face in a more unpleasant expression than she had worn before.

Epsom walked by Hugh's side, glancing nervously

around, as if wondering whether it wouldn't be better to say goodbye immediately and politely, and turn back.

'You look fine, Epsom,' said Lloyd. 'What bank did you break into?'

'Bank? I don't quite follow, Lloyd.'

'Same old Epsom. Still blinking like a mole at the facts of life. I was looking at your hat. It's a blemmer. With my collar and that hat, we look like two different sides of the same conspiracy.'

A hundred yards in front there was another entanglement of motor cars. The procession stopped. Lloyd rested his banner pole on the ground and lit a cigarette end. Epsom hurriedly offered them a fresh cigarette each, without smoking himself. He looked glad that he didn't have to march any further. He backed out from the rank in which he was standing and stood close to the kerb. Lloyd was irritated.

'Epsom, you've got about as much solidarity as a bloody scabby rat in a strike.'

'That's not very clean or decent language, Lloyd.'

'The man is hurt. Glory be! Don't mind me, Epsom. I'm training to be a road-sweeper. I'm getting myself dirty before I make my second application for the job. But I still think you lack solidarity.'

'Solidarity? I don't quite … '

'You don't quite follow. The only thing you did follow was superabundant rhymes. Now you seem to be going in for superabundant flesh-pots.'

'What are you fellows doing marching about like this?'

'We lack for work and food and hope. We're trying to get some fresh air to work off the giddy feeling.'

'Oh, that's a pity, a great pity.'

'He talks like a headmaster already,' said Lloyd. 'It's a pity, Epsom. That phrase covers one little aspect of the tragedy. I take it that you're working.'

'I'm teaching. In a Secondary School.'

'Where?'

'In the valley here.'

'How much did you have to pay for the job?'

'My mother's got a lot of influence.'

'She'd more influence than Merlin and his magic staff to get you a teaching job without palm-greasing around here.'

'There was a little payment involved.'

'Tell me how much. If it's reasonable I might start saving up to get myself a job.'

'My mother used her influence to get it cut-rate.'

The woman Epsom had left on the pavement started to call 'Alun, Alun'. Epsom said he'd have to go. Lloyd nodded towards the woman.

'That your mother, Epsom?'

'Yes. She's a very wonderful woman.'

'Many things are clear to me now that were dark before.'

'What d'you mean, Lloyd?'

'Nothing much. I was just thinking that when you see a woman who can hardly move for dignity, always look around for a couple of men with mutilated lives.'

'I can't stay to argue. Mother's getting impatient. Perhaps I'll see you again when you leave your banners at home.'

Epsom ran off with a dutiful crouch. Lloyd stuck his lips out.

'He'd better meet us when we leave the banners at home or he'll have this pole up his backside. What d'you think of him, Hugh?'

'Disappointing. That's the cleanest word I can think of.'

'Disappointing? Hellish! Mark Epsom down as one long lane that'll have no turning.'

The field on which the meeting was held was a large abandoned ash-tip with a flattened surface. In one corner of the field was a concentration of twenty or so policemen. They looked awkward, self-conscious and unable to determine what their attitude should be. The speakers were scattered about on half-a-dozen different platforms. Listening to the speeches was of less importance than the mere animal intermingling of thousands of people gathered together in one place for the same purpose. On the outskirts of the various groups, boys and girls acted the goat as they would at a fair.

Lloyd had left his banner propped against one of the platforms. He and Hugh stood in an open space, not far from the police concentration, talking.

'Those police boys know as well as we do that there's no possibility of disorder,' said Lloyd, 'yet they've got to stand there as if we were going to start a war. It isn't fair to them. It isn't fair to us.'

They noticed a man standing in the centre of the field. He was bleeding from a cut above the eye to which he was holding a bit of damp rag. He was talking excitedly. A large crowd was gathering around him. Hugh heard a woman shouting 'Shame, shame on them!' The people were leaving the platform to hear what the man had to say.

Lloyd and Hugh got to the edge of the crowd. Lloyd asked a woman what the fuss was about. The woman was young, pale and angry-looking. Hugh wondered whether her anger was fresh or momentary or fixed and long-standing. She let out a little string of curses before starting to explain.

'It was one of the smaller contingents who were coming over the mountain to join the main march. The police told them to turn back and go home. They told the police to go to hell. The police let into them. This bloke with the blood on him was there. He reckons they're still fighting.'

The man in the centre of the crowd had stopped talking. He was pointing his finger accusingly at the police in the corner. Another man, standing near him, strong in the legs and big in the shoulders, his eyes blazing around and his mouth strained and furious, flung both his arms out and started to shout.

'Come on, boys. Let them have it. Let the bastards have it.'

The crowd started to move in the direction of the police. Hugh ran like mad away from the path of the crowd. He got to clear ground and felt the people rushing past him. He saw Lloyd being hurtled along. He saw a young constable in the front rank of the concentration draw his baton and bring it down on Lloyd's forehead. As he looked his vision seemed more vivid than it had ever been. There was a throbbing in his head that he had previously felt only during thrusts of sexuality. He felt suprised that the baton hadn't seemed to come down on Lloyd's head as hard as it might have.

Lloyd was lost from sight on the ground. The police were beginning to retreat into a narrow back lane. The crowd were making to follow them. Hugh heard people bawling oaths, warnings, battle cries, laments, and saw them ripping stones from the black ground. The crowd were coming very close to the mouth of the lane. A strong body of stewards threw themselves between the crowd and the police, struggling to keep the crowd in check.

A loudspeaker van was roaring out instructions to the crowd to 'keep calm, keep calm, keep calm, keep calm'. The announcer was adenoidal. 'Keep calm, keep calm, keep calm!' The announcement had a slightly comic sound, at which the announcer himself seemed to be laughing. Hugh concentrated the attention of his ears on the loudspeaker van. He interpreted the instruction to be calm personally. He dug his hands into his pockets and his heels into the ground, to steady himself. He was sick to know what had happened to Lloyd.

The rain started to pour down violently. It helped the

stewards get the crowd back to the field. The police finished their journey through the lane in safety. The announcer from the van sounded more amused then ever. 'Thank you, ladies and gentlemen. Thank you, ladies and gentlemen.' Hugh saw the woman who had explained to them about the fight on the mountain standing quite close to him. She had her face lifted up as if letting the rain cool the hot anger on it. She was swinging her beret about, drying it. It had fallen in a puddle. Along the lane the police had taken, Hugh saw Lloyd being carried away by two ambulance men. He was sick and thirsty.

*   *   *

Hugh gathered in a pile the dirty dishes of the last two days. Herbert, sitting in his place at the side of the table nearest the fire, watched from above a newspaper.

'Alf was pretty bad,' he said. 'But at least he kept the dirty dishes in check.'

'Get him back here to teach me. Then with him and me doing well as handmaidens you could convert the place into an academy for teaching the unemployed a sense of responsibility.'

'Don't take that tone with me. I'll listen to you when you've got a job.'

'Listen now while you still can. If you wait till then old age will have defeated you.'

Giving up hope already?'

'I had to give up something to keep on moving. My back was getting bent. Hope was the first thing that came to hand.'

'Did you post off that last lot of applications?'

'I burned them.'

'What did you do with the stamp money I gave you? I work hard for that money, don't forget that.'

'I bought salt with it, to make the flames burn prettier.'

'Hugh, we are going to have a serious talk.'

'I heard a judge once. He spoke just like you're speaking now.'

'You make me feel like a judge.'

'Sentence me to dish-washing for life. Here's enough on the table to keep me going for the next ten years.'

'You need a sentence. Getting mixed up with rioters! How far do you think you'll get that way?'

'I wasn't mixed up. I wish I had been.'

'Keep up that attitude and you'll get no support from me.'

'I expect none.'

'You're getting it.'

'I just stand still. I've got no alternatives.'

'When I made sacrifices … '

'That holy word again.'

'You'll hear that word a thousand times a day whether you like it or not. When I made sacrifices to keep you at college, I did so on the understanding that you'd grow up to keep an orderly life.'

'Keep that line for the City Fathers. They'll lap it up.'

'When do you think you'll get a job?'

'Never.'

'Don't be daft, Hugh. I'm dead serious. When?'

'I can see you're serious. My answer's the same. Never. At least we can play with the idea of perpetual unemployment.'

'How long do you think I'll be willing to keep on helping you?'

'By your voice, I'd say not long.'

'You're right. Not for long.'

'You want to see the back of me?'

'I'd like to see you make a move.'

'Alf made a move. That made you glad. Now it's my turn.'

'Don't think I lack charity, Hugh. Things are not good as they are now. You're going to waste as you are.'

'Still thinking of that riot?'

'Not only that.'

'What else?'

'The friends you keep.'

'Alf?'

'Hell, no. Not Alf. He's your brother.'

'Coming from you that's news. What other friends?'

'That woman.'

'What about her?'

'She's married. Once, she was a woman with a respectable reputation.'

'As far as I go, she's still got it.'

'With you meeting her in back lanes?'

'That fact's got more to do with her marriage than with me. I'm all for light. It's she's for the dark, not me.'

'Back lanes! That's rotten.'

'Back lanes are for putting ashbuckets out and in of a morning. Taste my life and hers. They both remind you of ashes. There's some kind of justice about it.'

'Don't joke about it. It's worse than joking about the dead. The dead behave decently anyway. What in the name of God made you do anything so daft as to pick up with her?'

'I liked her.'

'That's no reason for anything.'

'All right. I'll give you a reason that will appeal to you. Why do you give me money?'

'I'm your brother.'

'I'm her lover. That makes me closer to her than I ever was to you. She gives me money. I take it. She's got more of it to give than you. I was making a temporary job out of her.'

'You'll have to stop it.'

'How?'

'Get away. It's for your own good, Hugh.'

'It sounds as if you stand to get something out of it, too.'

'I'd like to see you go.'

'Why the hell didn't you say so straight away? If you've got plans for yourself I don't want to hold them up. What are your plans?'

'I'm thinking of getting married in the spring.'

'You've kept it pretty quiet.'

'I'm marrying a quiet girl.'

'You'd like me out of the house before you marry her.'

'I've promised her myself and the house. You weren't part of the bargain.'

'I'd spoil it if I was.'

'Don't think I lack charity. Hugh.'

'You don't lack anything, Herb. You've been good at a time when being good doesn't pay so well. That's the nearest I'll ever come to thanking you. Don't forget that I said that. When do you want me to go?'

'When do you?'

'I won't be sorry to leave the valley. I'll go as soon as you like. But I can't just step out into the void. I wouldn't starve to please the angels.'

'I've got fifteen pounds saved. It's what I was going to use to get some things for the house to get it ready for Kitty.'

'Kitty?'

'Yes. What about it?'

'I had a notion you'd marry somebody with a name like Kitty. Sounds playful. She ought to suit you.'

'She will. I choose with care.'

'I can't take your furniture money.'

'I'll have a little left. And fifteen pounds should see you right till you find something. London's full of jobs.'

'When can you get the money?'

'Three days from now.'

'That's sooner than I thought.'

'Better to get it done with.'

'That's wise. In three days my life turns another page. Here's hoping the print gets a bit cleaner.'

'It will, Hugh, I'm certain it will. You're doing the best thing. You've got so much to live for. More than I have. I know you love the valley and the things inside it. I know you'd like to stay here till you die. But the valley's dying already, Hugh. There's nothing here any more. There's no need for you to die with it.'

'No, no. I don't suppose there is. There's no particular need for me to die at all, but die I will when I get my quota of thirty insurance stamps. And this money you're giving me, I'll pay it back with interest.'

'Don't worry too much about that.'

'It's healthy of me to worry at all.'

Hugh fetched a dish towel from the pantry. It was damp. He held it in front of the fire. He watched the steam rising from it. The sadness in his face was hard and sullen. In his mind there were two desires: the first to curse at Herbert like a maniac: the other to keep his mouth shut until the end of his days. He did neither. He shook the towel about in his hand to prevent the whole column of steam from rising into his face. He leaned his head against the mantelshelf and blew away some of the dust that lay thick upon it. He hummed a song that got so slow in his throat it finished as an angry moaning.

He wiped the pools of water from the table. He swished them away vigorously. Some drops splashed on Herbert's trousers. Hugh expected a stern caution. Herbert took no notice. He was preparing to go out. He was standing by the mirror, deciding whether the collar of his raincoat looked better turned down or up. Hugh asked him if the rain looked better, falling or evaporating. On his way out, Herbert stopped by the door and looked back. He said he had never liked Wednesdays. Parish relief customers, he added, got under his shirt.

'I'd like to get the whole damned smell of poor people out of my nose.'

He went on his way. Hugh waited for the table oilcloth to dry. The damp patches of it shone under the gaslight. He looked around at the walls. The walls were bad. In some parts, the paper hung from them. The landlord had promised to do some plastering ten years before. Since then a wave of family troubles had made the landlord other-worldly. He still collected his twelve shillings a week on the grounds that rent was not of earth but of heaven. The plastering was never mentioned. Hugh wondered whether Herbert would buy the house on his marriage-eve or devote all his marriage-eve to marriage and satisfy himself with negotiating a reduction in the rent.

Hugh switched on the wireless. For a moment he listened to part of a talk on what the church means to each and every one of us. Hugh smiled as he thought of what the speaker would feel like if he knew that he was speaking to at least one person to whom the church had never meant a thing. He wished he had arranged to see Mrs Beatty. She could always dry up his fears and launder his doubts. They had postponed their next meeting until after the rainy spell.

Making love in the rain, in a streaming, wind-filled backlane was death for passion. The only sheltered place that Hugh could think of where they might have gone as an alternative was a derelict bridge on the outskirts of the town. That was always congested with twenty to thirty courting couples, waiting with forty to sixty new styles of impatience for a chance to lean against the one dry patch on the wall that was no more than three feet across. Hugh damned the rain and the spell that had made it fall without cease.

He found a torn, blank sheet of foolscap paper in his

pocket. He threw it on to the table. He sharpened an indelible lead with the bread knife and wiped the blade clean on his coat. He sat down and began to write.

Mrs Beatty,
Dear Madam,
Dear Florence,

We have never spoken much to one another. The small, warm confidential details that are supposed to cement one person's love for another never came much into our conversations. A third person in our company might have considered both of us dumb. If we were ignorant of the way our friendship started and of the silent, groping intensity with which we sought to make it strong and indestructible, he'd have every reason to think that. It might have struck you that your friendship never meant more to me than a miserable little experiment in social self-adjustment.

It was more than that. It was a plan that involved a correct and intelligent analysis of present circumstances, and a prophetic reading of future possibilities. My love for you liquidated a part of the neurasthenia that grows like a hair shirt on the body of unused intellectuals. Our university masters, when they put us out on the market, should make a present: either of a woman like you or a five-year supply of headache powders. They could keep our degree certificates to paper their closets. Your love for me liquidated a part of the injustice that's wrapped up in a system which condemns your husband to become a cretinous coolie through overwork in the pay of the coal combines, and condemns me to become some other kind of cretin through having no work at all.

In transferring part of his wages to me you practised Christian Socialism, still with an inch or two of tragically primitive tail on it, but none the less Christian Socialism. In transferring the whole of your body from him to me you practised ordinary pagan common sense. I loved your body. He didn't. And if you had given it to him, you would have decreased his efficiency as a supervisor in the production of coal. That would have been an unpardonable sin in their eyes. The coal combines have no pity for those who slacken in the process of making them rich. They'd have fired him as passionately as you and I press our lips together ...

These words I am writing may seem stupid and ridiculous. I feel stupid. I feel ridiculous. My desire to keep alive is prompted only by my desire to accumulate enough dignity and strength to smash the crazy tragedy of my present shortcomings over somebody's skull. In a day or two I am going to steal away from you, and between now and then I don't want to see you. That intention may seem to put me on the level of a gutless, petty-bourgeois, ten-pound-a-week adulterer who gets a positive and quasi-revolutionary thrill from breaking his marriage pledge.

We made no pledge, you and I. There was never any tenderness of the ordinary sort. We were both rather silenced and frozen by a constant consciousness of the fact that the origin of whatever love we felt for each other was not mutually melting passion but the ugliest and coldest necessity. It was a curious friendship that lived always on the path that leads away from tragedy, and we never knew when the path would do a double jump and send us marching back towards what we thought we were leaving. Whenever we met I read and reread the thought in your eyes that perhaps we'd never meet again. You read the same thought in my eyes.

About every one of our meetings there was that sense of something bravely and unrepeatedly original. We should have learnt a couple of Greek tragedies apiece. We could have recited them interminably to each other. Thus we could have kept ourselves on a level of dignified and obstinate unreasonableness and far away from any bawdy, belly-tickling small talk that might have given society the idea that we were going down on our knees to ask for its scrutiny and approval. When and if I am ever driven to apply for Public Assistance to keep myself alive, I will submit to the scrutiny of society. Not until then ... The world that is capable of creating the relationship that existed between you and me must be properly damned and properly dying. It is. When its damnation ends and its death has been pronounced, and if your husband no longer exists, I will come back to you. I sometimes even permit myself the urge to have children by you. That urge reflects my sterility as a social unit. We would be plentifully fertile, you and I, in a day of vindication. But there's danger in that.

We have spent so much time in lightless lanes, slinking about like alley cats in search of satisfaction, our children might be all born blind. I have great faith in the lengths to which injustice in its present phase is prepared to go. But they would have a discontent of superhuman quality – a dynamic concentration of your miseries and mine ... I'm coming to the end of my page. I doubt if there's any more paper to hand. I have enough orthodox romance in me to fear that perhaps I might in some way have made you unhappy. If I have, suspend judgment till the present generation has reached the end of its time. Had I been allowed to function in the full range usually granted to human beings in determining their conduct, I'd submit to normal criteria. But I live against an abnormal background.

They should rip out the testicles and the tongue from the body of every unemployed person to complete his abnormality instead of leaving him with the illusion of effective life and robbing him of the substance. Don't consider me as a human being, capable of running luxury buses between the two distinct depots of good and bad. Mark me down as a historical force, a flesh and blood symbol of everything that unemployment is. As such, I am denied the majority of human rights. In return, I claim the abstract right to commit any crime, however vindictive, needless or brutal, on the head of any person, and feel no sense of regret or responsibility for it ... I won't ask you to forget me. I never intend to forget you.

Hugh.

He folded the paper as neatly as he could and looked about for an envelope.

Hugh made his way to Gwyneth's house. He was looking for Alf. The house was in darkness. Alf was wandering from room to room, walking fast one minute and slow the next, as if struck by a thought that griped him, twisting his face up as if he were in pain, reducing his pace to a helpless, hesitant crawl. He looked ill and outside himself. When Hugh came in Alf saw him and said nothing. He walked to the fireplace and spat into the cold ashes.

'Better take it easy, Alf.'

'What's the matter with me?'

'You look like a brainstorm.'

'Ugh! God Almighty! I'm sick, sick as a dog. What a happy bloody mess this is.'

'Where's Gwyneth?'

'Just gone.'

'How'd she go?'

'Private car. It'll take her to the gates of the sanatorium. The gates of men are narrow but the gates of heaven are wide. Remember that song?'

'Heard it when I was a kid.'

'Daft bloody song.'

'Daft … I thought she was going by train.'

'I decided to pay a fellow seven and a tanner to take her by car. Gwyneth's never been in a car before. She's been now. That's one happy thought she'll have to take into the dark with her.'

'She'll come back.'

'Not Gwyneth. I think she knows it, too. And if she does, what's for her?'

'You. You could get married.'

'The dole and two bob extra nourishment allowance to buy her a couple of Chinese eggs to stop her feet from paddling in the grave. Dying's a trip to Barry Island compared to that. We've been married ever since I came to live here a week ago. We went at it like a pair of mad people. We both had a notion that it was the last and only chance we'd have. God! You get some funny notions lying by the side of someone you know hasn't got very long to go. You do both lots of thinking, 'cause the other person isn't thinking of anything except just being alive. I was glad I got that car to take her away. When I pay the seven and six it'll knock my dole cock-eyed but it was worth it. I hope I get my dole.'

'Why shouldn't you?'

'I gave that supervisor at the Exchange a wallop. I flattened his ear for him.'

'What the hell'd you do that for?'

'He's a ... '

'What happened?'

'He's been bothering me to leave the district, get trained for another job. I told him to do that himself, because he's a bloody nuisance in the job he's doing now. He got nasty. He said, when the Act came in full force, either I'd go to one of those goddamn hardening centres in West Wales, or I'd go to jail as a vagrant or some bloody thing. I showed him how hard I was. I gave him a clout that nearly hit him over the counter!'

'That's fine. Is he going to prosecute?'

'Prosecute? He wouldn't miss the chance. He doesn't like the unemployed.'

'You sound as if you don't mind going to jail.'

'Who's going to jail?'

'If they take you to court, the fine'll be too stiff for you to pay.'

'I'm not going to court either.'

'You can't dodge that.'

'I won't be here. I'm getting out of the valley.'

'Getting out of the valley? You always said nobody'd ever get you to leave the valley.'

'It's different now, Hugh. I'm at the end of my piece of rope. I've had enough.'

'But Gwyneth … She'll be wanting to see you.'

'Gwyneth'll be wanting to see a lot of things she won't get. Me and her have got used to empty hands.'

'What'll she think.'

'When she first finds that I'm not coming to see her, she'll think a lot of bad things. The thoughts'll get sweeter as the light gets worse.'

'Don't be so damned cruel about it. Pity doesn't cost anything.'

'Pity? What's pity got to do with it? Five years I've spent pitying Gwyneth and doing the same good turn for myself. Pity festers quicker than anything I ever saw. I got Gwyneth that car to go away in because I knew it was the last thing I'd ever have the chance to do for her. It was the last minute of a dream that's crawling into a nightmare in the dirt on its hands and knees. What if I was a good little boy and went to see Gwyneth every Sunday and cried over her and told her how happy we'd be together when she'd leave that place, and take her one flower, one orange, one pear, because I couldn't afford any more? How'd you think that would make me feel? Best let the curtain drop on the whole damn thing and get it finished with. Anything long drawn out makes me feel sick.

'Things have happened to me for long enough. And they haven't been hitting me hard enough to keep me awake. They've been falling on me like soft rain, you know the sort of rain, the stuff that's more of a mist hanging on the mountain than anything else. I want to happen to things for a change. The first step's to get out of here. All around me I see chaps who wake up in the morning and find a little bit less in their lives than there was the day before. They're going grey and rotten. They are being sucked down into the earth before they've even found out the things they could do if they had the chance.

Not for me! This bloody place has done enough damage to me already. I'm for a change.'

'We can go together.'

'When?'

'Tomorrow.'

'Money?'

'I've got some.'

'Where from?'

'Doesn't matter where from.'

'Where to?'

'London.'

'What time?'

'Eleven in the morning.'

'I'll be there, shaved and clean.'

'Sure.'

'Gospel.'

Alf went over to the gramophone. The same record was still on the turntable. He gave the needle screw a sharp turn.

'This is bloody rotten music,' he said. 'But Gwyneth likes it. We'll play it, in honour of Gwyneth. Wherever she is we'll be joking she can hear it. If she can't hear it, that's her good luck, not ours.'

He put the needle down on the record. The music got on Hugh's nerves. He caught Alf's eye, waved his hand, said, 'Eleven o'clock, by the station,' and left the house.

* * *

On his way to the station, Hugh met Lloyd. Lloyd had a light bandage round his forehead. They walked down the hill together. They walked in the centre of the road to avoid the crowds of men who filled the pavements, on their way to and from the Labour Exchange. Lloyd was quiet and fidgety. His face was whiter than when Hugh had seen him last. They walked outside the station. Hugh kept looking round anxiously for Alf, Lloyd leaned against a thick pillar, chewing gum slowly and churning his hand among a mass of paper in his pocket.

'What are you leaving for, Hugh?' he asked.

Hugh put his case down and kicked his feet on the pillar Lloyd was leaning against.

'Had to. Got into a pretty nasty alley.'

'You should have stayed. Our struggle's here.'

'Our struggle's anywhere, Lloydie.'

'Coming back if you run into bad weather?'

' 'Course I will. I was born here.'

'You were born here and it's on the point of being born again. Something great and glorious will rise from this shambles. Poverty, unemployment, Means Test, hovels, filth … those things are just manure for the harvests to come.'

'I'll be back for the reaping. What about you?'

'My path is about to be sharply determined. So sharply I'll never be able to leave it. I'm due to appear in court on a charge of riot.'

'Riot? Riot? All you did was to get in the way of a baton.'

'The law's pretty elastic. They'll prove that my great-grandfather who did a bit of carpentering in Pembroke had a hand in making the baton. They'll send me down for a couple of months on a charge of conspiring with my ancestors to do violence unto myself. Mad, isn't it?'

'They can't do a daft thing like that.'

'They do dafter things than that every day and thrive on it. Chap three doors down from us hung himself yesterday. He had just been forced by the Public Assistance to sell the house he had spent all his life in buying, just to keep himself in food. A few months in jail is an adagio for flute and orchestra compared. You're wagging your head about like a bird.'

'My brother Alf.'

'Do you think he'll come?'

'I don't think so. He said he would. Last night he might have meant it. He's more chained to this valley than you are. Poor Alf. I always knew he'd see Gwyneth to the end of her trip. He was too good not to do that. He'll follow wherever life leads him. He'll keep on kicking it on the backside but he'll keep on following it. I was a fool to think he'd come away with me. I'll have to go. I wish he had come down though. I wanted to say goodbye to him.'

'You'll see him again.'

'Why not?'

Hugh got into the train. Lloyd stood on the platform by his compartment. Hugh leaned out of the window, thinking of what could be said in a hurry. A man sitting in the corner of the compartment poked his head into the opening between Hugh's thigh and the edge of the window. He said he had twenty years experience of first aid. Lloyd told him that that statement in itself meant nothing. The man pointed to the bandage around Lloyd's head. 'Too loose,' he said. 'Not a scrap of use, loose like that.' Lloyd told him he was giving the pain plenty of room to move about in.

The man sat back and laughed in a high tenor, saying that was the best joke he had heard during his twenty years experience as a first-aid man. Hugh had the impression that he was listening to something far away and crazy. Lloyd asked him for a penny to get some chocolate from a slot machine.

The train started to move. Hugh looked back at the station. Lloyd was lifting his chocolate to his mouth with one hand and waving with the other.

Hugh sat down. He looked to the left, then to the right. On both sides, the hills got lower. He was leaving the valley.